JILL SHALVIS

wrapped up in you

A
Heartbreaker Bay
Novel

AVONBOOKS

An Imprint of HarperCollins*Publishers*

Excerpt from *Almost Just Friends* copyright © 2020 by Jill Shalvis.

WRAPPED UP IN YOU. Copyright © 2019 by Jill Shalvis. All rights reserved. Printed in the United States of America. No part of this book may be used or reproduced in any manner whatsoever without written permission except in the case of brief quotations embodied in critical articles and reviews. For information, address HarperCollins Publishers, 195 Broadway, New York, NY 10007.

First Avon Books mass market printing: October 2019
First Avon Books hardcover printing: September 2019

Print Edition ISBN: 978-0-06-289778-7
Digital Edition ISBN: 978-0-06-289776-3

Cover design by Nadine Badalaty
Cover illustration by Shane Rebenschied
Cover photographs © Shirley Green (couple); © Dziurek/Lara_Uhryn/
Liliboas/Servet TURAN/istock/Getty images (4 images); © Anelina/
freedomnaruk/Kamenetskiy Konstantin gillmar/ PUSCAU DANIEL/
New Africa/nexus 7/YanLev/Artazum/tab62/MestoSveta/DMITRII
SIMAKOV/Rose-Marie Henriksson/Shutterstock (13 images)

FIRST EDITION

19 20 21 22 23   QGM   10 9 8 7 6 5 4 3 2 1

"I'm the law."

"The law can be dirty," she said.

"True." He let a teasing smile come into his voice. "And I can be very dirty, but only off duty, and only if you ask real nice."

She laughed out loud at that, the sound both soft and musical. "Okay, I'll give this to you—you're funny. And maybe also sexy as hell, but this isn't happening."

Sexy as hell? He'd take that any day of the week. "We're just talking."

"Uh huh," she said dryly. "But when men talk, they think they're flirting, and to them flirting leads to everything else, which is always a disappointment. And if I wanted to be disappointed," she said, "I could just go inside and watch *The Bachelor.*"

"How do you know I'd disappoint?"

"You're a man, aren't you?"

By Jill Shalvis

Heartbreaker Bay Novels

SWEET LITTLE LIES
THE TROUBLE WITH MISTLETOE
ACCIDENTALLY ON PURPOSE
CHASING CHRISTMAS EVE • ABOUT THAT KISS
HOT WINTER NIGHTS
PLAYING FOR KEEPS
WRAPPED UP IN YOU

Women's Fiction Novels

LOST AND FOUND SISTERS
THE GOOD LUCK SISTER (novella)
RAINY DAY FRIENDS • THE LEMON SISTERS

Lucky Harbor Novels

ONE IN A MILLION • HE'S SO FINE
IT'S IN HIS KISS • ONCE IN A LIFETIME
ALWAYS ON MY MIND • IT HAD TO BE YOU
FOREVER AND A DAY • AT LAST
LUCKY IN LOVE • HEAD OVER HEELS
THE SWEETEST THING • SIMPLY IRRESISTIBLE

Animal Magnetism Novels

STILL THE ONE • ALL I WANT
THEN CAME YOU • RUMOR HAS IT
RESCUE MY HEART
ANIMAL ATTRACTION
ANIMAL MAGNETISM

Whelp, as it happens, authors make mistakes. I think, I hope, the trick to forgiveness is to admitting those mistakes. What mistake, you ask? In a previous book, it's very briefly mentioned that Kel's mom passed away. That's not true. She is alive and well and causing some havoc in this book. Just wanted to let you know in order to avoid any confusion. Yes, I said she was dead. No, she's not dead. Consider it deleted.

:) Happy Reading!
XOXO, Jill

wrapped
up
in you

Chapter 1

Dig deep

"Stay down."

No, she would not stay down. Mostly because Ivy Snow didn't know the meaning of the words. Not once in her hard-knock, scrappy life had she ever "stayed down." So she popped back up, using a spin and a roundhouse kick to level her opponent.

Her kickboxing partner and friend hit the mat and grinned from flat on her back. "That's gotta be worth at *least* a donut. You're buying."

"Can't," Ivy said, eyeing the time. "I've gotta get to work."

"Well damn." Sadie sat up and yawned. "I've still got a whole hour and a half before I have to do the same, which means I'm going back to bed. And if I'm lucky, Caleb'll still be in it."

Caleb was Sadie's fiancé. Ignoring the little spurt of envy at the thought of having someone waiting in bed for her, Ivy hit the locker room to shower and change.

Fifteen minutes later, suitably beaten up by their four-times-a-week kickboxing session, she left the gym. It was six a.m., her very least favorite time of the day, and she shivered unhappily. It was two weeks before Christmas, which for San Francisco meant it could be any weather at all. Today it was forty-five degrees and she'd forgotten her jacket. She was on a budget, a tight one, but it wasn't worth freezing to death for a couple of bucks so she decided to forgo walking and hopped on a bus rather than turn into a human popsicle.

A guy in a suit, sneakers, and holding a huge energy drink took the seat next to her, giving her a not-so-discreet onceover. "Morning," he said with a charming smile.

And yes, she'd just felt a little wistful about not having anyone waiting for her in her bed, but that was fantasy, and Ivy was nothing if not grounded in reality. These days she prided herself on her sharply honed survivor skills, but in the past, she'd definitely failed herself in the man department. This was in good part thanks to a wanderlust lifestyle and a weakness for sexy grins that promised—and usually delivered—trouble.

Like this guy's.

But that was all behind her now. She'd promised herself. So she gave him a vague, not-interested smile and turned away to look out the window. Rude? Probably. But she was calloused, and—as every guy she'd ever let in too close had complained—a tough nut to crack. The words *cold* and *scary* had also been thrown around.

She didn't mind. She actually liked it, even if the image went completely against her Disney princess-like moniker, *Ivy Snow*. Maybe especially because it did. Her name had been a bone of contention for a long time, but it wasn't like she'd named herself. Her mother had done that, reportedly on some good prescription meds at the time.

At her stop, she exited the bus and walked the last two blocks to work, getting a little happier with each step because one, exercise was over for the day, and two, she loved her job.

For as long as she could remember, her entire life had been transient. This was mostly thanks to a dad who'd taken off a long time ago and a lounge singer mom who changed bar gigs like other women changed nail polish. As a result, Ivy had gone to a bunch of different schools, managing to slip through a whole bunch of cracks while she was at it. Luckily, she had been insanely curious and loved reading, and had taught herself most of the time. As a result, she was a pro chameleon and excelled at temporary. Temporary friends, temporary jobs, temporary life. It had suited her for a long time.

Until it hadn't.

She'd woken up one day about a year ago and had realized she'd changed. Moving around no longer suited her and she was over living out of a back-pack. So at the dubiously mature age of twenty-eight, she was trying a new lane. She'd settled in the Cow Hollow District of San Francisco, running a thing called The Taco Truck and living in an apartment that had her name on the lease.

Roots. After a lifetime of running, being invisible, and just barely getting by, she was growing roots. She was going for a life that until now had existed for her only on TV and in the movies, meaning friends and family, *real* family who'd stick with her through thick and thin. And maybe . . . maybe even someone to love.

Unnerving that she was actively working toward the very things that had terrified her for most of her life, but she'd decided she'd rather be scared shit-less than live with regrets. So she'd learned to put a smile on her face, because everyone knew you had to fake it to make it, right?

The Taco Truck was parked in the alley of the Pacific Pier Building. She kept it there at night thanks to the fact that the owner of the building,

Spence Baldwin, loved her food. And his grandpa, Old Man Eddie, who lived in the alley—by choice— had spent most of last year acting as a guard dog for her.

But just before winter had hit this year, Spence had finally talked his grandpa into taking an apartment in the building, so he no longer had eyes on her truck. Still, it felt safe here.

On work days, she pulled the truck out to the street at the entrance to the courtyard, always a gamble because her city permit hadn't yet come through. Permits were incredibly difficult to come by, but she'd been told she was finally going to get one, and hopefully that was true.

Just looking at the truck had put a smile on her face—a *real* one. She moved the truck and had just parked for the day when her day's deliveries arrived. She received her preordered inventory and eyed the time. Six thirty. She opened at seven sharp, so she got started chopping ingredients, frying up meats, arranging the makings for the day's menu. *Her* menu. She liked the work. Actually, she loved the work, and her boss wasn't bad either. She smiled at that as she worked because she was the boss. She owned the truck.

Okay, so she was making payments on it, but she was actually in the black these days. Everything about that thought improved her day on the spot.

Today she wasn't going to worry about bills or permits. She was going to enjoy herself, her food, and her new goals.

She was comfortable here in her small but mighty space of seventy-five square feet, working her magic, making what she liked to think were the most delicious tacos in the Bay Area. It wasn't an easy job. She spent just as much time prepping and being a mechanic as she did being a chef. And then there was the ordering and buying of all the necessary supplies, not to mention the bookkeeping, which often kept her up late into the night.

Her work was never done, but she was good with that. Hell, she was great with that. After spending most of her life at the mercy of others, she thrived on being independent and having no one tell her what to do or when to do it.

She was still prepping when she heard voices outside. She handled breakfast and lunch on her own, her two biggest meals. After that, her part-time helper, Jenny, came in the afternoons to handle the much thinner dinner crowd and closing. For now, Ivy still had her CLOSED sign up, but the voices stopped right outside her truck. Men, at least two of them, possibly three. With a sigh, she opened the serving window and stuck her head out.

A trio of extremely hot guys dressed in running gear and looking hungry as hell glanced up from the menu board posted on the side of her truck. Ivy knew two of them, Caleb and Jake, both currently off the market, so she felt free to give them her flirtiest smile. "Sorry, guys, not open for another twenty minutes."

Jake returned her flirty smile from his wheelchair while upping it another factor, which she knew was just a ploy to get his way.

"But you make the best food in the city," he said sweetly, as if Ivy could be swayed by sweet. "And we've all gotta be at work by seven."

Caleb stood at his side, and was a friend of Ivy's, and also a savior as he'd helped her navigate the purchase of her truck when dealing with the previous owner had gotten tricky. "I'm pretty sure you said you owed me a favor," he reminded her, always the negotiator.

Knowing the venture capitalist could talk anyone into just about anything, she laughed and gave in. "Fine. Figure out what you want and make it quick. But then we're even, Caleb."

They weren't even. She owed him much more than an early breakfast, and they both knew it. But having gotten his way as he always did, he smiled. "The usual for me."

"Me too," Jake said.

Ivy nodded and turned her attention to the third man.

She'd never seen him before; she most certainly would have remembered. Like the others, he was in running gear that fit his leanly muscled bod, which he held in a way that suggested military or cop. And just like that, the always-on-alert scared little kid she'd once been sent an automatic *danger* warning to her brain.

But she was no longer helpless, she reminded herself. She no longer had to pretend to be tough and brave. She *was* tough and brave. So she kept her smile in place, forcing herself to relax. She had nothing to hide. Well, almost nothing, anyway.

And it wasn't exactly a hardship to look at him. His smile certainly was heart-stopping as he added his charm to both Caleb and Jake's. And there *was* considerable charm. He had dark eyes and dark hair cut short, and in spite of his smile, when those eyes met hers, they gave away nothing of his thoughts.

Yep. Cop, she thought, which was a damn shame.

Kel O'Donnell stood there in front of The Taco Truck, starving and aching like a son-of-a-bitch. Pushing his body on a five mile, full-out run hadn't been the smartest of ideas after what he'd been through. But his more immediate problem was that if he didn't get food and fast, his stomach was going to eat itself.

The woman inside the truck looked to him for

his order. "And you?" she asked, her voice slightly amused, as if life wasn't to be taken too seriously, especially while ordering tacos.

But he was taking this *very* seriously, as his hunger felt soul deep. "What do you suggest?"

This caused twin groans from his cousin Caleb and their longtime friend Jake, which Kel ignored.

Not his server though. She quirked a single brow, the small gesture making him feel more than he had in months. Certainly since his life had detonated several months ago when he'd chased after a suspect on foot, only to be hit by the getaway car, getting himself punted a good fifteen feet into the air. That had hurt. But what had hurt more was his perp turning out to be a dirty cop. And not any dirty cop, but a longtime friend, which had nearly cost him life and career.

But hell, at least neither were on the line this time. It was just a pretty woman giving him some cute, sexy 'tude while waiting on him to decide between avocado and bacon tacos or spicy green eggs and ham tacos.

"You're going to have to excuse my dumbass cousin, Ivy," Caleb said. "Kel hasn't lived in San Francisco for a long time and doesn't know that you've got the best food truck in all of Cow Hollow. Hell, in the whole Bay Area."

"It's true," Jake said and nudged Kel, and with

Jake in the wheelchair, he got the nudge right in the back of the knee and just about went down.

"Everything on the menu," Jake said, "and I do mean *everything* is gold. Trust me, it'll melt in your mouth and make you want to drop to your knees and beg Ivy here to marry you."

Ivy sent Jake the sweetest smile Kel had ever seen. Then those compelling eyes were back on him, the sweet completely gone. She leaned out her serving window a little bit, bracing her weight on her elbows. Her hair was the color of fire, a stunning pile of red held back by an elf headband, which left a few strands falling around her face, framing it. Her apron read *I don't wanna taco 'bout it*. "What do I suggest?" she repeated.

"Yeah." Just looking at her, he could feel himself relax for the first time in . . . way too long. Something about her did that to him. Instant chemistry. He hadn't felt it often in his life and it always ended up a train wreck, so why the hell he felt relaxed, he had no idea. But it had him flashing another smile. "How about you pick for me."

Her lips quirked at that. "Fair warning—I like things hot."

"I *love* things hot," he said.

Jake just grinned. "Aw man, she's gonna eat you up and spit you out. I'm so happy."

"Shh," Caleb said. "I don't want to miss him getting his ass handed to him."

Ivy just cocked her head at Kel. "Think you can handle the heat?"

"Oh yeah."

"Five minutes." And she shut the window on them.

They moved to one of the two picnic tables at the entrance to the courtyard in front of them, where they sat to wait for their food. Caleb looked at Kel and shook his head. "Man, as much as I enjoy seeing you get your ego squashed, I feel duty bound to warn you. Whatever's making you smile, it's never going to happen. Ivy's not the girl you have fun with and walk away from. And plus, she hates cops."

"Agreed," Jake said. "You've got a better shot at stealing Sadie away from Caleb. And good luck with that. Your cousin's woman is batshit crazy over him, God knows why."

Caleb just smiled, apparently not feeling the need to defend his relationship.

Kel was happy for him. Very happy. Caleb hadn't given his heart away . . . ever. And for good reasons, which Kel had hated for him. "About time you found someone who deserves you."

Caleb was quiet a moment. "I like having you here," he said, kind enough to leave out the tone of recrimination. It'd been a long time, too long, which had been all Kel's doing. He'd spent the first ten years of his life here in the city, he and his sister and his parents. They'd lived next door to his aunt and her kids, including Caleb. Kel hadn't realized at the time, but they'd all been poor as dirt, even though his parents had always managed to make it seem like they'd had everything they'd needed.

Then his mom had destroyed that happy illusion with a single, shattering mistake, creating a huge rift none of them had recovered from. Two years later had come yet another blow. His dad had died, and Kel and his older sister, Remy, had gone to Idaho to be raised by their grandparents.

It'd sucked.

"You see Remy yet?" Caleb asked.

Kel's sister had moved back here to San Francisco after getting married last year. And no, he hadn't seen her yet. And yes, he was stalling.

"Okay . . . how about your mom?" Caleb asked.

Kel slid him a look.

Caleb raised his hands. "Hey, just asking."

"Uh-huh. Do you ask all your employees such personal questions?"

"No, just my brother."

"I'm your *cousin*."

"You're my *brother*," Caleb said with meaning.

Kel sighed and looked over at Jake.

Jake shrugged. "He likes to adjust facts to suit him. But you knew that already."

Ivy came out of the truck with three baskets. She served Jake first, then Caleb, and finally Kel. She handed him his basket and stood there at his side, a tiny pixie of a woman in that sassy apron, elf head-band, and painted-on jeans faded to a buttery softness. Her boots were serious and kickass, and because he was a very sick man, they turned him on.

Since she was clearly going nowhere until he tried her food, he took a bite of what looked like the most amazing breakfast taco he'd ever seen and . . . almost died. Spicy was an understatement. Holy hell hot was an understatement. But it was also the best thing he'd ever tasted, even if his tongue was numb.

Ivy smiled at him. "Still think you can handle the heat?"

Jake and Caleb were doubled over laughing, the asses. "I'm not a cop," he managed to wheeze, holding her gaze while he took another bite. And another. No doubt, he was going to eat her food the entire two weeks he was here. If he lived that long.

"He's a sheriff and ranch owner in Idaho," Caleb said. "So . . . *kind of* a cop."

"Also kind of a cowboy," Jake added ever so helpfully.

Kel rolled his still watering eyes. His grandparents had left him and Remy their ranch, which he oversaw, but had employees handling the day-to-day operations since his day job was more like a 24–7 job. "I'm just a guy on vacay," he croaked out. The more accurate term would have been assigned-slash-leave, but hell if he was going to share that. Or the fact that his still healing broken ribs ached like a bitch, as did the deep bone bruising he'd suffered down the entire right side of his body from being pitched into the air by a moving vehicle.

Caleb snorted. "You don't do vacay. As evidenced by the fact you agreed to work for me for the entire two weeks you're here. I needed him," he said to Ivy. "He's got serious skills. He's going to manage security on several large projects, including my most recently acquired building, the one being renovated into condos." He looked at Kel. "Ivy's going to buy one with her brother, who's an antiquities specialist. It's a great investment," he said like a proud parent, even though at thirty-two, he couldn't have been more than five years or so older than Ivy.

"Actually, it might just be me investing," Ivy said. "Brandon just got into a deal on the East Coast I was telling you about."

"The auction house job."

"Yes, and it's going to keep him busy for a while, so . . ." She shrugged. "I told him I'd go after this myself."

"That's too bad," Caleb said. "Was looking forward to meeting him."

Kel stopped chewing because something in Ivy's tone had just set off his bullshit radar. She was either lying or stretching the truth, but his eyes were still watering and his throat was burning or he might've joined the conversation.

Ivy reached out as if to take away his basket, but he held firm to it and kept eating. He was starting to sweat and he couldn't feel his lips, but he also couldn't get enough.

"Okay, cowboy, it's your funeral," she said, and he couldn't tell if she was impressed or horrified.

A few more people were milling around her truck now, and she eyed her watch.

"They start lining up earlier every day," Caleb said.

"Hey, Ivy," one of the guys who was waiting called out. "The fuzz! They're coming around the corner!"

"Crap!" Ivy ran toward her truck, yelling to the people standing in line, "I'll be back in ten minutes. If you wait and save my spot, I'll give you a discount!" And then she slapped the window and door closed and roared off down the street.

A minute later a cop drove by slowly, but didn't stop. When he was gone, the group of people who'd been lining up for tacos stepped into the empty parking spot Ivy had left.

Not ten seconds later, a car came along and honked at the people standing in the spot. "Get out of my way," the driver yelled.

No one budged.

The car window lowered and a hand emerged, flipping everyone the bird.

This didn't make anyone move either, and finally the guy swore and drove off in a huff.

"What the hell?" Kel asked.

"She's not supposed to be on the street before seven," Jake said.

"I'm working on getting her a city permit," Caleb said. "They're extremely hard to get."

Kel was boggled. "But . . . those people are blocking the street. They could get a ticket."

"Thought you weren't a cop," Caleb said, looking amused.

Kel shook his head and went back to his tacos, and for a guy who believed in the law, when the incredible burst of flavors once again hit his tongue, he thought maybe he could understand the flagrant disregard of it in this one case.

Chapter 2

Go hard or don't go at all

That night, Ivy stayed up late paying the bills that couldn't wait any longer, setting aside the ones that could, playing around with her credit card, doing the monthly money dance between bank accounts. Just the insurance policies alone—general liability, business owner, commercial auto, self-employed health care—nearly killed her.

But it was also an undeniable thrill to be legit.

For someone who'd grown up in dumpy trailers and motels across the southern states, living off her mom's cash tips from singing in lounges and crap bars, it was certainly surreal.

She even had a savings account, which made her smile every time she thought about it. A savings! She'd been in the city for just over a year now, living off next to nothing in order to put away every spare penny. She had eighteen grand put away, a fortune for her. But she was still two grand short of having enough for the down payment on a condo in Caleb's newly acquired and renovated building. The twenty thousand was only half the required down, but there was a first-time buyers program in play to ensure equality of housing, and the mortgage broker—Caleb—was going to match her down payment. The agreement was that she'd work that debt off by catering all of his business events, of which there were many. This was a good deal for both of them. Ivy didn't have to put up cash she didn't have, and Caleb was guaranteed her most excellent catering, if she said so herself.

For the first time in her life, she just felt ridiculously proud of herself. She was so close to having it all together. She wanted that condo. *Needed* that condo. It would be 1,600 square feet of home, and it even came with a parking space for her truck.

Right now, the owner of the Pacific Pier Building allowed her to park overnight in the alley, which was like having a golden ticket. But that was only temporary, and playing Russian roulette with the parking police wasn't easy. Plus, she really wanted to have the truck more safely stowed at night because she came from a world where your possessions could be taken away at any moment if you didn't clutch them tight to your vest.

Having it so far from her apartment was a constant source of stress. Other than her slowly growing savings, the truck was all she had. And both were thanks to the business plan she'd painstakingly put together when she'd taken over the taco truck.

She'd come so far. Granted, she still had a long way to go, but pride filled her. And as usual, right on the heels of that was an odd sense of loneliness because she didn't have anyone to show off to. Her mom was much more interested in her next singing gig than her children, so contact was extremely infrequent. As for Ivy's brother, he was sweet and charming and charismatic and . . . utterly incorrigible. He was one of those guys who could use their powers for good or bad.

He'd tried to choose good. It just hadn't worked out for him. It was always about the next get-rich-quick scheme. And unfortunately, along with those came trouble. She'd had to distance herself.

It'd hurt because in spite of all his faults, Brandon was blood, and he cared about her. In his own way. Which wasn't always the right way. Or any sort of legal way. The biggest problem they had was that she couldn't trust him to keep her safe. Or to put her first in a bad situation—which she only ever landed in when he was involved. Some of those memories were bad enough that they still haunted her.

So she'd gone west without a forwarding address,

and instead of wishing for her family to change, she'd gone after making new connections. She'd made friends here, and was happy. The only thing that kept her from enjoying her life fully was knowing she'd lied to everyone about her past.

But that was a problem for another day.

Leaning back in her kitchen chair, she looked around. Her apartment was a third floor walk-up, and she used the word *apartment* loosely. The building had once upon a time been a single family dwelling, and when the owners had renovated each of the floors into individual units back in the 1930s, they'd called the attic a "generous loft."

The two hundred and fifty square feet hardly qualified for generous anything, but she had a roof that leaked only in big rainstorms, decent electricity—if she didn't run her toaster and her blow dryer at the same time—and almost always could get hot water for a good three to four whole minutes at a time.

But the best part of the deal was that the landlord, a sweet old lady named Evelyn, adored her and gave her a huge discount on the monthly rent—in exchange for leftovers from Ivy's truck every day.

Tonight that had been brisket tacos, and Evelyn had been thrilled. She'd talked Ivy into having a seat and joining her as she'd eaten, telling stories about her kids, and her kids' kids . . . none of whom, at least that Ivy could tell, ever came and saw her.

Evelyn also always made Ivy tell her a story about

herself as well, and tonight was no different. Evelyn had wanted to hear about Ivy's famed brother, so she'd drawn a deep breath and did what she did.

She told stories.

She was good at it. She'd been making up stories about her family since she'd been little, each different, each more exciting than the last, and all as far from the truth as she could possibly get. Because the truth wasn't a story, it was a nightmare. Mentally sifting through a long list of fantasies, Ivy told her landlord all about Brandon the artist, who was living in Paris at the moment, becoming famous for his incredible oil landscapes. She left off the fact that he peddled stolen art instead of creating it, and it hadn't been Paris, France, but Paris, Texas.

Now, in the attic with her lights dimmed and the only sounds the creaking of the old bones of the building that had seen better days decades ago, Ivy shook her head and clicked on one of her open tabs to view her savings balance.

Still there, and she felt the smile curve her lips. A few more weeks and she'd be able to talk to Caleb about getting the paperwork started for the condo. Her condo. It was almost unreal to her, given how she'd grown up in a string of motels, each more roach infested than the last because Brandon, ever the fun-loving, trouble-seeking stoner of their threesome, had burned down the one halfway-nice trailer they'd had.

Ivy had left "home" at age sixteen to strike out on her own, couch surfing or living out of her car, working at whatever jobs she could get, mostly in bar kitchens, which was where she'd learned to cook.

Something that had given her purpose, and now a job she loved.

With a smile, she changed venues, moving to her office desk—which was really her bed. She fluffed her pillows behind her and stretched out her legs. She considered going to sleep. It was late, midnight, and she had to be up at five a.m. for kickboxing class.

Ugh.

Well-known secret: Ivy hated kickboxing class. She hated the gym. She hated to work out at all, but she hated the way her clothes fit when she didn't do it even more. And yet she still might've taken the extra hour to sleep if her exercise app hadn't texted her a notification with a picture of a guy working out, captioned: *This is Jack. Jack got up on time for his workout. Be more like Jack . . .*

Yes, her exercise app had shamed her into getting up. So here she was, being beaten up and paying for the pleasure. When she'd first come to the city, she'd been oddly lonely and sad. She'd gone to Google instead of a therapist she couldn't afford, and had learned that moving your body helped with depression. She still hated the gym. *Hated*. But she was a whole lot less sad.

But because she knew herself, she'd doubled downed and bought a gym pass knowing she was far too cheap to not go. So she tried to get to sleep, but couldn't. Something was niggling at her. Had she left something on in her truck? Had she left something plugged in? Had Jenny locked it up properly? She'd swear the answers to those questions were no, no, and yes, but . . . she couldn't shake the feeling.

There'd been many times in her life when her instincts had been all she had, and they'd never failed her. The first time they'd kicked in, she'd been fourteen years old, Brandon sixteen. Since their mom had worked nights, Brandon had been in charge. He'd had some new friends over to play darts in the yard—a hustle, of course. On a good night, Brandon could earn several hundred in cash.

But halfway through the evening, Ivy's instincts had kicked in, the hair on the back of her neck standing straight up. Not questioning it, she'd climbed out a back window of the trailer and huddled in the bushes, listening as some of the guys who'd become bored with losing money to Brandon had come inside to "have some fun with the hottie little sister . . ."

Brandon had been furious when he'd found out, and had promised not to bring them around again. And he hadn't. But that didn't mean the trouble stopped. A year later, this time in a seedy motel in Florida, Brandon had been selling pot out of their single room,

using the bathroom as his "office." He'd been open for
business when Ivy had gotten the same hinky feeling, complete with the hair standing straight up on
the back of her neck. Again, she'd sneaked out a window. She'd gotten across the yard when the police had
come, sirens screaming, into thc lot and confiscated
all their possessions *and* Brandon.

Lesson learned. She never ignored her instincts
now, never. Which meant she shut off her laptop,
locked up, and headed down the stairs. It was only
two miles to her truck. Normally, she'd just hoof it
over there like she did every morning, because calling a Lyft was a luxury she'd given up for her savings
account's sake.

But no matter how badass she liked to think she
was, she wasn't stupid. No way was she going to risk
walking that far alone this late at night. So though it
killed her, she opened her Lyft app.

Fifteen minutes later, she got out of the Lyft at
the southeast corner of the building, which housed
O'Riley's pub. The place was packing and thriving.
Music and laughter poured out of there as she walked
by and stopped at the front of the alley to eye her
truck.

All looked well. But unable to shake her weird
feeling, she moved closer, and then she was running
toward it because the back door was cracked, the
lock broken and dangling uselessly.

Chapter 3

Leave it all in the room

Kel heard something, a female cry maybe? It indicated fear and he immediately moved in that direction from the pub, where he'd been with Caleb.

They'd met up with a bunch of his cousin's friends for dinner and drinks, including Sadie, Caleb's lovely significant other. It'd been a sort of welcome back to the city thing, and though Kel had planned to lay low for the duration of his visit, being out tonight had been good. Caleb had toasted and roasted him—with "Kel the Cowboy Does the City" jokes, cracking himself up.

None of it had bothered Kel, it'd all been in good fun, and sitting there surrounded by Caleb's tight-knit group of friends and the exciting, urban energy of the city itself, made his own not-great reality feel a million miles away.

He'd left San Francisco when he'd been twelve years old, and it hadn't been under the best of circumstances. He hadn't given it much playtime in his brain in the nearly two decades since, but being back had definitely opened the floodgates.

Realizing that, and the fact that the pub had gotten too loud for him, he'd left just after midnight, escaping to the courtyard attached to the pub. It was peaceful out here and he'd taken in the incredible architecture of the old building, the corbeled brick and exposed iron trusses, the large picture windows on the retail shops, the cobblestone beneath his feet, and the huge fountain centerpiece where idiots the city over came to toss a coin and wish for love.

And all of it was decorated for the holidays with garlands of evergreen entwined with twinkling white lights in every doorway and frame, along with a huge Christmas tree near the street entrance, making it look like a Christmas card. It'd rained earlier, so the cobblestone pavers were wet and shiny.

He'd stood there looking up at a sky that was vastly different from the one he had in Idaho, all the old memories stirred up and causing havoc in his head, the ones he'd thought he'd put to rest a long time ago.

That's when he'd heard the cry and then muttered cursing. He ran down the courtyard, passing the pet shop, the coffee shop, the tattoo place, the hundred-plus-year-old fountain in the middle, a wedding shop, a paint and wine place, a stationery store . . . and ended up at the alley opening to the street. There he turned in a slow circle looking for . . . what, he had no idea.

He saw Ivy's taco truck. He'd noticed it earlier when he'd walked into the pub with Caleb. Catching movement in the alley, he stepped closer. The back door to the truck was open, and from inside he could see a beam of a flashlight moving around.

Pulling his gun was automatic, and he stepped closer, catching a shadow of a figure inside. "Hands where I can see them," he called out.

The figure jerked, gasped, and then whirled around. In the ambient lighting, he immediately recognized her.

Ivy.

He slid his gun away. "You okay?"

"Hell no, I'm not okay! Are you kidding me? You just gave me a freaking heart attack! What's wrong with you?" She had a hand to her heart. She'd startled hard, and for the beat before she'd recognized him, there'd been real fear in her eyes, something that had quickly turned into *pissed-off woman*.

"What are you doing here?" she demanded.

"I was at the pub." He took in her appearance. Camo leggings, untied boots, huge black sweatshirt that threatened to swallow her whole and hit her at her knees. No makeup. Eyes stricken, mouth grim, her wild hair loose around her pale face. And he got the feeling whatever had brought her down here, it'd been without warning. "I'm going to ask you again," he said quietly. "Are you okay?"

She exhaled a long shaky breath and then shook her head as she turned away from him. "Do you always carry a gun when you go out, cowboy?"

"Yes."

"Always?"

"Yes."

"How about during the day?"

He gave her a look, wasted because she still had her back to him. "Still yes."

"How about when you're in bed with a woman?"

He knew what she was doing. Stalling. Also clearly trying to annoy him. But he'd been to hell and back, and on the return trip he'd learned how to shut himself off enough that he didn't get easily annoyed. "Do you always answer a question with another question?"

Again she shook her head. She moved inside to an industrial refrigerator and dropped to her knees in front of the low pull-out freezer. When she went through the drawer, she made a sound of distress.

He was at her side in a second. "What is it?"

"Someone broke in. Took some money. Left my refrigerator and freezer door open, and it's been just long enough that nearly everything is ruined."

"Why did you have cash in here? And how much was taken?"

"It was petty cash, locked up in my cash drawer,

and it was around a hundred bucks. Which maybe doesn't seem like a lot to you, but to me it might as well be a grand."

Kel pulled out his phone.

This got him a reaction. She whipped around, eyes wide. "What are you doing?"

"Calling the cops."

The look on her face defied description. Incredulous disbelief and maybe instant wariness. "No, you're not."

Okay, definite wariness. Cops made her nervous. Interesting. "You have a problem with the police, Ivy?"

She tossed up her hands. "Why are you even here? *Go away.*"

He wasn't going to do that, for a bunch of reasons, the least being that she could be in danger. "Do you have something to hide?"

Ignoring him and his question, she pulled her phone from her pocket and sent a text. Then she went about turning on the lights. When a text came in, she read it, sighed, and slipped the phone away.

"Who was that?"

She looked at him as if surprised he was still there. "My employee, Jenny. She closed up tonight like always, and said everything was fine when she left, no problems." She began methodically taking everything out of her fridge and freezer. When he tried to help, she "accidentally" elbowed him in the gut.

"Oops, sorry," she said, sounding anything but. "Stand back. Better yet, get out."

"Not going to happen."

Turning to him, she went hands on hips and blew a strand of hair from her face. "Why not?" she asked in exasperation.

"Because someone violated your personal space." He softened his voice. "And you seem shaken by that, as anyone would be. You shouldn't be alone."

"I'll call someone."

"Okay," he said, calling her bluff.

She stared at him and then rolled her eyes. "I can't, okay?"

"Why not?"

"It's too late."

"A friend won't care," he said. "Neither will a boyfriend." He hadn't meant to say that, but she was both the most infuriating and yet fascinating woman he'd ever met.

Her gaze shuddered and again she turned away. "Even if I called the police, they can't do much. It was just some light vandalism, and missing cash is impossible to trace."

He knew this to be true, frustrating as it was. "If you're not going to call anyone, I'm staying."

"Fine." She gathered up her red waves of hair and tamed it into submission with a hairband she'd had around her wrist. Then she slapped a pair of latex gloves against his chest and donned her own pair. "You can make yourself useful."

He called a 24–7 locksmith, who showed up and replaced the lock, while Kel and Ivy dumped what had to be hundreds of dollars of food since they couldn't be sure it was still safe to serve.

Kel paid the locksmith, and in doing so pissed off Ivy. He hadn't meant to step on her pride, but he had the feeling she was already stretched thin, and the late-night cost of having the guy come out hadn't been cheap.

"I'm going to pay you back," Ivy said stiffly.

He hated that she was acting like an injured animal with her back up to the wall, so he did his best to give her lots of space. Not easy in the close quarters, but he deferred to her for what she wanted done and then quietly followed her example without pushing.

And he wanted to push. He wanted to know why she felt so . . . alone. Why she didn't trust anyone. But she wasn't exactly an open book, so he worked alongside of her, meticulously scrubbing everything down.

"People rave about your food," he said.

She looked up, and he could tell the statement gave her pleasure, but she kept her cool. "Everyone loves a good taco."

"Do you do it all yourself?"

"I've got part-time help. Jenny's a grad student

and helps serve the dinner crowd. But I do all the food stuff."

"You're a good cook." He cocked his head. "Or is the right word *chef*?"

She grimaced. "*Chef* seems a bit fancy for what I do."

"I've gone to upscale restaurants that don't come even close to what you manage to create inside this truck."

She bit her lower lip as if to hold back her smile, but those blue eyes lit. Nice to see the spark back. He hated what the break-in had done to them, leaving them hollow and haunted. "How did you learn to cook?" he asked.

"My earliest memories are of rifling through what was available to eat and making it seem better than it was," she said, and shrugged. Her head was down now, she was concentrating on scrubbing her counter as if its life depended on it. "I was four maybe?" She shrugged again. "Turns out, I like to eat."

His chest had gone tight, and he had questions, so many questions, but he worked at keeping his mouth shut because he wanted her to keep talking.

"As I got older," she said, "I realized I was good at it."

"Where did you grow up?" he asked, having detected a very slight, maybe Southern, accent in certain words.

"We moved around a lot, mostly the South though. My first jobs were cooking in bars. Eventually I worked my way up to restaurants, honing the skills. But once a city rat, always a city rat. Staying in one place made me itchy and anxious. I liked being on the move, never settling down."

"You could work at any five-star restaurant in the city," Kel said.

She shook her head. "I'm not that good."

"Yes, you are."

Their gazes met and held. He'd have sworn the air shimmered and heated, but that was most likely either exhaustion or wishful thinking.

She looked away first. "I've always liked being able to move around when I want to. Running a food truck's the natural progression for me." She smiled. "Old habits die hard and all that."

She'd carefully left off any mention of family, and while he wanted to know so much more, he didn't want to spook her either. "You've got a brother. Older? Younger?"

"Brandon's two years older." She was turned away from him now, still scrubbing. "He was fond of eating too, so he was happy that one of us was willing to cook." She paused a moment. "He was the dessert king though. We had quite the sweet tooth, and that was his job. Getting the sweets."

Her voice hadn't changed, but there was something

off about her body language. It was defensive, and didn't match her casual voice, and he realized it was the same way she'd acted when Caleb had mentioned her brother that morning. Wishing he could see her face, he asked, "What about your parents?"

She shrugged. "My dad was never around, and my mom worked nights singing in bar lounges and sleeping during the day."

"So you're self-taught," he said, and she laughed, although he wasn't sure it was with true mirth.

"Most definitely self-taught. How about you?" she asked, turning the tables on him. "Do you cook?"

"If I have to," he said, making her laugh again, which he enjoyed. "Not while I'm here though. I'm staying with Caleb. His fiancée, Sadie, has been cooking. My cousin's spoiled rotten and doesn't even know it."

"Oh, he knows it. Sadie's great."

"You know her?"

She nodded. "I was invited to the pub tonight, but I had work to do. You're here on vacation?" she asked, changing the subject from herself. "And to work with Caleb?"

Not vacation. More like a leave of absence while his superiors poured over his last case, the one case in all the years he'd served in law enforcement to go bad. They'd decide his fate, which, for the record, he hated. "I've got two weeks off and Caleb nagged me out here." His good humor faded some as he thought of that, of how upon going back, his life could go one of two ways.

"To handle security on the new building," she said. "Because Archer Hunt and his investigations and security company, who'd normally handle this, aren't available. Something about a government contract and being stretched too thin."

"You know a lot about Caleb."

"Everyone in this building are friends and coworkers. And most of them gossip like middle schoolers." She shook her head. "There aren't many secrets here."

"I'm getting that," Kel said. "I'm putting together security teams to manage and handle Caleb's new buildings. That, and setting up the security systems, getting them in place to run smoothly for after I'm gone. Caleb put some temporary contract workers in place to cover everything, but he needs someone in charge."

She met his gaze. "And you're good at being in charge."

A statement not a question, and he was pretty sure it wasn't a compliment of any sort, so he did his best to look harmless and innocent.

With a snort, she went back to work.

Okay, so she wasn't easily fooled. And she was most definitely not a slacker. It was two hours before she was satisfied they'd cleaned and properly sterilized everything. Then she took out a small menu chalkboard, wiped it clean, and wrote *CLOSED for breakfast, but will open at 11 for lunch*. She hung it on her closed serving window.

"I'll need the morning to restock," she explained as they exited the trailer into the chilly night.

"And maybe to sleep," he said, noticing the time.

She shrugged, like sleep wasn't as important as her job.

He could understand that. He'd made his job more important than his life for years.

San Francisco never closed its eyes. Even at three in the morning, the city was hopping. Traffic flowing. People moving on the streets. With what sounded like a bone-weary sigh, Ivy turned to the new lock on her truck. She struggled with it a moment, so he moved in close to help, once again making her jerk in surprise.

"Seriously," she snapped. "Stop sneaking up on me."

Her fingers were freezing. He pulled his gloves from his jacket pocket and handed them to her.

"I'm not taking your gloves," she said, shoving her hands into her sweatshirt pocket.

"Not taking," he said. "Borrowing."

Her shoulders slowly lowered from where they'd been up at her ears. "Okay, thanks," she said, almost begrudgingly, making him laugh.

"What?" she asked, eyes narrowed.

"You're as prickly as a porcupine."

She cocked her head. "Is that something you say on your ranch in Idaho?"

So she had been listening to his and Caleb's and Jake's breakfast conversation earlier. Interesting. In another woman, he might've taken that as a sign of interest. In this woman, he had no idea. "It's something you say anywhere," he said. "Especially when it's true."

"I'm not a big people person," she admitted in a tone that said sorry-not-sorry. "People are often my biggest pet peeve." She looked at him as if he might say something about that.

"Hey," he said. "I get it."

"What's your biggest pet peeve?"

He thought about that. "I guess being lied to. Gets me every time."

She didn't say anything to this, and he eyed her taco truck. "And you're sure you don't want to call—"

"I'm sure."

"A friend might be good about now," he said. "I know Sadie, or any of the women in that very close-knit group, would want to be here for you."

"It's fine, I'm fine. Someone just needed cash and food, and got sloppy. It's all cleaned up, no need to bother anyone about it."

He disagreed, but he knew enough about her already to know that pushing her into doing something she didn't want to do would only make her close off further. "Come on, you look done in. I'll walk you to your car."

She shook her head.

"You don't have a car," he said.

"I have a taco truck."

He smiled. "For which I'm incredibly grateful, since your food's amazing. How did you get here?"

"Lyft." She pulled out her phone but he covered her hand with his. "I'll drive you."

She looked at him for a long beat, her hood up now, covering her gorgeous hair, her face not quite as pale, those eyes seeming to see right into him. Finally, she nodded, and he had no idea why he felt as if he'd just won the lottery.

Chapter 4

Rise up and take the challenge . . .

Kel led Ivy to his truck, where he held open the door for her, waiting until she'd buckled up. When he walked around the front of the vehicle and slid behind the wheel a moment later, he felt the weight of her gaze. "Something on your mind?" he asked.

"Who taught you to be so polite?"

He laughed. He couldn't help it. His grandma would be laughing her ass off right now as well.

"Is something funny?" she asked a little stiffly. "And I take it back, by the way. You're not so polite at all."

"My grandparents practically had to beat manners into me," he said. "They'd be very amused to hear you say you think I'm polite."

"Your grandparents?" she asked. "Not your parents?"

"My dad died when I was twelve. My sister and I were sent to Idaho to be raised by our grandparents. They're both gone now."

Her smile faded. "I'm sorry. What about your mom?"

He concentrated on the road as he pulled into the street. "Where's your place?"

"The Tenderloin," she said, and gave him the address. "Are you not answering about your mom on purpose?"

"Yes."

She smiled at that, and he relaxed. "I like it when you do that," he said.

"What?"

"Smile."

She rolled her eyes and looked out the window.

They didn't speak again, just drove through the city lit within an inch of its life for the holidays with festive garlands and twinkling lights on every block.

Then the neighborhood changed. The decorations vanished, as did pride of ownership, each street more run down than the last.

Ivy had him stop at a very old, possibly falling off its axis Victorian that had seen better days—like five decades ago. It'd clearly been broken up into a few apartments, one per floor. He counted three floors, and what was possibly an attic. He didn't like the street and layout, and he especially didn't like the bushes and shrubbery that were overgrown and too close to the house. The ground floor was a security nightmare. Someone could climb into any window virtually undetected. The top floor was just as bad because there were gussets strengthening the angle of the structure that could easily be used to climb like a ladder up the corner of the place. "Tell me you don't live on the first or the top floor."

"I don't live on the first level."

He looked at her.

"But I do live on the top floor. It's the attic."

Shit.

Ivy unhooked her seatbelt. "Thanks for the help." She turned to him and in the soft ambient light looked at him. Like really looked at him, as if maybe she was seeing him for the first time.

"How did you know anything was wrong?" he asked. "How did you know to show up at the truck?"

"Instinct," she said. "Just a feeling, I guess." She held his gaze. "And now the same question to you. How did you know anything was wrong?"

"I heard you cry out."

She cocked her head, eyeing him like he was a puzzle and she was missing some pieces. "Most people would've run the other way, but you ran toward what could've been a dangerous situation."

"I'm the law."

Something flickered in her gaze at that. She didn't like that he was a cop. "The law can be dirty," she said.

As he well knew, but he wasn't going there. Instead, he let a teasing smile come into his voice. "True. And I can be *very* dirty, but only when I'm off duty, and only if you ask real nice."

She laughed out loud at that, the sound both soft and musical. "Okay, I'll give this to you—you're funny. And maybe also sexy as hell, but this isn't happening, Cowboy."

He'd take *sexy as hell* any day of the week. "We're just talking."

"Uh-huh," she said dryly. "But when men talk, they think they're flirting, and to them flirting leads to everything else, which is always a disappointment. And if I wanted to be disappointed, I'd just go inside and stream *The Bachelor*."

"How do you know I'd disappoint?"

"You're a man, aren't you?"

He slid her a look. "Coloring all of us with the same pen then?"

She shrugged and slipped out of his truck. He got out too, and there on the sidewalk, she put a hand to his chest. "You're not coming up until I invite you."

He liked the promise of "until," but he left it alone for now. "I'm not coming *in* unless you invite me," he clarified, extremely aware of the fact that even as they stood there, they were being watched by two homeless people sitting under a tree, a man smoking on the driveway next door, and two guys loitering at the corner. "But I *am* going to walk you to your door," he said firmly.

He waited for her response, still keeping vigilant on their peripheral audience. Even twenty years ago when he'd last been familiar with the city, this neighborhood was known for bad news and he liked to be ready for the worst.

Ivy tilted her head as she studied him. "You're different."

"Now you're getting it." He took her hand. "Come on."

They passed the tree, under which were two women, each huddled beneath a pile of dirty blankets.

"Hey, girl," one of them said.

Ivy smiled. "Hey, Jasmine. Too cold to work?"

"My corner flooded, thanks to a broken hydrant."

"Sucks," Ivy said. "Hey, Martina. Bad week?"

Martina uncovered her head and nodded.

Ivy handed over something from inside her big purse. It was some food from her truck that hadn't spoiled, but couldn't be served because she didn't know if it'd been handled.

"Thanks," Martina said. "Can Marietta still hang with you tomorrow afternoon?"

"Of course," Ivy said and led Kel up the steps to the building.

"Who's Marietta?" he asked.

"Martina's daughter. Martina's bipolar and schizo-phrenic. She lives at home with her elderly mom and her fourteen-year-old daughter, but sometimes when she goes off the meds, she goes to the streets."

"Isn't her daughter old enough to stay alone?"

"Yeah, but I'd have killed for a safe place to stay when I was fourteen," she said. "Plus, she's having trouble with math class and it's my strong suit. Not to mention, I've got heat and Netflix." She unlocked the front door, which led to a hallway and a set of stairs. The hallway had fake, cheesy holly strung along the walls, held there by duct tape. There were lights too, but they weren't working.

At least someone had tried.

They began climbing, with Kel eyeing Ivy with a newfound respect. He was getting an idea as to what her childhood had been like and why she wore an armor of toughness, but it seemed that shell of hers hid a tender heart.

The second floor landing had even more holiday decorations and he took a moment to admire the re-sourcefulness of someone who'd stacked Heineken beer cans—green and white—to make small Christmas trees.

"Why are you doing this?" Ivy asked as they kept climbing, sounding genuinely confused.

"Someone broke into your place of business. Maybe they hit your home too."

"I told you, it was random. Someone just needing food and money."

"Probably," he agreed as they came to the next set of stairs. She took off her hoodie and for a moment gave him a glorious view as he walked behind her on the steps. But then she tied the sweatshirt around her waist, once again covering a fantastic ass that had been perfectly showcased in her leggings. But now she wore only a tank top and that was nice too. "I just want to make sure you get home safe. Is that so odd?"

She didn't answer.

Which was an answer in itself. In her world, it *was* odd.

They hit the third floor landing. No holiday decorations here at all. The next set of stairs narrowed and steepened. At the top, there was a single door, and they had to stand very close together as Ivy unlocked it. Close enough that he caught the scent of her shampoo and the fact that she had a tiny, dainty tattoo scripted on the back of her right shoulder— *this too shall pass . . .*

Ivy turned on a light. Kel poked his head in and took a quick glance around to make sure it was all clear. The open loft could be seen all in one glimpse. The steep pitch of the roof meant slanted walls, which limited much of her space, but open rafters allowed for a large fan to drop down and stir the air. The wood floors were scarred and scuffed, and dotted with throw rugs. Furniture was sparse. A small couch and coffee table, a nook in the small kitchenette with a couple of barstools, and a four poster bed in the far corner, covered with a thick quilt and what appeared to be at least a million pillows. All of it looked like it belonged in another time period.

She shrugged. "The price is right."

His gaze slid to hers. "I wasn't judging you."

"BS."

"Okay, so I was judging all the pillows. How do you sleep with that many?"

She laughed, that same sweet, infectious sound from earlier, but she didn't respond, just shook her head. And remained firmly in her doorway, clearly blocking him from coming in any further.

Yeah. Serious trust issues.

"Can I see your phone?" he asked.

She narrowed her eyes. "Why?"

Afraid she wouldn't give it to him if he told her he wanted to enter his number in, he just wriggled his fingers in a "gimme" gesture.

She shook her head, but fished the phone out of her pocket.

"Unlock it?"

"Alright," she said, "but just so you're aware, that's *not* where I keep the nudes."

He smiled and thumbed his contact information into her phone.

"You really think I'm going to call you?" she asked, amused.

"If you have any more problems, I hope you will." He held out her phone. She reached for it, but he held firm for a second as their gazes met and held. "Ivy."

She stared at him, then lifted a shoulder. *Maybe,* the gesture said. Which was the best he was going to get.

Then, still maintaining the eye contact, she took her phone, retreated a step, and slowly shut her door in his face.

He stared at the wood, thinking she was possibly the most fascinating and frustrating woman he'd ever met.

"Why are you still standing there?" came her voice from the other side of the door.

"I'm waiting for you to lock the door and slide on your security chain," he said.

There was a beat of silence during which he imagined her prickly pride at being told what to do was warring with her common sense. But then came the sound of the lock and the chain sliding into place.

"Night, Trouble," he said, and then he had no choice but to walk away.

Chapter 5

Less chitchatting, more ass-kicking!

At five thirty in the morning, Ivy was flat on her back on the mats. With a groan, she rolled to her knees and got back up. She was in kickboxing class with her friends Tae, Abi, and Haley, and they were all lined up facing a row of punching bags.

Ivy's had punched back.

Sort of the theme of her life.

"Dig deep!" her instructor yelled.

"I'd like to go deep," Haley whispered on Ivy's left. Haley was an optometrist who worked on the second floor of the Pacific Pier Building. "*Deep* back into my bed."

"Less chitchatting, ladies, and more ass-kicking! If you never change, you'll never change!"

Ivy glanced at their personal trainer. Tina was

dark-skinned, dark-eyed, and thanks to sneakers with a three-inch rubber-soled heels and black braids piled into a mountain on top of her head, she was also well over six feet tall. Tina's day job was running the coffee shop at the Pacific Pier Building, and in the coffee shop she was all sweet and kind.

In the gym, she was a tyrannical drill sergeant.

Ivy turned to Tae, who was Jake's sister and a mathematical wizard and insurance adjuster. "I thought she'd be as gentle here as she is at her coffee shop."

Tae laughed. "She's about as gentle as my brother. And they both learned it in the same place—the military."

"That's right, sweet cakes," Tina said. "Don't be fooled by this gorg hair and figure. Back when I was Tim and right out of the army, I was a middleweight champion."

"Wow." Haley looked impressed. "So you kick ass for real, not just for show."

"Nah." Tina smiled. "I like my face too much now. So class it is. But there's something immensely satisfying about kicking the shit out of a bag, isn't there?"

"*Yes,*" Ivy agreed. If there was one thing she liked about getting up early and having to exercise, it was the satisfaction of beating the shit out of a bag.

"Then let's get serious," Tina said. "Come on, ladies. This isn't elementary school and you're not on recess. Look at Abi, she's brand spanking new here and she's kicking your asses."

Everyone looked at Abi, who ran the wedding shop in the Pacific Pier Building. She always looked perfectly together, but at the moment, she was drenched in sweat and breathing like she'd just run a 5K. But she waved cheerfully at everyone, looking like she was having the time of her life.

Ivy sighed.

"You're on Tina Time, ladies," Tina barked. "So start moving." She was hands on hips, back to serious tyrannical taskmaster.

And let's face it, Ivy needed a taskmaster.

"I want to see you go at it like you're eighteen again!" Tina yelled.

"I was stupid at eighteen," Ivy muttered.

"Hey," Tae said breathlessly. "If you can't look back on your younger self and say wow, I used to be stupid, you're probably *still* stupid."

"More energy!" Tina yelled. "Again! One-two punch, jab, cross, and then a big front kick!"

Ivy repeated the routine to herself as she went through the motions, her limbs liquefying.

"We're targeting your shoulders, triceps, and core, as well as the quads and glutes," Tina said. "You ladies want nice asses, right? Go hard or don't go at all!"

"Going hard isn't always what it's cracked up to

be," Tae managed to gasp out breathlessly, sagging against her bag, hugging it in order to stay upright. "I'm whupped."

"Leave it all in the room, ladies!"

Haley sighed. "I always do," she muttered. "Not that it's getting me anywhere."

"You gotta rise up and take the challenge, don't hide!"

Ivy managed to keep up with the nonstop punching and kicking to the rhythmic beat, barely, but she was with Haley. She'd rather be back in bed.

When the torture—er, class—ended, they all crawled out of the gym whimpering and sweating. Ivy hit the showers, dressed, and had to run to catch the bus. Sagging back on her seat, she took a moment to close her eyes. She was exhausted from too little sleep and spending much of the few precious hours she'd had staring up at the rafters and the ancient old fan that hung from them, slowly whirling round and round.

Worrying. Stressing . . .

Yes, she played at being the tough girl on the block, but the truth—her truth—was that she was really a big fat chicken. So the knowledge that someone had helped themselves into her truck, the one she'd worked her fingers to the bone for, the one she'd bled for, heart and soul, killed her. It was *her* personal space, the first she'd ever had, and she felt incredibly proud of it.

And yet someone had broken into it like it was nothing, destroying her door, a whole bunch of food, and stealing her hard earned cash.

And more . . .

She closed her eyes on that thought and shook her head, knowing it was far more than that. She'd played it off to Kel like it was no big deal because she didn't need his help, didn't need *anyone's* help, but it *was* a big deal to her. From a lifetime of living where creaks in the night meant something bad, she'd always had a hard time falling asleep. Living in San Francisco the past year in one spot, the *same* spot, even with the rough neighborhood outside, she'd somehow started to believe she was safe.

But she was *never* safe, and she was far too alone. And last night had seriously shaken her sense of privacy and security and safety. Except . . .

She hadn't been alone.

Kel had stood there in the opened truck door, gun drawn, eyes cool, calm, and sharp.

Shock had been Ivy's first emotion, and right on the heels of that had come a different emotion altogether.

She still wasn't ready to put a name to it, but she did know one thing. With a panic attack looming and a helpless rage making her shake, she'd felt backed into a corner and she'd never been good at that. So of course, she'd reacted predictably, which meant she'd been cold and rude.

He hadn't deserved it. Not when he'd gone over and beyond, helping her clean up. The image of him at two in the morning, on his knees wearing pink latex gloves, helping her scrub the truck floor like it was the most important task in the world brought a reluctant smile.

With a sigh, she got off the bus two stops early to hit the market, and grabbed some fresh supplies to replace what she'd lost, along with some extras that she had plans to use to apologize to Kel with. Then she walked to her truck, shivering in the morning chill. She'd always thought California was the land of the eternal warm sunshine, but whoever had coined that phrase had never been to San Francisco in December.

Inside her truck, she left the CLOSED UNTIL LUNCH sign in place and took a quick moment to access her bank app. She robbed her savings account to cover the unexpected costs of restocking for the week, then got to work.

Last night she and Kel had disinfected everything, but she was obsessive about the kitchen and needed to put her stamp on it all. So she filled her extra-deep sink with hot water, and added in some of the gentle cleanser she used to clean the expensive copper pots and pans that she'd spent more money on than her clothes with no regrets.

When she'd finished, she put everything back in

its place and cleaned and dried the sink. Then she pulled all her ingredients down from their various shelves. She'd organized everything perfectly and could find anything in seconds. She knew what she had at all times, which was how she'd been able to tell so quickly what had been taken last night.

And in spite of what she'd let Kel think, it hadn't been just food and her petty cash.

Beneath the petty cash box had been another box, filled with a few things that represented the only happy spots in an otherwise terrible childhood. A postcard of the Golden Gate Bridge framed by the California hills and the azure blue of the bay. She had no idea where she'd gotten it, but she'd had it for years and years, and was a big part of the reason that when she'd decided to settle somewhere, she'd landed here.

She also had a picture of her mom on a stage at a piano, singing with a melancholy look on her face that made Ivy ache, though she had no idea why. She'd rarely seen that soft side of her mom.

The third and last pic she had was of her and her aunt Cathy, her mother's sister, at a state fair. Ivy had been five, her hair rioting in wild red waves around her face. Her *smiling* face, because she'd been in Cathy's arms in front of a Ferris wheel. Cathy, the only true mother figure Ivy had ever had, had died from cancer the year after the photo had been taken.

She didn't remember a whole lot of that time, but she could still remember Cathy always telling her:

Be smart.

Be brave.

Be vulnerable.

Her heart pinched at the memories. She'd hopefully done the smart and brave parts, but she'd actively done her best to never be vulnerable. She figured Cathy would understand.

There were also a few trinkets: a teeny little notebook she'd used as a journal for a few years. A Beanie Babies bear dressed as a chef, given to her at her first cooking job by her boss, one of the few positive male role models she'd had up until that point. She'd been fifteen. Of course, he'd thought she was eighteen, but that was the story of her life. Pretending to be what she wasn't in order to get what she needed.

The last thing in the box had been a gold and diamond necklace, the one she'd taken with her when she'd run away from home. It'd been given to her by her aunt Cathy who'd worn it every day of her life. About six months before her death, she'd carefully coiled it up and put it into Ivy's palm. "For when you need me," she'd said quietly.

It'd been years after her death before Ivy had understood what her aunt had meant. The necklace had turned out to hold not just sentimental value, but was worth several thousand dollars. Aunt Cathy had known that if Ivy ever needed money fast, she could sell it.

She'd been wearing it until recently, when the clasp had broken when she'd been at work. She'd been meaning to bring it home, but it'd slipped her mind. And now it was gone.

And she hadn't told Kel. She didn't know why.

Okay, she did know why. Because although it could've been just a random thief who'd stumbled upon it, she wasn't feeling that explanation. Nothing was ever that simple, at least not in her life. In her mind, there was only one person on the planet who'd known she had that necklace.

Her brother.

She had no idea what that meant. Had Brandon found her? And if he had . . . what did he want?

She got out the utensils and cooking implements she needed and then quickly started measuring and mixing dry ingredients. She preheated a pan, added the wet ingredients into the dry, mixed everything, and then gently folded in fresh blueberries.

While the pancakes cooked, she put everything meticulously away and got out some eggs and a thick slice of ham. She preheated another pan and flipped the pancakes. Cracking the eggs in a perfect break—so satisfying—she put them in next to the ham that was almost hot all the way through. She slid the pancakes onto a plate. Toast went down.

Then she slid the eggs and ham onto another plate. Turned the pancakes, buttered the bread, and quickly and efficiently cleaned up after herself before packing the prepped food up in a special to-go protective container, slinging the strap over her shoulder.

She opened the back door and found several people standing there waiting, most of them her regulars. "I'm so sorry, I'm closed until eleven," she said, pointing to the sign.

"But you're making bacon," Sadie said. "I could smell it across the courtyard. I'd kill for bacon."

At Sadie's side, Haley and Tae both nodded.

"We earned bacon this morning at the gym," Tae said.

"I earned bacon in a much more satisfying way," Sadie said with a smile.

Sadie was possibly the only person Ivy had ever wanted to be her best friend. She'd never really had one, so she wasn't quite sure. But she imagined that Sadie would be a perfect BFF. She was a tattoo artist at the Canvas Shop, the tattoo parlor on the other side of the courtyard, and was no-holds-barred, tough in her own right. She was kind, but she was also a sarcastic smartass, which Ivy related to on a core level.

"I'm sorry," she told them. "But the truck was broken into last night and—"

They gasped in tandem and Ivy shook her head,

holding up a hand, which didn't stop them from all talking at once.

"Was anything taken?"

"Are you okay?"

"What can we do?"

"I'm fine, it's all fine," Ivy said, admittedly a little surprised and also warmed by their obvious concern. "They got some petty cash, but the fridge was left open and a bunch of the food spoiled. That's why I'm closed this morning."

Sadie reached out and took her hand. "I'm so sorry. You're really okay?"

"Yes. I wasn't here when it happened."

"That doesn't mean you can't be freaked out," Haley said, pushing her red-framed glasses farther up on her face, looking like the cutest little book-worm worrywart Ivy had ever seen. "I was robbed once, and even though it was my ex-girlfriend, it was still terrifying."

"Need some cleanup assistance?" Tae asked, always the efficient, calm one.

"I've got it handled, but thanks." The genuine out-rage on their faces, along with the empathy, was new for Ivy, and she wasn't quite sure what to do with it all or how to respond. And they did seem to need a response. "Thank you," she tried, relieved when they all nodded. "But it's really okay. Kel helped me clean up the mess."

The three women's necks swiveled sharply as they looked at each other and then back at Ivy.

"Kel?" Sadie asked. "Caleb's sexy cousin Kel?"

"He is sexy," Haley said. "I mean, men aren't my thing, but if they were . . ."

"He was walking across the courtyard yesterday," Sadie said. "And I saw a woman walk right into one of the lampposts when he smiled at her."

"What is it about a cowboy, I wonder," Tae mused.

"Everything," Sadie said and everyone looked at Ivy expectantly.

"Hey, I'm off men," she said.

"Forever?" Haley asked. "And what about women?"

"For the foreseeable future, and yes, women too," Ivy said. "And anyway, you deserve someone who isn't as colossally messed up as I am."

"Apparently, I'm attracted to messed up," Haley said morosely.

"It's not your fault girls are crazy," Sadie said.

Tae laughed. "Someone once gave me some good relationship advice," Tae said. "Make sure *you're* the crazy one."

"Ha," Haley said. "And done."

"Is that why you're not in a relationship?" Sadie asked Tae.

"I'm not in a relationship because both Liam and Chris Hemsworth are taken."

They all smiled at the truth of that, but Ivy had sat

next to Tae at the pub a few times. She knew Tae had recently come out of a really bad relationship, but in what way exactly, she wasn't sure. What she was sure of was that Tae was most definitely haunted by it.

And skittish.

Something Ivy understood at a core level, which made her incredibly sympathetic to what she suspected Tae was feeling about allowing anyone to get close ever again. Ivy wasn't opposed to an actual relationship instead of a quickie. In theory anyway. But in reality, she didn't know the first thing about what a relationship might entail or demand from her. She suspected it might be things she couldn't provide, like pure honesty, transparency, and the like.

"I just haven't found what I'm looking for," Tae told Sadie.

"And what's that?"

"I don't know." Tae shrugged. "Maybe warm brown eyes, messy hair, cute nose, and four paws." She smiled. "A golden retriever would be perfect."

They all laughed and Ivy hitched the food pack higher on her shoulder. "I'm sorry about breakfast. I'll make it up to you guys at lunch, okay? But I've got to go."

"Don't forget tomorrow night's full moon midnight hike," Sadie said. "Elle sent out a group text yesterday to everyone."

Elle was the building manager, and she took her

duties very seriously, organizing social events for the group of them that either lived or worked in the building. Ivy had gone to a few, but usually begged off, feeling like the odd man out because everyone was so tight with one another, and she was the new kid on the block.

Okay, not new, not exactly. She'd been there a year. And though Tae was Jake's sister, she'd only recently come back to town, which technically made her newer than Ivy. But Tae had a natural way with people and she'd fit seamlessly in.

Ivy had never fit seamlessly into anything, including her own skin.

"Did you not get the text?" Haley asked Ivy.

She'd gotten the text, but she'd ignored it, thinking Elle probably automatically included everyone to be polite.

"Please come," Haley said. "You're usually too busy, but we'd so love to have you."

"I thought maybe the text was just for the core group of you."

"Of which you're a part," Sadie said so easily that Ivy knew she meant it. "So say you'll be there."

Surprised and touched that it mattered whether she went or not, Ivy found herself nodding, even though she wasn't 100 percent sold on it. "I'll try."

It was still early by the time she got to Caleb's newly renovated condo building in North Beach. She'd been there before, a couple of times now, walking through with Caleb, Sadie, and Keane Winters, the general contractor in charge of the project.

Ivy's condo wasn't a corner unit, or on the penthouse floor, or anything that stood out at all, and that was what she loved about it.

That, and the fact that it would be all hers.

She walked through the underground parking garage to the security office and found Kel there with a few other people, all standing around a table with a bunch of blueprints spread out before them.

Kel introduced her to the room; Keane, Carly, and Roberto—both supervisors on Keane's renovation team—and then Arlo and Stretch, who worked under Kel as building security.

Ivy smiled and made nice, but she couldn't concentrate on anything but Kel, feeling the weight of his gaze. Unable to resist, she turned to him and felt her pulse kick.

Ridiculous.

He was dressed as always, in rugged and well-worn jeans, work boots, a T-shirt with an unbuttoned shirt over the top of it, and a ball cap worn backward. Casual clothes, but there was nothing casual about the lean, hard body hinted at beneath those clothes, or, for that matter, the man himself.

And then there was how he moved with the careless grace of an athlete, his body suggesting it could handle just about anything thrown at it.

He smiled and she felt a kick in the gut—a fact that told her two things. One, she was still stupid when it came to men. And two, he was going to be trouble for both her peace of mind and her heart.

Big trouble.

Chapter 6

The range makes the change

"Hey," Ivy said to the room, sounding annoyingly breathless even to herself. And who was she kidding, she wasn't talking to the room, she was talking to Kel, who couldn't look any finer. "I don't want to interrupt, but I . . . brought you something."

Kel turned to the others. "Give us a minute."

It wasn't a question, and the sound of authority in his tone was unmistakable. If she'd been one of the guys, she might have given him a smartass salute, or at the very least rolled her eyes on principal, but none of these people did that. They respectfully filed out and left them alone.

Kel was watching her with a small smile curving his mouth. That was the thing about him. He was never in a hurry. He went at his own pace, and with slow, easy purpose. In direct opposition to that, she was always in a rush to get anywhere. She wondered if he was like that in bed as well and then pictured him doing just that, moving over her with slow, purposeful intensity while she writhed in pleasure—

"Earth to Trouble," Kel said.

She actually jumped. And blushed. *Blushed.* Unbelievable, but she definitely felt the heat of it flash across her face. And once that happened, once she was aware that her cheeks were on fire, they got even worse.

He chuckled softly.

"Not helping," she said, putting her palms to her fiery cheeks.

"I'd pay big bucks to know what you were just thinking."

"Nothing! I'm thinking nothing!"

He grinned. "You're pretty cute when you're embarrassed."

No one had ever called her cute, not once in her life. Feral, yes. Untamable, also yes. Cute? No . . . She closed her eyes. "I don't get embarrassed."

He leaned in and put his mouth to her ear. "Then you're . . . aroused."

"Oh my God. I need you to stop talking for a minute."

Still smiling, he slid his hands into his front pockets and rocked back on his heels.

"And stop smiling," she added.

He clearly gave it a shot, but the smile was there lurking in his dark eyes, and she sighed. "Never mind! Are you hungry?"

"Always."

At the low timbre of his voice and the heat to go with it in those eyes now, parts of her quivered. Parts of her that had no business quivering. "For food," she clarified. "Are you hungry for food?"

"That too."

Oh good God. He was unrepentant, and she couldn't say it wasn't one of the sexiest things about him, because it was. Ignoring the flutters in her belly, she slipped the bag off her shoulder and handed it to him.

He held her gaze for a long beat before taking the bag and unzipping it, finding the dishes she'd put together for him. "Not tacos," he said in surprise.

"Making tacos is my job," she said. "This was for something else."

"And what's that?"

"An apology for being . . . grumpy last night."

"You weren't."

She gave him a *get real* look and he smiled. "Okay, maybe a little. But it was understandable. You'd just gotten an unfortunate and unfair surprise." He gently tilted her face up to his. "You doing okay this morning?"

"Yes," she said. "Of course."

"Of course," he repeated and shook his head. "Smart, tough, *and* resilient," he murmured, his gaze on her face.

Now it was her turn to smile. "Some might say stubborn, impulsive, and doesn't know when to quit."

"Yeah," he said. "But I find those things very attractive."

Honestly, she didn't know how to take half the things he said. They made her feel both terrified and exhilarated at the same time. "You're a strange man."

"So I've been told." He looked over the food. "You poison any of it?"

"No, but only because I'd never waste food." To prove it, she grabbed the fork she'd packed and took a bite of her eggs. "Mmm," she moaned before she could stop herself, but hey, she'd worked out and been on the move ever since, and she was starving. Plus, she made damn good eggs if she said so herself.

Again their eyes met, and that now familiar spark went right through her. She wanted him. Quite badly, if her racing pulse meant anything. He was so . . . *what*, exactly? Steady? Tough? Intense and yet somehow easygoing, not to mention also extremely easy on the eyes?

"You didn't have to cook something special for me," he said, sounding touched.

"You helped me last night. I repay my debts."

"I didn't do it so you'd feel indebted to me," he said and cocked his head as he studied her for a beat. "Someday you're going to have to tell me about the apparent assholes who've been in your life to make you so wary of me."

"Oh, don't flatter yourself. It's not just you. And it wasn't just me paying back a debt," she admitted. "I wanted to cook for you." And because that made his smile warm, which in turn made something inside her warm as well, she shrugged and backed up a few steps, needing breathing room. "I also wanted to thank you for your help," she said, feeling annoyingly awkward as he shoved stacks of plans to one side of the table and started pulling everything else out of her bag with a deep male hum of pleasure when he caught sight of the pancakes.

"Are those blueberry?" he asked very seriously.

She nodded.

"Fair warning, if they're as good as the eggs, I really am going to drop to my knees and ask you to marry me."

That startled a laugh out of her. "Fair warning, if you drop to your knees, I'm going to use my considerable kickboxing skills on you."

"Scared of marriage?" he asked.

She shrugged that off. "I'm not scared of much."

"Everyone's scared of something, Trouble."

"Is that right?" She cocked her head. "Then what are you afraid of?"

His eyes shuttered and he diverted his attention to how he was carefully buttering his pancakes, like it was a very important job. "Lies."

That had her silent for a beat. "You've been burned."

"I have." He drowned the pancakes in syrup and dug in. With a passionate sigh, he closed his eyes. "Oh my God."

Good Lord, watching him eat was turning her on. "Good?"

Not opening his eyes, he shook his head and chewed, his expression saying he was in heaven. "I can't talk right now. I'm having a sexual experience all by myself, just me and these pancakes."

She laughed. "Take your time. Like I said, I just wanted to thank you."

He took several more bites before saying anything more. "You thanked me last night," he said.

"Yes, but I thought I'd try again without being a jerk."

"Ivy. You weren't."

She gave him a long look.

"You were unnerved and maybe a little bit frightened," he said softly. "Definitely not a jerk." He kicked a chair away from the table, and then another, sitting in one and gesturing for her to sit in the other.

"Oh, I'm not staying."

"Sit," he said. "Please?"

Apparently she was a sucker for the *please*, because she sat and together they mowed their way through the food. "Amazing," he said on a moan, eating with the same laid-back easiness he did everything else. "Been a long time since someone cooked for me."

"No girlfriend?"

"Been a long time for that too."

She smiled. "You expect me to believe a guy like you is celibate?"

"I didn't say celibate."

He laughed when she rolled her eyes. Okay, so he was seeing people. And why wouldn't he be? Look at him.

"What did you mean, a guy like me?" he wanted to know.

She snorted. "Not touching that one, cowboy."

He smiled, but it faded. "I'm not a good bet," he finally said, answering her "no girlfriend" question. "Always on call, and the job comes first. Apparently, that's annoying and frustrating, and I get it. My life hasn't exactly lent itself to relationships."

Made sense. Up until this year, her life hadn't lent itself to relationships either. It made her wonder if he ever felt the same loneliness she did, and if so, maybe she'd invite him along to the hike tonight.

No, that made no sense at all. After all, she was changing her life, settling down . . . and he wasn't.

In fact, he was temporary here, very temporary, and he'd just admitted he wasn't relationship material. "There's a midnight full moon hike tomorrow," she heard herself say. Apparently her mouth wasn't taking direction from her brain.

His eyes cut to hers. "Yeah?"

"Yeah."

He just held her gaze.

He was going to make her ask him. "Do you want to go?" she asked.

"With you?"

She narrowed her eyes, her "never mind!" on the tip of her tongue, but she caught the glint of humor in his eyes and realized he was teasing her. "No," she said. "With Santa Claus."

He laughed, and . . . still didn't answer.

"You know what? Forget it." She stood to gather the plates. "It was a dumb idea."

He put his hands over hers to stop her and then took over the job of repacking everything up, doing it with greater efficiency than she could've managed. "I'd like to go," he said. "Thanks for thinking of me."

Good thing he wasn't a mind reader or he'd know just how much she'd been thinking of him.

Reaching for her hands again, he drew her closer and bent his knees a little so he could look right into her eyes. "And thanks for breakfast."

She nodded and then licked her suddenly dry lips,

which were shockingly close to his. At the movement, his gaze dropped to her mouth. And like magic, hers trembled open.

That's when someone cleared their throat from the doorway.

Caleb.

Ivy yanked her hands from Kel's and grabbed her bag, flinging it over her shoulder. "I was just leaving."

Caleb didn't move from the doorway. Instead, he divided a gaze between the two of them. "Interesting."

"Nope," Ivy said, lips still tingling from the near kiss that she'd wanted shockingly badly. "Nothing interesting to see here."

Caleb, eyes on his cousin, just grinned. "Uh-huh."

Kel didn't grin back, or react at all. Nope, the cowboy was calm and stoic, giving nothing away. Apparently they taught 'em well in Idaho.

"Thought we decided you should go see your sister and your new baby niece tonight," Caleb said. "Or your mom."

"Thought we decided you were staying the hell out of it," Kel replied.

"Fine." Caleb lifted his hands. "Staying out of it."

"If only I could believe that," Kel said.

The banter was light. There was an ease to their interactions that spoke of a very long and very close relationship.

Ivy both envied that and felt the need to run far

and fast. Because she didn't have that kind of easy affection with . . . anyone.

Although in the deep, dark of the night when they'd been in the small space of her truck, side by side in the mess, working together in a way that had seemed shockingly intimate . . . that had felt very intimate.

And so did right now in an office where they weren't even alone.

Scary stuff. Really scary. So much so that she could feel a mini freak-out coming on. She was good at that, very good. So while Kel and Caleb were still exchanging barbs in the way that only men seemed to be able to do without getting their feelings hurt, she made her escape.

See, look at that. Something else she was good at.

Chapter 7

I promised sweat, let's see it

The next morning Kel ran with Caleb and Jake while it was still dark outside. *And* drizzling. His body felt less achy about it though, which was a good thing. He wasn't fond of running, or early mornings, but Caleb was.

His cousin was a nut. So was Jake, who raced alongside of them in his wheelchair, arms pumping.

It was possible Kel was just tired. He'd been restless the night before and had gone for a drive. He'd thought about going to Ivy, but after the way she'd abruptly left his office that morning, he knew she needed space.

Or maybe that was him.

He wasn't sure. But he did know that right before she'd left, she'd flashed a vulnerability, like she was surprised to find that she liked him.

Too much.

He recognized it only because it was the exact same for him. Which meant they were at a bit of an impasse. Maybe with a little distance, they'd both come to realize it was just physical attraction. They could explore that—in great detail, he hoped—and then when he left, there'd be no bad feelings.

So he'd driven up to Sonoma to visit an old friend. He'd gone to middle school with Donovan, and even back then, the guy had always wanted to move outside the city and have a horse ranch. He'd recently bought property, and when Kel got there and rode around with him over his hundred acres, he got it. The rolling hills were rich and lush and gorgeous, but more than that it was about being on the land with the horses. There was a peace to it that was missing from his life. They'd stayed up late talking about old times, and Kel'd had a hell of a time getting out of bed at the butt crack of dawn.

Caleb hadn't had a single ounce of sympathy, dragging Kel's half-dead body out anyway. "Thought you were a country boy. Country boys are hardy," he said, pushing Kel hard.

Kel'd had just enough spare energy to flip him off. But it was his own fault. He'd not told Caleb, or any of his family, how badly he'd been injured.

"So," Caleb said casually. "What's going on with you and Ivy?"

Kel nearly tripped over his own feet. "Nothing."

"Is that because you think you're relationship jinxed, or because she's not interested in you?"

Oh, there was interest. Lots of it. And that wasn't ego. It was fact, and it went both ways, and it was seductive and hot as hell.

And just a little terrifying. "You know my job gets in the way of my personal life," he said.

"It's not your job," Caleb said. "It's you."

His sister, Remy, had said that to him on numerous occasions. So had the last two women in his life. It rang in his head more than it should. *It's you . . .*

He'd ignored all of it.

"Ivy's a five-foot-two-inch dynamo of a cook with a personality much bigger than her petite frame," Caleb said, not struggling to breathe and run and talk at the same time, the bastard. "And she's one of the rare good ones."

"I know."

"She's independent, savvy, fearless, creative, street smart, and has some serious authority issues."

Kel snorted at the truth of all of that.

"You can count on her to give it to you straight up."

Kel thought maybe this wasn't necessarily true. He saw Ivy slightly different. He believed she was a chameleon, and good at figuring out what people wanted to hear.

Which meant he wasn't 100 percent certain why

she appealed to him so very much. And there was appeal. So effing much appeal . . .

After the run, they stopped for breakfast tacos. It was seven straight up and there was a line at Ivy's truck, but she served quickly and efficiently, exchanging an easy banter with everyone in front of them in line.

When it was Kel's turn, she met his gaze, her own hooded.

Yeah. She didn't know how to handle this thing either.

"What'll it be, cowboy?" she asked.

Thinking he was being cute, he smiled and said, "What do you suggest?"

She rolled her eyes. "You're a glutton for punishment."

"I'm not," Jake said. "My usual, please."

Caleb nodded the same. "We need it to go, cutie, we've got a meeting." And as they stepped aside to wait, his cousin eyed Kel. "You screw things up?"

"There's nothing to screw up."

"I really thought you'd have more game than this," Jake said.

When their order came up, Ivy handed out their baskets, again serving Kel last. Their fingers brushed and she sucked in a breath.

"Thanks," he said quietly, not pulling his basket from her hand, but holding it with her, stalling . . . "How's it going?"

Their eyes met. She didn't answer, but gave him a small—and, he'd like to think, just for him—smile, before walking away.

Jake and Caleb were staring at him.

"What?" he asked.

"There was enough heat in the air between the two of you to light this whole city up in flames," Caleb said.

Jake just gave a slow nod. "Guess you do have some game after all."

Caleb's and Kel's phones both buzzed at the same time with a reminder of a meeting in thirty minutes. Their entire day was full.

The story of his life, of course. He hadn't been kidding when he'd told Ivy his life didn't lend itself to relationships. But it was the first time he'd ever *wanted* to put personal stuff ahead of work. He wanted to take the time to talk to her, and see what might happen next.

This of course led to some fairly creative fantasizing, none of which he had any business doing. Didn't stop him. And it wasn't all sexual. He thought about taking her out on the water in one of Jake's boat. Sans Jake, of course. Or walking Pier 39 and sightseeing. Or going out on the town for the night.

The entire duration of his and Caleb's meeting with the city inspectors, he nodded when necessary and spoke when he needed to, but in spite of the importance of the meeting, he'd definitely done what he'd never thought he could—relegated brain power to his personal life.

To Ivy.

He'd hoped to get some time later in the day to go talk to her, but that didn't happen. And right after work, he had something else he had to do first, something he'd put off.

He wasn't even sure why. He loved his sister. They had a good relationship. She'd been in Idaho just a few months ago and had stayed with him. Plus, he couldn't wait to see the new baby. But he knew it wasn't going to be just a catch-up visit. It wasn't going to be that simple. His sister wanted family unity, including his mom.

And Kel wasn't sure he was ready for that. Or if he ever would be. So he stood on the porch of his sister's small Victorian house in the Soma District, hands shoved in his pockets, feeling more jumpy than he'd ever felt at work in Idaho, and that was saying something.

He knocked, but he could hear a baby wailing away at high decibels inside, so he doubted anyone could hear him. But just as he lifted his hand to knock again, the door whipped open and his sister, Remy, stood there with a baby in her arms, red face and crying.

The baby, not his sister, though Remy looked like she was on her way to doing the same. "Oh, hello. Has hell frozen over?" she asked.

He grimaced. Yeah, he was really good at pissing off all the females in his life. "Sorry it took me so long."

"Harper's three months old."

"I know," he said softly. "I'm sorry. I let work rule my life and I suck." No way was he going to tell her he'd nearly ended up six feet under, especially when she looked so close to losing it. "I missed you. Can I come in?"

"I'm trying to decide," she said, her brown eyes looking suspiciously shiny, her voice hitching.

Shit. He knew what that meant. An impending storm. He slowly stepped into her, forcing her to back up a step. Shutting the door behind him and hitting the bolt, he turned and pulled Remy and the baby into him for a hug.

Remy clung for a long beat and he knew they were going to be okay. He kissed Remy on the top of her head and then nodded to the still squalling bundle. "May I?"

His sister handed the baby over, and at the exchange, the little thing hiccupped and took a shuddery breath, holding off on the sobs for a beat as she took in her new carrier. Huge drenched eyes stared up at Kel, her skin blotchy and mottled from her temper tantrum. "Hey, Harper," he said softly, staring into her sweet little face.

A face that started to scrunch up again, because

clearly the kid knew the score. He wasn't packing warm, soft curves. Or her next meal. "You're not going to cry on me, are you?" he asked. "Because you're way too special to be so worked up. In fact, I promise you right here and now, if anyone ever makes you cry, they'll answer to me."

The baby blinked, her face still half scrunched up like she couldn't decide whether to cry some more or to lay low.

"I get it," he whispered. "You don't know me. But I'm your errant uncle Kel, the one who was on a case when you decided to show up four weeks early. I'm sorry I couldn't get here until now, but I've gotta say, you are worth the wait." His chest tightened up just looking at her. "You're beautiful."

The baby cooed at him and then projectile vomited all over him. Stunned, he lifted his face to Remy's.

Who no longer looked like she was going to cry. In fact, she burst out laughing. "Welcome back."

Thirty minutes later, he was showered and sitting shirtless in Remy's kitchen while she washed his shirt. Remy's husband, Ethan, called to say he'd picked up dinner on his way home from work.

He showed up with tacos from Ivy's truck.

Kel stared at The Taco Truck bag as his sister squealed in delight and started pulling out the food with one hand, a sleeping Harper in her other arm, the baby looking sweet and innocent and not at all like the she-devil she was. "Oh my God," Remy moaned, leaning over the bag to give her husband a big fat thank-you kiss. "Kel, you've got no idea how good these tacos are. I make Ethan go miles out of his way at least once a week to bring them home. The cook's amazing."

Kel let out a low, ironic laugh. Seemed he wasn't the only member of his family Ivy had made a big impression on. "I've eaten there. And you're right, she's amazing."

And elusive.

And sassy, funny, smart, and a taker of absolutely zero bullshit.

Some of his favorite things.

Ethan snagged his wife and cuddled her into him. "How are my two babes doing today?"

"Great," Remy said. "One of us had a whole bunch of colic and gas earlier."

"Is it the one of you I sleep with?"

Remy lightly smacked Ethan's chest. "No! But then she threw up all over Kel—like seriously threw up, it was a horror flick. After that, she felt much better."

Ethan grinned at Kel. "Welcome home, man. And thanks for taking one for the team. Usually she does it to me."

"Someone could've warned me."

"I wouldn't have had to if you'd come sooner," Remy said. "You'd already know to duck."

"How long are you going to be mad at me for not coming sooner?" Kel asked. Only Caleb knew what had happened at work, minus the part about him being injured. He hadn't wanted to freak anyone out, and anyway, he was fine now.

Mostly.

"Are you going to see Mom when you're here?" Remy volleyed back.

Kel took another taco.

"Uh-huh," Remy said. "Then I'm going to stay mad until you're no longer a dumbass."

Ethan winced. "Remy—"

"Don't even try to take his side," she warned her husband. "I can only handle one stupidly stubborn male ego at a time."

"It's not about ego," Kel said.

"Fine. It's about your inability to come to terms with the fact that family forgives family. You move on from the past and accept what is."

Kel shook his head. She didn't understand. And how could she? He'd been ten years old when he'd walked in on their mom and a man in his parents' bed.

A man who hadn't been his dad.

Wanting to protect both his sister and his dad from what he'd seen, he'd kept his mom's precious secret, but watching her live a lie had scarred him as a kid.

Even more so when his dad had died of a heart

attack two years later without ever realizing his wife had betrayed and lied to him.

Worse, after they'd buried him, his mom had gone off the deep end, losing her mind with grief.

And actually, that was Kel's biggest problem. It wasn't her lies necessarily. Adult relationships were complicated and he understood that now. What he didn't understand, what he would never be able to understand, was how his mom had abandoned him and his sister in Idaho, where they'd been raised by their grandparents on their small ranch in Sunshine, a town at the base of the Bitterroot Mountains.

Back then, he'd been told his mom would come for them when she could get it together.

That had never happened.

Instead, his mom had moved on, he'd found out years later, with that same guy she'd cheated on his dad with, Henry something or another.

At the time, Kel had felt lost in his grief, which he'd had to shove deep because Remy had needed him and so had his grandparents. Being so far from home in a new place with nothing familiar around him had been hard.

He and his mom had talked about it once, years ago now, when he'd point-blank asked her why. She'd said he wouldn't understand. And she was right about that. The few times they'd seen each other since, he'd done his best to not talk to her at all.

"You think you know everything," he said to Remy. "But you don't."

"So tell me."

He couldn't do that. Remy and their mom had come to a sort of peace and had a real relationship. He wouldn't jeopardize that.

"Want to know what I think?" Remy asked.

"No."

She ignored this. "I think that you *think* you know everything, but you don't."

"Then please enlighten me," he said.

"Oh hell, no. You'll have to talk to the source for that intel," she said. "It's not my story to tell. But I can say this . . ." She paused and softened her voice. "Mom's happy, Kel. Really, truly happy. Henry's a great guy—" She broke off at the look on Kel's face and sighed.

After an awkward, tense silence, Ethan spoke. "Why do you suppose Harper never cries when we need her to?"

Remy reached for the plate of tacos. Kel ducked.

Remy rolled her eyes. "I'm not going to throw them at your stubborn face."

"Well it wouldn't be the first time."

"Whatever," Remy muttered. "I'm mature now. I've got a kid."

"Right, because you didn't throw shit at my head when you were in labor," Ethan said.

"Hey, you were eating French fries and I was starving," she pointed out. "You're lucky I didn't gnaw your arm off."

"The mother of my child," Ethan said fondly, and kissed Remy's cheek.

She shrugged. "Fine. I have my moments. But at least I know how to forgive." She sent a meaningful look in Kel's direction and then passed him the hot sauce before he asked for it because she remembered he loved hot sauce.

Apparently, he was forgiven for being a dumbass. And that was the thing with his sister. She always forgave him, no matter what. He wouldn't mind having the ability to do that. It wasn't like he wanted to be harboring resentment for their mom. Or for anyone who'd hurt him in the past. "Thanks for not throwing stuff at me," he said softly.

"I must really love your dumb ass," she replied back just as softly.

Chapter 8

*"If you don't squeeze your bum,
no one else will!"*

At midnight, Kel found himself on the moonlight hike up Lands End. He'd picked up Ivy and they went to O'Riley's pub in the Pacific Pier Building to meet the others.

Caleb introduced him to everyone by ticking off the names of his friends. "Elle, Archer, Spence, Colbie, Lucas, and Molly . . . Sadie, who you already know . . ."

Sadie, her dark hair with its purple tips, which matched her nails and lipstick, bowed with a smart-ass smile.

Caleb blew her a kiss and went on. "And Haley, and her date, Dee; and then Ivy, who you appear to know better than I thought . . ."

He rolled his eyes, but Ivy ignored Caleb's statement entirely. He figured it was her default setting, ignoring things that made her uncomfortable, and their attraction to each other definitely made her uncomfortable. He hoped to get her past that tonight.

They took three cars, and Kel landed in Caleb's vehicle along with Sadie and Ivy. Caleb drove, smiling like he knew something no one else did.

"What?" Kel asked.

"Nothing."

Bullshit it was nothing, but Kel also knew it most likely wasn't anything he wanted to discuss in front of Sadie and Ivy. When they parked, Kel pulled Ivy aside.

"Hey," he said.

"Hey."

"Everything okay?"

"Sure."

Since she was avoiding eye contact, he tilted her face up to his. "Okay, different question. Do we have a problem?"

"No."

"Ivy."

She lifted a shoulder. "We don't have a problem. You don't have a problem. *I* have a problem."

"Which is?" he asked.

"Personal."

"Personal as in there's something going on between us and you don't know what to do about it?" he asked.

She looked a little startled. "Are you always so forthright?"

"Yes."

"Hey, are you guys coming or what?" Caleb called to them from the trailhead. "Or do you need a room?"

Kel looked at Ivy. "I hope you don't mind that I'm going to have to kill him. I'm sorry for your loss."

She laughed, which made him smile.

"Zip it," she yelled back to Caleb, eyes still on Kel. "We're coming." She turned to go, but he caught her hand.

"So we're okay?" he asked.

"We're not a *we*, but yeah, we're okay."

He'd take that. For now.

Everyone hit the trail along the coastline and up to Eagle's Point Overlook. The walk was punctuated by light conversation and laughter in the way only a tight-knit group could.

Kel had spent his first twelve years in San Francisco, but his memories of the city were like having photos on shuffle in his mind, just flashes of time and place. He was pretty sure he'd been to Lands End before, but he had no specific memories of it.

That was forever changed now. He wasn't easily impressed by scenery. After all, he'd spent the past two decades in the Bitterroot Mountains, which was heaven on earth as far he was concerned. The sharp, jagged, rugged peaks with their blanket of gorgeous forestland that went on as far as the eye could see was unparalleled.

But he was surprised by what he saw. It was a mile and a half moderate hike up to Lands End and it wasn't taxing. He started to get impressed when they walked past the Sutro Baths. But then they hit the coastal cliffs and bluffs, the sweeping views of the Golden Gate Bridge under the soft glow of a full winter moon, and it was stunning.

At the top, it was even better. Apparently one didn't have to drive all the way to Big Sur to catch the gorgeous landscape of the Central Coast. Lands End offered that, along with the drama of windswept cypresses and cliff faces descending into the crashing ocean surf below.

Lucas looked at Molly. "I think we found our place."

"For what?" Sadie asked and then gasped. "To get married? You two want to get married up here?"

Molly was eyeing the view, but she nodded and sent a sweet, dreamy smile to Lucas. "Definitely."

They stood there for a while, everyone in awe of the beauty.

"We need to promise to always do this," Elle said, staring out at the view.

Her husband, Archer, slipped an arm around her. "Feeling nostalgic?"

She just smiled.

Sadie stepped in closer. "I'm with Elle. We have to keep this up. All of us." She turned and faced everyone. "I'm serious." She thrust out her pinkie finger and waited.

"You want us to pinkie promise?" Caleb asked, sounding amused.

"Yes. I want all of you to pinkie promise."

Caleb touched his pinkie finger to hers without hesitation. "You know I'm with you babe, anywhere, anytime."

She smiled goofily at him.

Elle, Archer, Spence, and Colbie added their pinkie fingers to the mix. Lucas, Molly, Haley, and Dee did the same. Kel drew a deep breath. "I don't think there's going to be another full moon before I go back to Idaho," he said. "But I'll pinkie promise to visit when I can and come along on whatever I'm here for." And with that, he touched his pinkie to the others.

The only one now not in the circle was Ivy, and everyone looked at her.

She shrugged, but remained back a step. "Sorry, I don't make promises I can't keep."

"Not a fan of midnight hikes?" Elle nodded. "No problem, we take turns deciding on our adventures. You can pick whatever you want when it's yours."

Ivy shook her head. "It's not the venue. It's the commitment."

"You don't like us enough to keep dating us?" Molly asked in a teasing tone.

"I'm not the going steady type of girl," Ivy said, teasing back, but there was something in her eyes now. She wasn't actually kidding.

"You know you fit right in with us, right?" Haley asked.

"And we all adore you," Sadie said. "And I think you adore us too. Come on, say you'll do it, babe. Say you'll date us."

Kel watched Ivy take in her friends' expressions, and he realized she was processing the fact that these women were showing that they gave a damn about her.

He wondered if she'd never really understood that until now.

"You don't get it," Ivy said. "Until this place, I've never lived anywhere for more than a few rent cycles at best. Making friends and keeping them . . . it's not my strong suit."

"That's okay," Sadie said. "It's our strong suit. We got you."

Ivy didn't look convinced and Haley took her hand. "Tell us the truth. It's because we're pushy and nosy, right?"

Ivy choked out a laugh. "I've got you all beat to hell there." She shook her head. "But fine. Whatever.

I'm in." She thrust out her pinkie and the girls all hooked theirs with hers. "To more adventures."

Kel couldn't take his eyes off her. She was smiling sweetly and openly and it was a good look on her. She wore faded jeans that fit her like a glove and a white long-sleeved tee with an army green puffy down vest and her usual work boots. She'd let her hair free and it flowed past her shoulders in thick rich red waves that he wanted to sink his fingers into.

Yeah, he was in trouble when it came to her.

They all continued walking, the girls ahead, arms linked, chatting and laughing and talking the whole way.

"Nice view," Lucas said.

"Oh yeah," Spence said.

Kel took in the row of great asses in front of them, his gaze locked on those faded jeans, and had to agree. Great view.

The night had gotten cold enough that their breath crystalized in front of their faces, but seeing wasn't a problem. The moon was a huge ball in the sky directly overhead, lighting the world in a blue glow that cast through the night and banished the shadows to the distance.

At the top, they sat at the ledge and ate the homemade cookies that Haley's date, Dee, pulled from her backpack. Dee was a waitress at O'Riley's pub, and apparently also a talented baker. "I hope no one's allergic to warm, soft chocolatey goodness," she said.

They then ate the most amazing chocolate chip cookies and watched the world go around. Or everyone else watched the world go around and Kel watched Ivy, sitting at his side. He could smell the scent of her shampoo and he kept straining to get another sniff. Their arms were touching and so were their thighs, and—

"Which constellation is that?" Molly asked, pointing up at the sky. "I recognize it from astrology, but can't remember."

No one seemed to know, and in unison, turned to Caleb.

"What?" he asked.

"You're the resident genius," Sadie reminded him. "You've got more degrees than I can count."

"Yes, but I was mostly busy studying girls."

Sadie rolled her eyes, but looked at Ivy. "Didn't you say once that your brother's an astronomy wizard?"

Ivy froze for a beat and then seemed to forcibly relax. "He's three hours ahead."

"You could just text him a pic and if he's awake, he'll solve our problem."

Ivy hesitated and then nodded, and for some reason, Kel's bullshit meter started to hum.

Ivy pulled out her phone and shifted very slightly,

just enough that, accidental or not on her part, he couldn't see her screen.

"Brandon's an astronomy wizard?" he asked casually. "I thought he was an antique dealer."

Ivy shrugged. "Astronomy is a hobby for him."

Okay, he thought. Interesting. But then he caught a quick glimpse of her phone.

She wasn't texting her brother. She was Googling constellations.

"Just sent him a text," she said lightly, still working her phone, most definitely *not* texting but scrolling through images of constellations. "He says it's . . . Orion." She slid away her phone, took a breath, and looked up. She smiled at Kel.

He managed to return it, but . . . what the hell had just happened? She'd just lied right to his face and he had zero idea how to feel about that. No. Correction. He knew *exactly* how he felt about it.

Shitty.

He stared out into the night and wondered why the hell she'd lie about her brother? And it wasn't like this was the only time either, he would swear she'd done it that first morning to Caleb. And just like then, no one else seemed to notice. How was it that he, the one who'd known her the least amount of time, was the only one who knew she was making shit up?

Turning his head, he went to look at her and found

her eyes on his. He caught a brief flash of incredible vulnerability before it was gone.

And in that quick beat, he knew. Whatever she was up to, it had nothing to do with him. Or her friends. It was about self-preservation, and damn.

He understood that.

But for the record, he still hated it.

"Last one back to the cars buys drinks," Haley said.

Dee smiled at her.

Haley blushed.

And just like that, it was a race. But Kel wasn't too surprised to find everyone else immediately slowing to a walk so they could talk on the way back down.

Not Ivy though. She was still flat-out running like demons were on her heels. Kel caught up with her and then had to laugh when her response was to speed up. Competitive to her sexy core. But it turned out laughing and running at the same time was a bitch on his still healing ribs, and at the bottom, he stopped and bent over at the knees to breathe through the pain.

Ivy made a point of touching the trailhead in victory before turning to him. Her smile faded. "You okay?"

"Just an old injury not fully healed."

"Old injury?"

"It's nothing," he said.

"So . . . I win fair and square?"

"Yeah. You win not buying everyone drinks." He laughed. They'd left everyone else way back in their dust. "I take it you like to win."

"Of course. Don't even try to tell me you don't."

"Oh, I do." He stepped closer. "I also like to know things. *All* the things."

She cocked her head. "Such as?"

"Such as why you didn't really text Brandon even though you said you did."

She was good. She didn't show any physical reaction to this. And that in itself made him feel a little sick, because she was *very* good. Which not only gave him bad flashbacks to Gina, his friend and a longtime coworker who'd betrayed him without a qualm, but also his mom.

And it made him wonder what else Ivy had lied about.

"I didn't bother texting Brandon because he never gets back to me," she finally said and leaned back against the trailhead, letting her gaze drift down to his mouth.

He had to very carefully ignore that. "It sounds like your brother's a guy of many talents."

"Mmm-hmm."

They were standing close, very close. Somehow his feet had taken him there so that they were nearly touching. Clearly his brain and body weren't in sync. His body didn't give a shit that she'd lied to him. "And how about you," he murmured, watching her eyes go to half-mast from . . . his closeness? His voice? The way their bodies were straining to touch each other? "Are you a woman of many talents as well?" he murmured.

She shrugged and then reached out to brush a fallen leaf from his shoulder. Her fingers remained on him. "Maybe that's something you should find out for yourself."

He caught her hand in his and dipped his head to see into her eyes. "Are you trying to distract me?"

"Is it working?"

Hell, yes. "I've got a question," he said.

"Okay."

"We're not a we?"

She bit her lower lip. "As already established, I don't really do . . . we."

"But we're . . . *something*," he said.

After a long hesitation, she nodded.

They were a something. He could work with that. "So let's make a pact. No more half-truths or misdirections from either of us."

Her gaze was on his mouth. "Are you accusing these lips of lying?"

He let out a low laugh. "There's a whole bunch of a lot of things I've been thinking about doing with those gorgeous lips of yours, Trouble, but accusing them of lying wasn't on the evening's program."

"Good." Her free hand slid up his chest and around the back of his neck. "It's my turn to ask a question now." Her fingers slid into his hair and fisted. "I bet you're a good kisser."

"That wasn't a question," he pointed out.

She smiled. "Are you a good kisser?"

"I'm an awesome kisser."

"Prove it," she said, "and I'll answer another question."

Best deal he'd heard all day. Hell, maybe all year. He slid one arm low around her hips and his other hand up her back to cup the nape of her neck. "Just to be clear," he whispered a fraction of an inch from her lips. "You want me to kiss you."

"Yes."

"Okay, but just so we're straight . . ." He held her gaze. "No regrets."

Her mouth quirked. "I'm not making that promise until you've proven you're any good."

He was laughing. He'd thought there was nothing he'd not seen or done, but laughing while kissing someone . . . that just might be a first.

He released her, his fingers sliding through her hair as he brought her forward for a kiss. Cupping her face in his hands, his thumbs lightly brushing against her cheeks, he kissed her. Light at first, his lips just grazing hers as he absorbed her shiver before deepening the kiss. She tasted like Dee's chocolate chip cookies and warm sexy woman, and she was delicious.

When he broke off, she made a soft sound that

might've been a whimper for more. But that could've been wishful thinking on his part. It'd been a hell of a kiss, and he'd have liked to take it much further, except that the rest of the gang was coming; he could hear their footsteps crunching through the fallen foliage and leaves, maybe a hundred yards back.

He'd have liked to have more time, a lot more time. Seemed as if maybe she felt the same. Her pulse was beating frantically at the base of her throat, but she shrugged casually.

"Not bad," she said.

He laughed.

And she smiled. "Okay, better than not bad."

"I know. And now I get to ask a question."

"Okay," she said slowly, not sounding exactly enthusiastic.

"Your friends love and adore you. Why lie to them about your brother at all? They'd understand."

Her smile faded. Mood killed. But that was okay, because his mind had wrestled the controls back from his body.

"You don't know what you're talking about," Ivy said.

"Unfortunately, I do. You're good at compartmentalizing your life. Work in one box. Friends in another. You've built walls, not allowing anything to get all the way through." He paused. "How am I doing?"

She turned and started to walk off.

Guess he was doing pretty good then. "Ivy."

She kept going.

He caught up with her and gently turned her to face him.

"You're a hypocrite," she said.

"What?" he asked, surprised. "How's that?"

"When I asked you what you were in town for, you said you were here on a break from work, helping out Caleb."

"Yeah, and that's true," he said.

"You didn't mention your mom, or that you were here to see your family."

No, he hadn't mentioned either of those things. But Caleb had, right in front of her, clearly making her feel like he was hiding things.

"It's a small thing," she said. "I know this. And we're . . . strangers. So why would you tell me?" She shook her head, talking to herself. "Of course you wouldn't tell me. I'm no one to you."

Shit. The last thing he'd meant to do was make her feel unimportant. "Ivy—"

"No, it's fine. It just felt like for a guy who hates liars, you weren't honest with me about why you were here. And I get it, I really do. It's none of my business. It's just that I have some issues, and—"

"It's not fine, I did lie by omission," he said gently. "And I'm sorry. It's just that sometimes it's easier to avoid a topic than bring up old painful memories and family issues."

She stared at him and gave a barely perceptible nod.

"I *am* here to help out Caleb. But yeah, there's another reason too, and it's one I haven't wanted to face, much less talk about it. My family is . . . complicated. And it's a little bit ugly. I've been pretending to myself that it was okay to ignore it all and just hope it goes away. I'm sorry if I came off like a jerk."

She looked up into his eyes and he did his best to project the fact that he was being as honest as he could be.

After a few seconds, she nodded again. "I understand. A whole bunch, actually. I do a lot of pretending to myself too." She grimaced. "And much of it is about Brandon, who isn't the stand-up guy I like to pretend he is."

His chest tightened, his heart aching for her. For the both of them as they stared at each other for a long beat. He wasn't sure where they stood exactly. He wasn't sure of anything, except that he wanted his mouth on hers again.

But with everyone else catching up with them, the moment was gone.

Chapter 9

It's not nap time

A few days later, Ivy took a kick to the back of her knee and went down.

"Oh my God," Tae said, sounding utterly pleased with herself. "That actually worked!"

"Told you," Tina said from above Ivy.

Ivy blew her hair from her face and pushed herself to her knees. "No, really, I'm alright, thanks for asking."

Tae offered her a hand up. "I'm surprised I was able to catch you by surprise."

So was Ivy. Once again, she was at the gym with the girls in kickboxing class with Tina, the gorgeous barking tyrant.

"Get up, ladies, it's not nap time."

Tina moved them to a row of hanging bags, which

they had to kick-kick-punch in tune to one of Tina's favorite songs—"Push It" by Salt-N-Pepa. It was a show to watch Tina sing and boogie as she moved through the room yelling encouragements at them.

"If you want to see results, you've got to stay with me!"

Kick-kick-punch.

"If you're not turning up the tension, you're only cheating yourself! I promised sweat, let's see it!"

Kick-kick-punch.

"This is what you came for! The range makes the change!"

Ugh. Kick-kick-punch.

"Make this the best one yet!" Tina hurtled this last comment at Haley, who was drenched in sweat and looking worse for wear.

Haley gave Tina an I'm-trying smile.

"Sugar, hold up a minute."

Haley stopped and sagged against one of the hanging bags with gratitude.

"You're wearing a certain . . . glow," Tina noted.

"It's dehydration."

Tina shook her head, studying Haley closely. "No, that's not it."

"I'm working my ass off?"

"Still not it." Tina walked in a slow circle around everyone's favorite nerdy optometrist. Suddenly, Tina smiled. "You got some."

Haley opened her mouth and then shut it, her face much redder now. "Um . . ."

Tina grinned and high-fived her.

Then she turned on everyone else. "Okay, your girl here's slacking cuz she used up all of her good energy in bed last night. You guys are going to pick up her slack. Kick-kick-punch!"

They all groaned and went back to burning calories.

"You slept with Dee?" Ivy whispered to Haley as she punched her bag. "The night of the hike."

"And the two nights since." Haley bit her lower lip. "But there's been very little sleeping involved."

They all laughed, genuinely thrilled for Haley, who'd had a tough time in the love department. And Ivy loved how blissful Haley looked. She'd never begrudge anyone finding some holiday cheer, never would, but she sure wouldn't mind some of her own.

With Kel, the guy she'd told they weren't a "we."

And she meant it, she reminded herself. *You need to let go of the idea of having him in your life.*

"Make this your best one yet," Tina yelled at them. "Especially you, Ivy Snow, you're slacking."

She was. Because while Haley had been getting lucky since the hike, all Ivy had been doing was thinking about getting lucky. It was all Kel's fault. He'd kissed her, really kissed her, and apparently all her brain cells had leaked out.

It was the only explanation she could come up with for why she couldn't stop thinking about him.

Or the kiss.

She hadn't seen him since. The night before last she'd taught her once a month cooking class at the rec center, which she did for extra cash. Last night she'd had dinner with Sadie, who'd said Caleb and Kel were up north in Sonoma on a friend's horse ranch.

Just as well.

She'd lied to him and he'd caught her at it, and while he'd said he understood, she knew he couldn't really understand at all.

Or forgive.

He wasn't that guy.

So it was for the best that she not see him again. She just wished . . . hell. She wished it wasn't for the best.

"Hands up!" Tina yelled. "Bust it out with every ounce you've got left, and you'd better have lots of ounces left since we've still got twenty more minutes to go."

Oh goodie. Twenty more minutes. Ivy tried to concentrate, but there was a lot tumbling around in her head, and though she always, *always* had reasons for doing the things she did, this time she was having trouble remembering why she'd ever thought letting Kel get close was a good idea.

And that kiss . . .

She sighed. Yeah, it'd been *her* idea, but when he'd teasingly boasted about his skills, she'd dismissed his promises as pure—and stupid—male ego. And then one touch of his mouth and she'd just about forgotten her own name. He'd truly dazzled her.

Only she hadn't dazzled him quite as much if he'd still been able to keep his wits, enough to call her out on her lies about Brandon.

It was second nature, making up stories. Hiding in plain sight was what had always kept her safe, like when they'd been living just outside of Atlanta through one very hot, humid summer. Her brother—charismatic, charming, and actually very sweet—had been chasing one get-rich scheme or another as always. He had the best of intentions—or he tried anyway—if not a gray moral code. So mostly when Ivy would get home from school, her mom would still be sleeping and she'd be on her own. Truth was, she liked those hours alone best. But that day in particular, being alone had worked against her because when Brandon screwed over his new—and scary—associates, they'd of course come looking for him.

They'd been conning drunks at the pool for weeks. But Brandon had gotten greedy and stupid at the same time, and thought it'd be a good idea to turn the con on his guys, stealing the whole pot for himself.

Good thing she'd been skinny back then, because

once again she'd been able to escape out of a window and run.

Just one of many, many times.

It'd never occurred to her to call the police for help. The police were the ones who brought her mom home late at night after she'd started a fight in a bar. Or her brother when he'd done something stupid. He usually ended up in juvie. Such as when he stole her new principal's car and crashed it. They'd had to move, which they'd done a lot, but Ivy hadn't minded that time because she liked where they'd ended up.

Until Brandon had gotten high with some friends and burned their trailer down, leaving them homeless.

So it was really no wonder that she'd learned to have her own back because there was no one else to have it for her.

Hence the kickboxing class.

They'd lived in their car for a while after that, in a different town. Just par for the course. It'd been about survival, with things like material possessions and friends being a luxury she couldn't afford.

Besides, even if she'd been the sort of girl who easily made friends, she never could've had them over or let them into her world. What if Brandon, or one of his guys, did something stupid and someone got hurt? And the odds were in favor of him doing just that. She couldn't risk it, so she hadn't.

When she'd run away to go off on her own, she'd

actually thought she'd never have to worry again. But she'd made mistakes. She and her mom kept in casual touch every few months and Ivy hadn't thought to tell her mom not to pass her current whereabouts on. So just about every time she'd started over, working in bar kitchens mostly, Brandon had shown up, flashed his forgive-me smile, and played the family card. Lonely and anxious for a friendly face, she'd usually fallen for it and let him suck her into his vortex, where he'd then ruined everything. Like the time she'd been in LA working at food services at one of the studios and Brandon had talked his way in to see her and then stolen a bunch of costumes. He'd sold them for big bucks and got her fired and nearly arrested as an accomplice.

After that, she'd gone back to moving around more often so no one could pull the rug out beneath her. She'd still been underage, but had portrayed herself as legal so as to not get social services on her ass. She'd stuck to kitchen jobs and lying low.

But that had gotten old, and she'd yearned for more. It'd been a few years since she'd seen Brandon, so . . . She told herself it was okay to settle down and make a place for herself, including friends. And she'd done just that here in San Francisco. She loved her life here, loved being her own boss, loved the people in her life, loved everything about it. But . . . even she knew you didn't lie to those you cared about.

But how else to protect herself from her past and keep this new life she wanted so badly? Telling little white lies about where she'd come from and the people in her past was what kept her safe.

And her friends.

And she was okay with that.

But she hoped to God whoever had broken into her truck was a stranger felon and not her brother the felon . . . Yes, sometimes she actually missed him. He'd always done his best to take care of her, by whatever means possible, and in spite of all his screwups, he was family and she cared about him. And sometimes, she was just damn lonely for family.

But he'd come in like Hurricane Brandon and blow up her life in some manner, she knew that for a fact. So yeah, her brother was a much better brother from far away. Very far away.

"Unleash your inner athlete!" Tina yelled to the class. "Bring it out with every ounce you have left."

"Uh, I have negative ounces left," Sadie whispered to Ivy.

"Just one more!" Tina yelled at her, apparently having superpower hearing. "Okay," she said when Sadie and Ivy did the extra. "Two more. Make it three. Leave it all in the room!"

Tina said that a lot, leave it all in the room, and it was actually pretty great advice. She was going to go with that. *Leave it all in the room* . . . She would concentrate on the things she knew she could handle. Her taco truck. Saving every spare penny for the condo's down payment. Strengthening the ties with her friends.

She didn't include Kel in this list. Much as she craved him, he wasn't for her.

Not even a little bit.

She'd decided on permanence in her life, and Kel—sex-on-a-stick or not—was just about as temporary as they came.

When class was finally over, they crawled to the showers and shared an Uber to the Pacific Pier Building where they all worked. Halfway there, Sadie's phone buzzed an incoming call from Caleb. She answered, listened, smiled, and handed the phone to Ivy.

"Need a favor," Caleb said without preamble. That was Caleb. Busy 24–7, he liked to get right to the point.

"Whatever you need," she said.

This broke him out of business mode enough to snort. "The Ivy I know doesn't give anyone that kind of power."

"True," she said. "But you went through your better half to get to me so I'm not worried you're looking for anything icky. Plus I owe you, we both know that. We also both know you won't ask me for anything I can't do, so . . . spill it. You're wasting the day away."

He snorted again. "I'm going to take you up on the 'whatever you need' thing in spite of the fact that I happen to know you're not going to like it. But tough, you already said you'd do it."

"Okay," Ivy said slowly. "But now you're scaring me, so start talking."

"I need you to cater an event tonight."

This was not anything unusual. It was part of their deal. Part of the deal of him matching her down payment on the condo was that she pay him back by catering his fancy events at cost. And even then, she got way more out of it than he did because he was high-powered and high profile. Catering events for him always led to other gigs. She'd tried to tell him he was only helping her out even more, but he said he got what he needed out of the deal and was glad she got something out of it as well.

If he wasn't already taken, and wasn't a complete control freak, and didn't wear clothes on a daily basis that cost more than her annual worth, she could've fallen in love with him. "Short notice," she said. "For how many?"

"A hundred."

She sucked in a breath and remembered there was *another* reason she didn't fall in love with him. Because she also usually hated him. "Seriously?"

"Seriously. It's going to be at a private residence in Nob Hill. Your truck won't be able to get up the driveway. Get Jenny to help you prep and I'll cover her hours. I'm sending someone to pick up you and the food at six p.m."

"Alright," she said. "Sure. And thanks."

"No, thank *you* for the amazing food," he said.

"You don't know yet if it will be amazing."

"Yes, I do," he said. "See you tonight."

He disconnected in her ear, and still smiling at his confidence in her, she handed the phone back.

"If he hadn't put a better, bigger smile on my face just this morning, I'd be jealous," Sadie said. "But I'm too done in from kickboxing to be anything but a limp rag doll."

Ivy laughed and set her head on Sadie's shoulder. She had no idea how she'd gotten so lucky to count them both as friends, but she was grateful.

Those warm fuzzy thoughts faded when she got to her truck and her very busy day started in earnest. She had to call Jenny in early to handle the truck customers while she prepped for the evening ahead. She was still feeling anxious and harried when her chariot arrived in the form of a Ford truck, and Kel got out.

And suddenly all her resolve to let him go faded, replaced by warm fuzzies—until she reminded herself that he was not for her.

He was not for her.

And she'd just keep repeating it to herself like a mantra until it took.

Chapter 10

Make this your best one yet

Ivy stood standing hands on hips watching Kel approach, all long, loose limbed, easy stride, as if he didn't have a care in the damn world.

Well good for him. But she had a care, a whole damn bunch of them at the moment, not the least of which was that she'd just talked herself out of him, and at just the sight of him, her resolve was melting faster than the ice caps. "What are you doing here?" she asked.

"I gave you my number to call if you needed me."

"I don't need you. I didn't call you."

"Caleb called me for you," he said. He was in dark jeans, an untucked white button-down, and a sports coat, looking incredibly . . . well, incredibly incredible. Damn him.

She grappled with her reaction to him for a moment, along with the fact that Caleb had clearly interfered. "Your cousin is dead rich guy walking."

This got her a curve of his lips, which she now knew tasted like heaven on earth. Ivy knew herself well. She was almost always in a rush to get from point A to point B. But in exact opposition to that, Kel tended to move with slow, easy purpose. He kissed like that too, and she'd spent a shocking amount of time wondering what else he could do with that slow, easy purpose.

He helped her load all the food, and when he stretched to carefully set his armful into the back, his jacket stretched taut across broad shoulders, allowing her to see the outline of a shoulder harness and a gun. "I don't think I need an armed escort to a party."

He shrugged. "I came straight from work."

"Caleb needs armed guards at work?"

"On some of his projects, yes."

"What kind of projects?"

Instead of answering, he held the door open for her, waiting until she buckled up before shutting the door. When he slid in behind the wheel, she gave him side eye.

Which he ignored. He simply steered them into traffic, remaining in his zone as he drove them across town.

She didn't feel in her zone. She felt . . . awkward.

They'd fought. They'd kissed. They'd retreated to their own corners—okay, so *she'd* retreated to her own corner, but she had no idea what to do with him now. The smart thing, of course, would be to stay on track and do nothing. She told herself she was going to be very, *very* smart.

"I take it we have another problem," he said, voice calm. Like he hadn't a damn care in the world.

"No, not at all," she said in her best PMS voice.

His mouth curved.

And she couldn't just let it go. "Okay, yes, there's a problem. It's you, actually."

"Me."

"Yes, you."

He pulled up to a gigantic house near the top of Nob Hill, from which one could basically see the entire world in all directions. The mansion had to be fifteen thousand square feet, which was a whole lot of house to clean and keep warm, but hey, who was she to judge. She started to get out of the truck, but Kel put a hand on her arm to stop her.

"The problem," he said. "Tell me about it."

She blew out a sigh.

He just looked at her. "Let's say that I don't understand female loaded silences, so maybe you could translate for me. What exactly have I done?"

She looked at him.

He merely returned the look, his own calm but

curious. Patient. And it was that, the patience, that utterly disarmed her. She opened her mouth . . . and then had to shut it. Because what had he done besides buy her food, help her clean up her truck after the break-in, drive her home, make her feel safe, and oh yeah, kiss the thoughts right out of her head . . . "Why did you really kiss me?"

"Because you wanted me to kiss you." He gave a slow negative shake of his head. "But that's not the only reason why I did."

"Then why?"

He smiled the sort of smile a man gave a woman when he was thinking incredibly dirty thoughts, and certain parts of her body stood up at attention.

"Because I wanted to," he said. "Very badly, in fact."

Suddenly, it was hot in his truck. Way too hot. So she shoved open the truck door and got out. Before she could load up her arms with the first of many trips she'd have to make into the house, Kel had come around, and with a knowing smile took twice as much as she could have and was on the move.

"But I've got this," she said to his back.

He didn't bother to respond. Because they both knew the truth. She didn't have this. At the moment, she didn't have anything. He had her all discombobulated and upside down and inside out.

The event was not much different than any of

the others she'd catered for Caleb and his associates. Huge, gorgeous house that had probably cost more money than most developing countries' annual yield. Important people milling around in their couture finery; men in costly suits, women in gowns looking like they hadn't eaten in weeks to fit into said gowns.

But as she'd learned the hard way, people at these things tended to eat like ravished vultures no matter how they looked, so she always doubled her per person portions when figuring out how much food to cook.

The following hours flew by in a whirlwind of restocking trays and keeping everything fresh and looking good. Before Ivy knew it, it was ten o'clock and the party was winding down. She was gathering her now empty trays when Kel reappeared in the kitchen.

She hadn't seen him since he'd dropped her off. She'd assumed he hadn't stayed. "What are you doing here?"

"That's the second time you've asked me that tonight alone. Not exactly trusting, are you." He took the huge stack of trays from her and turned to the back door.

"I already told you that *trusting* isn't in my vocabulary," she said to his back.

"We'll work on that," he said without slowing

down or turning to face her. "And I'm here for you, to take you home."

His calm thoughtfulness made her feel curmudgeonly. "Caleb needs to mind his own business."

"Caleb didn't ask me. I'm here of my own free will." And then he walked out the door, only to return a minute later, arms empty. He took another stack of trays and gave her a challenging look, like *what would you like to fight about now?*

She gave another heavy sigh. "I'm sorry."

"For what, your sweet, sunshine-like nature? For assuming the worst of me? For apparently not knowing how to retract your claws?"

She had to laugh. "All of the above."

He smiled, and she got the feeling he liked the sound of her laugh, which also made her all warm and fuzzy again. Dammit.

He merely bowed his head in acceptance of her apology and vanished outside again. She followed with the last of the load and got into his truck. She'd just buckled her seatbelt and he'd done the same when her stomach rumbled so loudly it echoed off the windshield.

Kel turned to her, brow up.

Horrified, she pressed her hands to her belly and pressed hard. "Ignore that."

Kel flashed a grin. "You made all that amazing food and didn't feed yourself, did you."

"I was busy."

He started driving. Ten minutes later, he parked at an all-night diner in the Marina District.

"What are we doing?" she asked.

"Feeding the beast."

The diner was mostly empty at this time of night. It looked like it'd been opened in the 1950s and not renovated since. Black-and-white linoleum, steel tables, bright red booths. It was, however, done up for the holidays within an inch of its life. The walls and every available surface were twinkling with multi-colored strings of lights and decorations.

It was a seat yourself sort of situation, so Kel gestured for her to pick a spot and she headed toward a booth, stopping short when she realized that hanging in front of each booth was a sprig of mistletoe.

Kel stopped too, and toe-to-toe with her, they both looked up.

"Don't even think about kissing me again," she warned.

He grinned.

"Because *I'm* not thinking about it," she said. "So you shouldn't either."

"Honey, I've done nothing *but* think of it."

Something deep inside her hummed in pleasure at that, but she ignored it and slid into the booth. Grabbing two menus sticking out of a holder, she tossed him one. "Have you been here before?" she asked.

"No. But the flashing sign in the window says BEST PANCAKES EVER, and I'm planning on testing out that promise."

"Do you eat a lot of pancakes?"

"Whenever I can. None as good as yours though."

She tried and failed to not be secretly pleased by that and eyed his leanly muscular build. "Where do you put it?"

"Good metabolism," he said.

"Plus hard work," she guessed. "You, Spence, and Jake go for miles every morning."

"Do you ever run?"

"Only if I'm on fire."

He laughed. "A coworker and I used to run in the mornings, then hit up a local diner. We won the pancake eating contest three years in a row."

"If I ate pancakes every day, I'd weigh two tons. Is your coworker off work for these two weeks too?"

Kel looked at her for a long moment. "My coworker's in jail," he finally said.

She gaped before she could stop herself. "What happened?"

"She was dirty." He suddenly seemed to find the menu engrossing. "They have French toast too."

Her heart squeezed hard and she put her hand over the menu and waited until his gaze met hers. "Are you okay?"

"Why wouldn't I be?"

Right. He was a male. She gave him a *get real* look and he blew out a breath, pushing his menu away. "I'm the one who turned her in. She tried to frame me. For a while, she nearly succeeded. And then she nearly killed me. Hence my forced leave. Seems my superiors need a little space and time."

"But that's not fair," she said, a little surprised by her own vehemence. But she knew him, or she was starting to, and she knew the people who cared about him. She didn't take the time to freak out about that. There was plenty of time for that later. "You're innocent."

The smallest of smiles almost crossed his lips. "You don't know that."

She looked right into his brown eyes, eyes that she knew could be razor sharp with focus and intensity, or soft with affection and heat. "I feel like I do," she murmured, even more shocked by her easy admission.

He seemed just as shocked. "Look at you going all sweet on me." He paused. "You're a surprise, Ivy."

And because he didn't sound necessarily happy about that, she snorted. "Yeah. I hear that a lot. So what do all the women in your life think of your two weeks in San Francisco?"

"My women?"

"The people you're seeing," she said casually, eyes on her menu.

He flashed another smile, which she caught because he put a finger on her menu and pushed it down. "Are you fishing?"

Dammit. Yes. She lifted her chin. "In your dreams, cowboy."

His smile slowly faded and he leaned in, eyes on hers. "Putting aside the fact that you know my life doesn't lend itself to relationships, you really think I'd kiss you like I did if I was kissing anyone else?"

She stared at him, heart suddenly thundering in her ears. "Lots of men do."

He gave a single shake of his head and brought his hand over the top of hers on the table, squeezing lightly. "Ivy?"

"Yeah?"

"I don't want you to take this the wrong way, but the men in your past really sound like a bunch of assholes."

Unable to deny that, she shrugged. "There haven't been that many, to be honest. But I do tend to . . . pick the ones who are bad for me."

"How so?" he asked.

She was surprised to hear herself answer, and truthfully at that, especially since she very purposely never thought about this particular time in her life. "My last relationship was my longest. I met Dillon in LA, where I was living at the time. We stuck a whole year."

"What happened?" Kel asked.

This was embarrassing. And embarrassingly revealing. "I'd moved in with him. Then he got a promotion he'd been hoping for, but his new position was in New York."

"You didn't want to move?"

She turned her head and looked out the window, not wanting to see his face. Or have him see hers. "I would have. But he took the job and gave up his apartment without asking me to go with him."

"Leaving you homeless?" he asked with a whisper of disbelief.

She shrugged. She'd been homeless before. And hey, she'd had a few weeks' notice from the building super to get out.

"That was a real dick move, Ivy." She felt his hand take hers in his bigger, warmer one. "I'm sorry that happened to you. You deserved better."

"It wasn't meant to be," she said. "And anyway, I ended up getting something out of it."

"What's that?"

"I realized I wanted to make some changes in my life. I wanted my own place. And real friends. I wanted a sense of permanence. And I came here, where I'm working at making it happen."

"By buying the taco truck and one of the new condos."

She nodded.

"The first round of owners are moving in next week," Kel said.

"I'm not in the first round." But she was hoping to be in the second. "I'm still working at getting my down payment. When I was there bringing you breakfast, they were doing finish work on the ground floor around the lobby, the offices, business center, and gym."

"It's nearly all done now. We just got the office and business center fully furnished and equipped. All the computer systems are up and running, and the state-of-the-art gym will be finished by tomorrow. There's now more money spent on that floor alone than most developing nations."

A waitress appeared at their table. She was midfifties with a trim build and a kind face, her gray-tinged brown hair pinned to the top of her head. She looked up from her pad and stilled, staring at Kel in shock.

Kel looked just as shocked. "Mom."

Mom? Ivy stared at the woman, able to see it now. They had the same dark brown eyes, the same set to their jaw, and currently the exact same expression of *oh shit* on their faces.

Neither of them spoke.

"Wow, you have a mom?" she asked Kel in a teasing tone she hoped might defuse the awkward silence. "You were once a little kid? Somehow I can't imagine you as anything but a smartass cop."

His mom smiled a little. "He was a cute little boy. And sweet, so very sweet. He always held my hand when we went anywhere. He was my dragon slayer, even when he was barely three feet tall."

Kel had recovered from his surprise. His expression was now completely blank.

"It's been a long time," his mom said quietly, her eyes on her son. "I know you didn't expect me here. It's a new-ish job since the last time we talked . . . When was that?" she asked.

"Grandma's funeral last summer."

Her smiled faded. "Right. I'm sorry about this. I didn't expect you either, but I'm . . ." She paused to take in a deep breath. "I'm so happy to see you, baby."

Kel didn't say anything. He didn't have to. His eyes did it for him. He was seriously regretting offering to feed Ivy's beast.

She wondered what his and his mom's relationship was to cause him this much pain.

"I left him," his mom said to Ivy's unspoken question. "When he was twelve. I couldn't help it, and I can't take it back, but I regret it. I've deeply regretted it every day since. Especially because . . ." She turned back to Kel, her eyes swimming with unshed tears. "I know that you had to step up and work the ranch with your grandparents, and when they got older, you had to take over the entire operation. I know you put aside your own childhood to make sure Remy had hers. I know my selfish act meant you giving up your life to be the head of the household when you were way too young, which caused you to shut down your emotions and hold yourself in tight control at all times, something you never should've had to do."

Kel's expression didn't change.

Cue another awkward strained silence, and Kel's mom's smile faded. "Well. You didn't come here for this. You came to eat. What can I get you?"

As they placed their orders, his mom nodded, but never took her eyes off Kel, like maybe he was Christmas and summer vacation all in one. "It really is good to see you," she told him softly.

Kel closed his eyes and shook his head.

His mom straightened and nodded. "Right. I'll get your order in." And then she was gone.

Chapter 11

Don't let your head sell you out

Kel couldn't believe it. Of all the pancake joints in all the world . . . He'd had to find the one where his mom worked. He'd watched the light in his mom's eyes fade before she headed back to the kitchen and told himself he didn't owe her a single damn thing.

But he still felt like a big bag of dicks. There was a time in his life when he would have welcomed her wanting to see him. But when she'd waited until he was nearly an adult to try to explain to him why she'd never come for her own children, he'd decided he no longer wanted to know.

Did that make him an asshole? Yeah. Probably.

And never in a million years had he thought he'd run into her like this, by complete accident. He'd purposely avoided the places he thought there might be a chance of seeing her.

Fat lot of good that had done him because here she was, and she'd looked at him as if he'd been the best thing she'd seen all year. When he'd been little she'd looked at him like that, like he was the sun and the moon. Her entire universe.

But he was no longer young and everything had changed.

"You okay?" Ivy asked quietly.

"Why wouldn't I be?"

She didn't break eye contact or let him get away with answering the question with another question. In fact, she—unlike anyone else in his life—never let him get away with much. "Obviously, there's a problem between you two," she said.

"The problem is that when I needed a mom, I didn't have one."

"And now you, what, don't need a mom?"

"No."

She nodded, accepting this easily, more easily than anyone he'd ever told. "She seems really sweet," she said.

Kel let out a low, mirthless laugh just as his mom reappeared with hot chocolate, which she set in front of him.

He looked down at the steaming mug, his chest pinching at all the memories that slammed into him. This had been a tradition. On cold days when he'd come home from school, she'd make him hot chocolate. Up until the day he'd come home from school to *no* hot chocolate because she'd been in bed with another man. He pushed the mug away. "I didn't order this."

She clasped her hands together. "It used to be your favorite."

"Yes," he said. "When I was ten."

His mom's face flushed with embarrassment. Across the table Ivy slid the mug toward herself. "Well, I'm not ten, but my mom never once made me hot chocolate. No sense in this going to waste, right?" She took a sip. "Wow."

His mom beamed at her. "You like it?"

"It's the most amazing hot chocolate I've ever had," Ivy said.

Kel rolled his eyes and Ivy kicked him beneath the table. Hard.

"I added my special secret ingredient," his mom said. "A pinch of cinnamon."

"It's delicious. Thank you."

"You're so welcome." His mom turned to him and shyly pulled something from one of her apron pockets.

Her phone. Which she opened to her photos.

Perfect. "Mom, this isn't really a great time—"

"Aw," Ivy said, eyes on the picture of Remy and the new baby. "So cute! Who is this?"

"That's Kel's sister," his mom said. "And her new baby, Harper. This was taken right in the birth room. Harper was two minutes old."

"Precious," Ivy said softly, looking and sounding very sincere.

Kel had seen the picture. Remy had sent it, and he'd thought the same thing then that he thought now. The baby was red, mottled, and covered in . . . well, he wasn't sure exactly what. Some sort of goop. *Precious* wasn't exactly the word he'd use.

"And this was yesterday," his mom said, thumbing to the next pic. "In her daddy's arms."

And okay, the baby was pretty cute now. She had Remy's eyes and Ethan's smile. And just looking at her made Kel smile, which was a real feat at the moment.

Then his mom slid her finger across the screen to the next pic, which was of her and Henry wearing *Best Grandma Ever* and *Best Grandpa Ever* T-shirts, holding Harper.

"Love the shirts," Ivy said.

They were smiling down at the baby like real doting grandparents. The only person in the family missing from the photos was Kel.

His own doing.

His mom gently touched his arm, making him realize he'd frozen in place, staring at the phone. "My break's in thirty minutes," she said. "I could come and sit down, maybe catch up a little."

"Can't," he said. "I've got to get Ivy home."

His mom's smile faded a little bit, and for the first

time he didn't feel the usual resentment and anger. He felt . . . guilt.

This time when she headed back to the kitchen, silence reigned at the table. He looked over at Ivy. "Sorry about that."

She stood. "Excuse me a minute?" She headed to the restroom.

He eyed the hot chocolate on her side of the table. Fighting—and losing—the battle, he pulled the mug in close and took a sip. He didn't know what he expected it to taste like—broken hearts and destroyed dreams? But it tasted like hot chocolate. *Delicious* hot chocolate.

Five minutes later, Ivy still hadn't returned, but their food arrived. His was a huge stack of pancakes that he'd wanted only a few minutes ago, but his appetite was gone.

A few minutes later, his mom slid into the booth where Ivy had been sitting. She pulled Ivy's plate toward herself, much as he'd done the hot chocolate.

"What are you doing?" he asked. "Ivy'll be back any minute."

"Will she?"

"What does that mean?"

She gave him a slightly pitying look. "Son, she climbed out the bathroom window about ten minutes ago."

He blinked. "What?"

"Yeah, I think she thought we'd communicate better without an audience."

"That's . . . oddly specific." He narrowed his gaze. "You talked to her."

"No." She took another bite. "She talked to me. She called a Lyft."

Kel couldn't believe it. She'd ditched him.

His mom took a few bites of pancakes and moaned, closing her eyes. "Sorry, I've been on my feet for eight hours and I'm starving." With a long sigh, she finally pushed the plate away. "Don't worry, I know you're not interested in talking to me. And for the record, I did try to tell Ivy that. And I'm not going to take up your time. I just wanted to give you this." She slid an envelope across the table.

"What is it?"

"An invite to Remy's surprise baby shower. It's on the night before Christmas Eve." She paused. "I know you're still mad at me, but it's for your sister. You know that Harper was a preemie and we had to cancel the original shower. She'll be over the moon if you come. The whole family together in one place."

It was what he'd wanted every single day of his life during those years he'd been grieving his dad, stuck in Idaho, his mom gone from their lives, nothing of his dad's to remember him by. All he'd wanted was his family together again.

But he was no longer a kid, and he no longer yearned for such things.

When he remained quiet, his mom nodded as if she'd expected it and stood up. "Okay. So you still don't want to talk to me. I have to respect that. I hurt you, and we can't come back from the past. But I hope you'll at least think about it. I'd hate for you and your sister to miss out because you're still mad at me."

"I'm not mad at you, Mom."

She just gave him a sad smile and walked away.

Chapter 12

*If you're not turning up the tension,
you're only cheating yourself*

For the next two days, Ivy went through the motions at kickboxing, at work, everywhere, all while braced for Kel's inevitable appearance.

Because she'd sneaked out on him at the diner.

It'd been for a good cause, she reminded herself. She'd done it for him. And yet at that thought, she rolled her eyes. She couldn't even sell the lie to herself.

Family drama made her nervous and anxious and extremely uncomfortable. Add that to what she was feeling for Kel, a guy who was the opposite of a keeper—hello, he was leaving town soon—and she'd just run scared.

Not cool.

But . . . she'd also wanted Kel and his mom to talk, for their sakes, and she was no one to them. She hadn't needed to be there.

It wasn't hard to keep herself busy. Work had picked up, having her considering upping Jenny's hours. She'd procrastinated on doing that up until now because of the cost. And getting bigger meant putting more of herself out there, and that was terrifying. What if she failed?

In the past, she'd always positioned herself to be able to get out quick if needed. From anything. There'd been years where all her belongings had fit into a single backpack.

That was no longer the case. For God's sake, she'd spent two hours last night deep into Pinterest, looking for ideas on how to decorate the condo she didn't yet own. Her board was filled with her hopes and dreams, and she'd only stopped when she'd literally dropped her phone on her face.

Now it was the end of a shift and she was getting ready to leave her truck in Jenny's hands for the dinner service. But Jenny was on the phone blowing smoochie kisses to some guy, and finally, out of patience, Ivy gave her the *wrap it up* gesture.

Jenny slipped her phone in her pocket and gave what could only be called a dreamy sigh.

"You've gone out with him *once*," Ivy said.

"Twice. And he's The One, I know it."

"That's what you said about the last guy."

"The last guy had me fooled," Jenny said. "But this time, this guy . . . he's going to stick. He is," she said to Ivy's look of worry. "I know it."

"Yeah? How can you be so sure?"

"Because my heart says so." Jenny rubbed the middle of her chest.

"Might just be indigestion."

Jenny laughed. "So cynical. What has love ever done to you?"

What had love done to her? Name it. She'd sacrificed plenty in the name of love. Believing time and time again in her mom, that this move, this job, would be the one and they'd settle somewhere and be a family. Hadn't ever happened. Believing in her brother and his stupid get-rich-quick schemes that never turned out to be anything but trouble. And then there'd been Dillon. Yeah, she'd actually believed he might be The One, and she'd probably sounded just like Jenny. Hopeful. Excited. Happy.

But that had ended in not only heartbreak, but also losing the place she'd come to think of as home, and the small community of his friends as well. To her, love meant her making stupid sacrifices. And yet in return, no one had ever sacrificed for her in any way.

The bottom line, love offered nothing but pain. "Just . . . be careful," she said to Jenny.

"What's the fun in that?"

Sadie showed up just then with a carload for Ivy. Her trays.

Ivy began unloading them with Sadie and Jenny's help, feeling the weight of Sadie's gaze. "What?"

"You know what," Sadie said.

Ivy blew out a breath. Yeah, she figured she did. Sadie wanted to know why Kel hadn't returned the trays himself. "It's complicated."

"Uh-huh," Sadie said dryly. "He's a man, isn't he? Men are complicated."

Jenny laughed. "Agreed. But then again, the very best things always are, aren't they?"

"One hundred percent," Sadie said. "But to be fair to men everywhere, women tend to be the ones to make everything so complicated. I certainly did with Caleb. Good thing he's a patient man. Also good thing he had the sense to know I was worth all the trouble. Anyway, yesterday Kel asked Caleb to return the trays for him. Said something about you probably not wanting to see him, since you'd ditched him on a date by climbing out a bathroom window to escape him."

Jenny turned and gaped at Ivy. "You dined and ditched on the hot cowboy? Seriously?"

"Oh my God. *No.*" Ivy closed her eyes and shook her head. "That's not how it went down." She gave it some thought and sighed heavily. "Okay, that's pretty much exactly how it went down. But it wasn't a date."

Jenny shook her head. "Wow."

Sadie just laughed in amazement. "So it's true." She bit her lower lip. "I overheard them talking. Caleb really had to drag it out of Kel. I bet you anything he's not used to being ditched on a date, not a guy like that."

"Meaning?"

"Meaning," Sadie said. "Kel's . . ."

"Sex walking?" Jenny offered helpfully as she walked off to serve some customers.

"I was going to say tough," Sadie said to Ivy. "And steady as a rock. And he's also a real good guy all the way through." She said this last with fierce affection, and Ivy felt another stab of regret.

"I didn't ditch him . . . exactly," she said quietly. "I was giving him some space." And that was the truth. Because that night, sitting there in the diner watching Kel and his mom, she realized the stoic, always in control Kel was a master at hiding his emotions. Maybe even as good at it as she was. He'd had to be in order to be strong for his sister and grandparents, to help run the ranch, to be the man of the house.

Which meant they had more in common than she could have ever guessed. And maybe . . . maybe *that's* why she'd crawled out a tiny bathroom window and run like hell.

Without a word.

It'd been so rude. She knew this. She felt bad for it.

But she couldn't say she'd surprised herself. She had a long history of not looking back. So it was doubly annoying that this time, with Kel, she wanted to.

Sadie stared at her and then suddenly smiled. "Wow. I didn't see this coming, but I should have. You like him. You *really* like him."

"Woman, bite your tongue."

"Tell me I'm wrong and I'll shut up," Sadie said, and when Ivy just snorted, she rolled her eyes. "Okay, so I don't know how to shut up. Tell me anyway."

Ivy shook her head. "I . . . can't." And because Sadie looked hurt at that, she confessed her truth. "I'm flying blind here. I haven't been able to put words to my feelings yet."

Sadie nodded in understanding. "I can understand that. But I worry. I worry you don't think that you deserve happiness. Because I didn't, not until all too recently. I don't want either of you to get hurt."

"We're tougher than we look."

Sadie laughed at that. "Don't worry, you both look tough as hell. Impenetrable. And that's another thing I worry about, because you're not. You're sweet and kind, and just a really great person, Ivy."

Ivy scoffed.

"No, I mean it," Sadie said fiercely, surprising Ivy with her vehemence and grabbing her hand, holding on tight, apparently not willing to let her joke this away. "Sometimes I can feel the weight of your . . . I don't know." Sadie tossed up her hands. "Your past maybe? And it makes me ache for you, Ivy. You hold so much of yourself in. I want to be there for you. Let me be there for you, like you always are for me."

"You *are* here for me," Ivy said softly. "You brought me my trays back. That was really nice of you, and—"

"Best friends are more than nice to each other."

Ivy stilled. "Best friends?"

Sadie gave her a *well, duh* look, and at the sheer irritation in it, Ivy felt emotions flood her. Warmth, gratitude . . . affection. "I didn't know that's how you saw it."

"Well it is," Sadie said. "And if you don't know, it's because you hide behind your walls. And bee-tee-dub, it'd be really great if you stopped doing that. I mean, hide from the world if you want, but not me. I'm here for you. Okay?"

Unable to speak, Ivy nodded.

"You promise?"

"I'll try."

"Pinkie swear," Sadie demanded and help out her pinkie.

Ivy managed a laugh. "You and your pinkie swears—"

"I'm dead serious," Sadie said. "I know you never make promises you don't keep. So if you mean it, you'll promise me."

Ivy stared at the proffered pinkie. "Wow, I'm sorry, but I just got unexpectedly blinded by your twenty million carat diamond ring . . ."

"Of course you are, and it's three carats," Sadie said so loftily that Ivy laughed and hooked her pinkie with her apparently best friend.

"Sadie," she said, suddenly serious.

Sadie narrowed her eyes. "So help me God, if you're going to back out now—"

"No. I was just going to say that I've never had a BFF before."

Sadie shut her mouth. Her eyes went suspiciously shiny. "Okay, now you're just trying to make my mascara run." And she hugged Ivy so tight that she couldn't breathe.

Ivy tried to tap out, but Sadie just squeezed harder.

"Air," she gasped dramatically.

"Oh, shut up." And she kept hugging Ivy.

What seemed like a year later, they left Jenny in charge and walked through the courtyard to the pub. Sadie slowed at the fountain in the center of the courtyard.

"You know . . ." she started.

With a rough laugh, Ivy shook her head. The Pacific Pier Building had been built in the 1800s for a very large ranching family's central compound. Back then, there'd still been cows in Cow Hollow. Today there wasn't a single square inch of the San

Francisco district that hadn't been built on, but here in the center of the courtyard, the original ranching family's fountain still stood.

The legend associated with that fountain went that if one made a wish with a true heart, then true love would then find you.

Ivy thought she had a better chance of Santa Claus leaving her a few presents on Christmas Day.

Sadie looked at her. "You're not even curious what might happen if you wish?"

"No."

"Really? You're not interested at all?"

"In true love? Given all that love's ever done is destroy me, I'd rather make a pact with the devil," Ivy said.

"But if it destroyed you, it wasn't true love." She pulled out a quarter and held it out.

"You don't expect me to believe that true love costs only twenty-five cents, do you?"

Sadie laughed. "Maybe it's on sale, just for you. One time offer only."

Ivy thought about what Sadie had with Caleb, how real and deep it was, and for the first time in her life she wavered.

Sadie did a little flourish with the quarter, once again offering it up.

Ivy snatched it and tossed it into the fountain. She stared at the coin as it slowly sank below the surface, finally clinking on the bottom, shining up through the water.

"What did you wish?"

Ivy tore her gaze off the coin. "I can't tell you or it won't come true."

Sadie grinned. "See, you *do* believe!" She turned and started walking again.

Ivy stayed still a moment longer, staring into the water. *I wish I could believe,* she whispered to herself.

When she caught up to Sadie, her friend was smiling.

"What?" Ivy asked.

"Nothing." She took Ivy's hand. "You scared?"

Terrified. "Of course not."

"It's okay. True love's worth the fear."

"I'll take your word for it," Ivy said. "Now hurry up, it's freezing out here."

Tonight was Dare to Dart Night at the pub. The dart tournament was a monthly occurrence, and there was a bracket and stakes to go with it.

Ivy was on a team with Jake and his sister Tae. They were up by a whole hell of a lot for several reasons. First, Ivy had grown up in bars so she rocked darts. Second, Jake's throwing arm was big league ready. Oh, and three, Tae looked dainty and fragile, but she could hit a bull's-eye without even trying.

Kel showed up about an hour into the tournament.

Ivy immediately went into plan mode. She decided to play it casual, but she'd find a way to apologize to him later, in private. Maybe. Depending . . .

Depending on what exactly, she really had no idea. She was hoping it'd come to her in the moment.

But then she got a good look at his face. His mouth was tight and especially grim. She kept an eye on him as she finished her round. He'd sat at the bar with Caleb and Sadie, and she was pretty sure he hadn't even noticed her presence.

Until he lifted his gaze and unerringly met hers across the boisterous, nosy, crowded bar. Even from their distance, her heart gave a stupid flutter, but that took a backseat because there was something in his gaze, a hollow, haunted look that clutched her heart and made the air in her lungs whoosh out. The guy had been through a rough spell. He was recovering from nearly being killed at work, and had just unexpectedly run into the mother who'd abandoned him, and then the girl he . . . liked? . . . had skipped out on him.

She was a jerk.

Excusing herself, she made her way across the room, watching as Kel continued to interact with Caleb and Sadie, who were both smiling and chatting easily, making Ivy frown.

Couldn't they tell something was wrong with him?

When she got to the far end of the bar where they

were gathered, she stopped, suddenly feeling extremely awkward.

"Hey, you!" Sadie said in greeting and gave her a hug before grabbing Caleb by the hand. "We're going to kick some serious ass in the dart tourney."

"But it's not our turn yet—" Caleb started and then zipped it at Sadie's long look in his direction. "Well clearly I'm mistaken," he said smoothly, making Sadie beam at him as she pulled him away.

"She's matchmaking," Kel said without any inflection or indication of his thoughts.

"Yes," Ivy agreed. "I'm not sure she can help herself. Happy people are like that. They want to spread the cheer, when what they don't get is that it's horribly annoying to those of us who just want to be left to our misery."

That got her an almost smile. "You're happy in your misery then?" he asked.

"Exactly." But more than anything, Sadie's efforts were misguided because she and Kel didn't have a shot at the long-lasting happiness Sadie and Caleb were clearly destined for. But it didn't mean that she couldn't still apologize.

Kel was sprawled comfortably on the barstool, one hand on a bottle of beer, watching her with that same small smile he'd had with Caleb and Sadie. The one that didn't quite reach his eyes.

"How did things go with your mom the other night?" she asked.

He shrugged.

"Don't want to talk about it?"

He took a pull of his beer. "If you'd stuck around instead of sneaking off, you'd already know."

She winced. "Kel—"

"Before we start this conversation neither of us wants to have, why don't you do what you do and walk away. There're windows in the bathrooms, if you feel more comfortable with that exit strategy."

Chapter 13

Get your head in the game

Ivy blew out a breath and faced the clearly angry Kel. "I'm not leaving." She took the vacant barstool next to him. Because of how he was turned toward her, this put his long legs in close contact with hers. He could have pulled back, but he didn't. She decided to take that as a good sign. "I need to apologize to you."

"For?" he asked with a shrug as if whatever it was didn't matter to him one way or the other.

"You know what for," she said quietly.

"Oh, you mean when you dined and ditched me?"

"That's not—" She took a moment and another breath. "Okay, yes, fine. I did that, and I was a jerk. But I had a good reason, Kel."

"Which was?"

"I wanted to give you time to talk to your mom."

He just looked at her.

"Look, I didn't start this story with an I'm-proud-of-what-I-did. Because I shouldn't have left like that without thanking you for the ride and the help at the event. At the very least, I could have sent a text."

He raised a brow.

"What? I don't like talking on the phone."

"Not that," he said. "Interesting apology . . . since there wasn't one."

She grimaced. "I *am* sorry, okay? You deserved better, much better. But I really did think that you and your mom needed to talk."

"We didn't," he said flatly.

It was her turn to cock her head and study him. He was most definitely doing a good job at deflecting and misdirecting, but she was no longer surprised by their odd connection and ability to see right through each other's bullshit. And see right through him she did. "What happened?" she asked softly. "What's wrong?"

"How do you know something's wrong?"

"I don't know exactly. I guess I can read it in your eyes and body language. I can . . . feel it. It's about your mom, right?"

"We're not . . . close."

"I'm getting that," she said carefully. "She just seemed so sweet, and so happy to see you. She was proud of you, and that was special to see. Not that I've had my mom look at me like that." She shook her head. "Honestly? I was a little envious."

"Don't be." Kel ran a thumb over the condensation on the bottle of beer in his palm. "We haven't had any sort of a relationship for a long time."

"And that makes you . . . sad."

"Maybe. I don't know. For a long time, I resented her for having to lie for her." At her clear surprise, he nodded. "When I was ten, I caught her having an affair. I kept her secret for her. Two years later my dad died, and my mom sent me and my sister to Idaho to live with our grandparents."

"And you haven't spoken much since."

He shook his head. "At first, that was her doing. But around the time I turned eighteen, she started coming around, trying to make things right."

"And . . . ?"

"And by then I wasn't interested."

Her heart had squeezed hard when he'd first started talking, and it didn't unclench at the thought of him feeling so abandoned for so long. "So although you knew she lived here in the city, when you saw her last night . . ."

"It was a total surprise."

"And you don't like surprises," she murmured, adding up what he'd said and what she knew of him, all of which now made a lot more sense. He'd been burned by people in his life. His mom, his coworker . . . "I'm starting to understand your comment about not liking liars."

He gave a low snort, and relaxed a little bit. From talking to her, she realized. Not Caleb, his cousin and best friend, but *her*. This gave her a rush of both pleasure and terror. Pleasure because she felt proud of being the one he'd chosen to trust. And terror because . . . well, she was the exact kind of person he hated.

A liar.

"I'm sorry I left like that last night," she said quietly. "I shouldn't have. Was it awful?"

"She gave me an invite to a surprise baby shower for my sister," he said. "Remy missed her own first baby shower because she went into early labor with Harper. The party's on the night before Christmas Eve."

"Which is right before you go back to Idaho, right?"

He nodded, which had a little stab of anxiety going through her, but it was also a good reminder as well—he wasn't for her. "Are you going to go to the shower?"

He lifted a broad shoulder and finished his beer. He still wasn't giving much away, but there was a sense of longing in him that she imagined was much like her own longing for the kind of family she knew existed but had never experienced. "You should go to the shower," she said softly. "You could reconnect with your family."

"My sister and I are fine."

She thought of how his mom had looked at him at the diner, soaking up his face like she'd never seen anything more important to her in her entire life. The way her fingers had shaken as they'd gripped her order pad and pen in a death grip. "I know this is none of my business," Ivy said cautiously. "And yes, your mom had an affair. That sucks. But as awful as it sounds, lots of people do it. Not that it makes it okay, I'm just saying, maybe there's a lot more to her staying away so long before trying to have a relationship with you than a ten-year-old could possibly understand."

He shook his head, but she gave it one more try, from another angle. "Your sister won't understand you not being there."

"Probably not, but I'd have to be around my mom and stepdad."

"I'm assuming there'll be a lot of people there. You wouldn't be alone."

"It's a baby shower."

"Yes. And?"

"And that means stupid games like making clothes out of diapers and guessing the baby food." He shuddered.

She had to laugh. "Maybe, I don't actually know.

I've never been to a baby shower." She thought about the horrors of that and grimaced.

"See?"

"Yeah, but Kel, if I were invited to one, especially by my own sibling, I'd go."

"Brandon doesn't have kids yet, I take it," he said.

She shook her head. But in truth, she had no idea. In the two years since she'd seen her brother, anything could've happened. "Just seems like family should go to that sort of thing for each other."

He looked at her for a long moment and then surprised her when he said, "I'll go if you go."

She gave a startled laugh. "That's not how it works, Kel. You don't bring a stranger to a baby shower. I don't know your family. I barely know you."

"Fine." Standing, he shoved his hand into his pocket and came out with some cash, which he tossed onto the bar, giving the bartender a nod in thanks. "Let's go."

"Where?" she asked, baffled, even as her heart started a slow, heavy beat.

"You just said you barely know me. We're going to fix that."

Oh boy. Her knees wobbled. "Um . . . the dart tourney—"

"They don't need us. A date, Ivy," he said, looking amused by her panic. "We're going on a date to get to know each other."

"That's pretty extreme just to get me to go with you to the baby shower."

"It's not just for that," he said.

Their gazes locked and she swallowed hard. "Where to?"

"You're the one who lives here in San Francisco now," he said. "You pick."

She stared at him, at the unspoken but unmistakable dare.

"Afraid?" he asked.

"Of course not." Only petrified.

"Then . . . ?"

She took in the challenge in those dark eyes and felt the tingle of excitement and adrenaline flood her. *What the hell*, she thought. She'd bluffed her way through most of life, this was nothing, right? Ignoring the nervous little butterflies in her belly, she led him out of the pub and across the dark, quiet cobblestone courtyard.

She wanted this, whatever this was. She wanted to take him out of his own head, wanted to see him smile that slow, sexy smile he had, wanted to experience Kel when he'd let loose and was having fun. Or better yet, lost in pleasure.

That last thought had her tripping over her own two feet. She would've gone down too, except Kel caught her, held on to her until she got her bearings.

They stood at the center of the courtyard now,

right in front of the beautiful hundred-plus-year-old fountain, the water tinkling into the copper bowl the only sound in the cold night.

She stared into the water, wondering which coin was hers. Kel's hands were still on her hips, his eyes locked on hers.

"What?" she whispered, careful not to move because she liked the feel of the heat of him warming her from the inside out.

He pulled a quarter from his pocket and she froze. "Um . . ."

"Do you know the legend of the fountain?" he asked.

"You mean the lie that harbors false hope? Yes, and put that quarter away."

He laughed. "So you know if you make a wish for true love, that true love will find you."

"Have you ever noticed how legends and fairy tales are really sort of nightmares?" she asked. "And anyway, I don't believe in true love. Plus I've already made a wish—sort of."

He went brows up.

"I can't tell you," she said. "Or it won't come true. But it wasn't for love." Nope, all she'd asked for was the ability to believe. Believe in love.

Her aunt Cathy's words swam in her head.

Be smart.

Be brave.

Be vulnerable . . .

Kel tossed the coin up and down in his palm. "If you already wished for something, then you know you've got nothing to worry about. Especially if you don't believe."

But . . . did she truly not believe? Or was she just afraid? "What I know is that it's stupid to tempt fate," she said.

This got a chuckle. "If you could see your face right now." He tossed the quarter into the fountain and she stopped breathing.

He smiled. "Before you stroke out, I wished for Harper to have true love in her life."

She nearly sagged with relief and tore her gaze off the rapidly vanishing quarter to stare at him. "That was mean."

He just smiled.

"Like the meanest of all the mean."

"So I take it you wouldn't make a wish for one of your family members."

She turned back to the fountain and pretended to be fascinated by it.

"You know, you never say much about your family," he said quietly.

"Because we've known each other all of a week."

His mouth quirked and he gave another slow shake of his head. "You do that a lot, deflect with sarcasm and wit. Your mom's a lounge singer. Your brother's bad at keeping in touch. Tell me more, Trouble."

Again her heart started with a heavy drumming. She didn't do this. Not here, not now. Not ever, actually. She didn't share, and he was right, instead she deflected and she was good at it. "I thought I was going to show you a good time."

"You are. This first."

She rolled her eyes. "It's nothing exciting. Just a normal upbringing, really." *If normal was hell on earth* . . .

"There's no such thing as a normal upbringing," he said. "You were pretty adamant about me talking to my mom. Tell me more about yours."

She could hear her own heartbeat in her ears. "Nothing to say, other than what you know. I left home when I was sixteen."

This didn't make him happy. "What about school?"

"I tested out and got my GED," she said.

"How did you survive? Did you go to other family members?"

"No. And I did okay." If okay was being scared and alone all the time.

He shook his head, eyes troubled for her. "I can't imagine how rough that was for a young girl. You mentioned that your dad wasn't around," he said.

"Nope. Not at all."

"You never knew him?"

"No. I could pass him on the street and I wouldn't even know it." And when Kel just looked at her, eyes solemn and sympathetic, she admitted something she'd never said out loud before. "I used to look at faces in crowds to see if I resembled any of them."

"His loss," Kel said with a quiet intensity that made her throat feel tight. He slid a hand down her arm to entangle their fingers, which he used to tug her into him. "I'm going to kiss you now, Ivy. Tell me if that's okay."

She stared up at his mouth. "Are you always going to ask me that question before you kiss me?"

He pressed into her, that long, hard, hot body against hers. "Until I can read you better and be sure of what you want, yes."

Why did she find that incredibly sexy, as in maybe one of the sexiest things she'd ever heard? Her hands found their way to his chest and slowly slid up. "I know I'm not very easy to read," she whispered, going up on tiptoe so that the words ghosted over his lips. And then, against her best judgment, she whispered one more word. *"Yes . . ."*

Kel framed her face with his hands. Ivy didn't dare breathe for fear that it wouldn't happen, because at some point in the past sixty seconds, she'd come to want his kiss more than anything she could think of. It was an ache working its way through her, twisting her up into a ball of hunger and desire.

Without breaking eye contact, his fingers slid into her hair and he held her gaze for a long beat, until finally she whispered *"please."* In the next beat, his mouth closed over hers. She had no idea which of them deepened the kiss after that, only that she heard her own soft moan as a white-hot wave of need rolled through her. When his tongue touched hers, she shivered, pressing closer for more because he tasted amazing and she wanted to taste the rest of him, wanted to taste every single inch of him.

But he slowly pulled back and ran a thumb along her jawline. "I knew you were going to be trouble the very first moment I laid eyes on you."

"*Hello*, I've been trying to tell you that very thing!"

Snatching her hand in his, he grinned at her, a very sexy, very naughty grin, as if maybe he thought she was the very best kind of trouble, and led her through the alley to his truck.

Chapter 14

Unleash your inner athlete

Kel and Ivy were on the sidewalk in front of the Pacific Pier Building, walking toward his truck when someone called his name. It was a female voice, and one he recognized. In surprise, he turned just in time to catch the soft female form who threw herself into his arms.

"Wow," Janie said, hugging him tight, smiling up into his face. "It's a small world! I'm here for a conference. What are you doing in the city?"

"Working," he said, still stunned to see her. Janie was a middle school librarian he'd dated three years ago for six months. Until she'd dumped him, frustrated at the fact that he always put work ahead of her.

He'd deserved it.

But also . . . she'd been in love with him, and he

hadn't been able to return the feelings. It'd sucked. He returned her hug briefly, but then stepped back.

She was slower to let her arms fall from where she'd flung them around his neck.

"Sorry," Janie turned to Ivy with an embarrassed smile. "Didn't mean to interrupt anything. I'm Janie, Kel's ex."

Ivy gave a small but genuine smile. "And I'm Ivy. Not his ex."

At that, Janie grinned at Kel. "She passes the tough-enough test. I like her. You should try harder to keep her than you did me." She looked at Ivy. "When he won't give you more than skin deep, just don't let him tell you it's work. It's him."

Kel grimaced. At the time, he'd cared for Janie, deeply. At least as deeply as he'd been able to, but he was well aware he'd fallen short of expectations. "Janie—"

"Nope," she said with an easy smile and a shake of her head. "We're all good. Don't ruin it now." And with that, she blew him a kiss and walked off.

Ivy slid him a look. "Sort of brings new meaning to 'it's not you, it's me,' huh?"

"It was me."

"I know. Because in my experience, it's always the guy."

He snorted and opened the passenger door of his truck for her. "You still want to go out with me?"

"For tonight anyway," she said.

He slid behind the wheel and felt the weight of her gaze. He turned and faced her. "Let's hear it."

"Hear what?"

"Whatever's on your mind."

"So you screwed up, huh?" she asked.

"Yeah."

"Did you cheat on her?"

"Yes. With my job."

She looked at him for a few beats. "So . . . we're both messed up."

He nodded. "Yeah."

That made her laugh. "At least we both know it."

"True," he said on a smile. He hadn't had much to smile about in a damn long time, but something about Ivy, hell, *everything* about Ivy made him feel . . . lighter.

A problem, of course. But not one he had to solve tonight. Not after that kiss. And for sure not before he let her show him that good time she'd promised. "Where to?" he asked.

She gave him directions, but refused to say where they were headed. "Should I be worried?" he asked, amused at her secrecy.

"Do you have any allergies?" she asked. "Are you opposed to heights?"

He slid her a glance and realized she was just teasing him. And he liked it.

"I'll tell you this much," she said. "Where we're headed is one of the first places I ended up when I landed here in San Francisco last year. It was entirely by accident. I was walking around to get my bearings, trying to wrap my head around how much I loved it here. As in *instantly* loved," she emphasized, shaking her head with a small smile. "And for someone who'd never stuck anywhere for more than a year, it was more than slightly terrifying. I was so nervous and anxious all the time, but I also knew I wasn't going anywhere. I'd found home. And early on, late at night, I'd be too restless to sleep. My mind wouldn't shut up with the onslaught of questions and worries about things like how expensive everything was here, and how I'd possibly manage to make ends meet. So I'd go walking. The first night I did that, it was storming. I was cold and wet and hungry, and . . . I got lost. I ended up at . . . well, you'll see in a minute."

Sometimes she doled out little tidbits of herself, little insights that had him horrified for how she'd grown up, but also made him admire her all the more for what she'd made of herself.

It also made him want her. A dangerous road to go down for a whole bunch of reasons, not the least of which was that he didn't want to hurt her.

Or be hurt.

In the past, he'd done a real bang-up job of holding

himself back, always. Mostly because a part of him didn't trust love. But he was having a hard time holding back with Ivy, and that it'd only been a week made it all the more difficult to understand.

He pulled up at the address she'd given him and stared at the building. The sign read THE TROUGH. It was a country Western bar. "Interesting choice," he said, idling at the curb.

"Cowboys are welcome. And you're a cowboy, so . . ."

"Not exactly, no." He had to park a block down and across the street, at least tonight. Apparently cowboys were popular.

"I thought you were raised on your grandparents ranch in Idaho."

"And you think that makes me a cowboy?" he asked, amused.

"More than anyone else I know."

That was probably true.

"And maybe you're missing Idaho and all the wide open space and big skies and all that." She waved a hand to indicate there was more to miss but she didn't know what exactly. "Right?"

No. Being back in San Francisco was reminding him of a time when he'd been a young city rat, and a happy one. He loved the constant motion of the city, how he could get Thai food delivered at two in the morning if he wanted. He loved being with Caleb, like nearly two decades hadn't gone by. The only thing to miss about Sunshine, Idaho, was feeling like he had a handle on his future.

But that was gone now too.

"They've got a mechanical bull in there," Ivy said.

Scrubbing a hand over his face, he had to laugh. "You do realize that no real cowboy would be caught dead on one of those things."

"You're going to be," she said confidently.

"Oh yeah?" He turned to her and found her with a smug smile that was utterly contagious. "And how do you know that?"

"Because I'm going to ask real nice and sweet," she said, making him laugh again. "Okay," she admitted. "So maybe I'm a little short on nice and sweet. But let's just say there'll be a prize for whoever stays on the longest."

He held her gaze. "You have my full attention."

"Winner gets to pick their spoils."

And just like that, he was in. "I could take you outside the city to a working ranch in Sonoma that Donovan, a buddy of mine, runs," he said. "We could ride *real* horses."

She looked horrified. "What, are you crazy? No way."

He arched a brow. "Let me get this straight. You'll get on a mechanical bull, which by the way is actually very dangerous, but not a real horse?"

"I'm not riding anything that's got a mind of its own."

He sidled her a glance. *"Ever?"*

She grimaced. "Well I walked right into that one, didn't I."

He grinned. "Want to take it back?"

She looked him over, slowly and with great interest. "I'll get back to you on that one."

"I look forward to it."

They got out of the truck. Ivy held his hand, tugging him off the sidewalk and into the street.

"Jaywalking's illegal," he said.

"You can give me a citation later."

He liked the sound of that. He found himself smiling as she tugged him along, in her usual impatient hurry to get to everything.

The bar was every cliché of a cowboy bar imaginable, down to the saddles for seats and wagon wheels on the walls, and let's not forget the mechanical bull. Kel was still taking it all in when their drinks were served.

Ivy tossed hers back and stood. "Watch and learn, cowboy."

She strode to the mechanical bull. Someone gave her a cowboy hat and when the bull began to move, she was one hand on the hat, the other on the rope, her body moving in sync with the bull.

Kel's mouth went dry.

She lasted a respectable ten seconds before being tossed and landing in a graceful pile on the mats.

Then she was in front of him again, grinning with pride, still wearing the hat. "Beat that, cowboy."

Her excitement and love for life was contagious as hell, and against all his own personal boundaries and sense of dignity, he stood up. He did a brief internal inventory of his still healing injuries, but he was feeling good. Good enough to do this. "Winner gets to pick their spoils," he reminded her.

She looked at him for a beat. "Within reason," she amended.

He smiled, thinking he could work with those odds, and strode to the damn mechanical bull.

It was possibly the most ridiculous thing he'd ever done in his entire life, so why he was still smiling as he mounted the thing, he had no idea.

When the bull began to move, the crowd went wild while he held on for dear life. He could hear Ivy chanting "cowboy, cowboy, cowboy!" making him laugh and nearly fell off.

He lasted ten point five seconds before he was flung into the air, landing flat on his ass in an undignified heap. Before he could get up, Ivy jumped on him, laughing as she straddled him, slid her fingers into his hair, and—to the crowd's delight—kissed him. Then she pulled back and rose, offering him a hand. He let her pull him to his feet before he stole another kiss, this one more aggressive than hers. "I won," he said against her mouth, hands gripping her hips, enjoying the satisfaction of watching her eyes heat.

She removed the cowboy hat and set it on his head. "How about that for your spoils?"

He shook his head. "I won more than the hat," he said, and bought her another drink. They sat thigh-to-thigh watching the dance floor, talking easily, laughing, and seeing her relax with him was a gift he hadn't realized he wanted. He couldn't tear his eyes off her. "Want to dance?" he asked.

She looked at him in surprise. "You dance?"

"I grew up in a tiny town in Idaho. We had to dance for PE during snowy winter days in the auditorium."

She laughed.

"It's true."

She eyed him more closely. "Like the salsa and the cha-cha kind of dancing?"

"All kinds," he said.

"Do you do the silly white boy boogie, where you just sort of rock back on your feet and look like you might be having a seizure?"

He smiled. "Want to double down on our wager?"

She laughed. "Hell, yes, I'll take that challenge."

"Okay," he said. "But if I win again, we change the terms of what you owe me."

"How?"

"The 'within reason' clause gets eradicated."

She stared at his mouth and nibbled on her lower lip like the idea excited her, a lot, and the temperature in the bar seemed to spike about a hundred degrees. He led her to the dance floor just as "Thriller" came on, and when he began to make the moves with pinpoint accuracy, she started laughing. "Okay," she conceded, "you really can move on the dance floor."

"I'm even better off the dance floor," he promised.

She laughed some more and moved in closer, until they were up against each other, writhing to the beat. And damn, she could move too, and feeling all her sweet curves rock to his was driving him crazy in the very best of ways.

They danced until Ivy had to take off her shoes. Then they ate bad bar food and laughed and talked some more. It was midnight when he drove her home.

Still in the truck outside her building, he turned to her. "That was the best date I've ever been on."

She stared at him. "It was?"

"By far."

She squirmed a bit and then removed her seatbelt. "Thanks for tonight," she said softly. "It's late, and I've got to be up in a few hours, so—"

Leaning in, he took a nip at her bottom lip. "You're worried I'm going to claim my spoils tonight."

"No."

"Liar." He laughed when she narrowed her eyes at him. "Don't worry," he murmured. "I'm not collecting my prize tonight."

"You're not?" She sounded a little breathless, and . . . disappointed. He got out of the truck and came around for her.

On the sidewalk, Ivy called out a greeting to both Jasmine and Martina, who were huddled in their blankets. "Ladies," she said, and handed them over her bar leftovers. Waffle fries.

"Your breakfast tacos were real good this morning," Jasmine said. "I like the new seasonings."

Ivy smiled. "Thanks, I've been changing some things up."

"You should try a pinch of cocoa powder," Martina said. "My mama used to use it as her secret ingredient."

"I will," Ivy promised.

He and Ivy took the stairs and when they got to the top landing, she glanced up at him. "Kel?"

He looked into her pretty blue eyes and smiled. "Yeah?"

"It was my best date ever too," she said very quietly and she turned toward her front door.

And then froze, stopping short so fast, he nearly plowed into her back. He took one look at her pale face and immediately went on high alert. "What is it?"

She sucked in a breath and squatted low to stare at the door handle.

He crouched next to her. "What are we looking at?"

"After the truck break in, I got paranoid," she said softly. "I put a piece of tape on here from the handle to the wood of the door every time I leave so I can tell if someone's tried to get in."

The implication being that if someone had so much as tried to turn the handle, the tape would break off.

The tape was broken off.

Rising to his full height he pulled her up with him. The lock didn't appear broken or tampered with, but it was a cheap lock, one that anyone could pick with relative ease.

She tried the handle and it opened. "Shit."

Pulling his gun, he nudged her back and entered first. He walked through the entire place, checking behind doors, her closet, under her bed, the window ledge—which didn't take more than thirty seconds.

While he did this, Ivy stood in the middle of her apartment, hands on hips, expression carefully blank as she stared at him. "I know most women would disagree with me, but I like your cowboy costume better than the cop costume."

"It's not a costume," he said, slipping the gun away. "It's who I am. What's missing?"

She shook her head. "I don't think anything's missing."

He moved toward her until they were toe-to-toe, and gently tilted her face to his. Her eyes weren't soft and warm now. They were iced. "Ivy—"

"I don't need to call the cops. I'm looking right at one, and I don't even know what to tell you, so there's no reason to have them out here for nothing."

"The truck break-in was one thing," he said. "But this is now a pattern."

She turned away from him. "I live in a shitty area and we both know that. It's random. Just let it go. It's late and I have to be up soon, so I need to go to bed."

"Want me to stay?"

"No."

She was holding herself rigid. Her entire body one big stubborn nerve. "I could take the couch," he said. "No pressure."

"No, it's okay." Her back was still to him, but she was hugging herself now. "I'll be fine."

He gently turned her to face him. She wasn't fine. She was pissed and shaken, and that was all over her face. But she was also obstinate and full of pride and hated to accept help of any kind. Pushing her would get him nowhere. Which meant that he was going to spend the rest of the night in his car watching over her from there.

Chapter 15

You've got more in you

At kickboxing the next morning, Ivy was working her newfound frustrations out on the bag. She was in a zone when she realized everyone was looking at her.

Stopping, gasping for breath, Ivy relaxed her stance and stared at Tae, Sadie, and Haley. "What?"

"You seem a little . . . fierce this morning," Sadie said.

"She means kickass," Tina piped up from the front of the room. "Seriously kickass. And speaking of that, who's ass *are* you kicking this morning?"

Whoever had broken into her truck.

Whoever had broken into her apartment.

And then there was the serious frustration bubbling just beneath her skin. Sexual frustration. Which was all on Kel, so maybe she was also kicking his ass a little bit too. Metaphorically anyway. "Just burning calories," she said, swiping her sweaty forehead with her arm. "Now if you don't mind, are we having tea or working out?"

Tina laughed with sheer delight. "Working out, sweetness, and you're right. Let's do double time."

Everyone but Ivy groaned.

The sun had made an appearance when she left the gym and took the bus to her food truck. She'd been there maybe three whole minutes when she heard footsteps outside. They were easy and unhurried, and recognizing the quiet unruffled energy, she stuck her head out the back door.

"'Morning," Kel said.

She hadn't slept a single wink, she felt like she'd been run over by a Mack Truck, *twice, and* she had a headache from said lack of sleep. So no, it wasn't anything close to a good morning.

Until he held out a coffee. The ridiculously expensive coffee she treated herself to only *very* occasionally. She stared at it and then at him. He didn't look like he needed caffeine in spite of the fact he'd played bodyguard, staying in his truck in front of her building last night. All night.

He took in her expression and waited with calm patience, clearly not willing to let her get away with *not* voicing her thoughts out loud. She sighed. "Why are you doing this?"

"Doing what exactly?"

She gestured to the coffee she hadn't yet taken from him.

"You mean being nice to you?" He shrugged. "I like you."

She just looked at him.

"Blame your sunshine-y sweet nature," he said dryly. "And don't worry, I'm not expecting anything in return. Take the coffee, Ivy."

She did, and sipped cautiously but didn't burn her tongue. It was the perfect temperature for gulping, so she did exactly that. A minute later, she drew a deep breath and slowly let it out. "Thank you," she said, refraining from letting him know that in that very second, she'd have given him anything he wanted.

"Was there any trouble after I left last night?" he asked.

"Yeah, some guy was parked out front of my place all night."

Their gazes met. His easygoing expression never changed, and she realized that though she'd thought *she* was the master of hiding in plain sight, she was nothing but an apprentice, because the real master stood right in front of her. "I almost called the cops," she told him. "But they don't like to go out to that area if they don't have to."

"A good reason to get into that condo in Caleb's new building sooner rather than later."

"I'm working on it. And the neighborhood's not *that* bad," she said. "I've—"

"—Lived in worse," he finished for her. "Yeah, I know."

She laughed a little, not sure if she was flattered or uncomfortable at how well he'd come to know her in such a short time. She began prep work for breakfast. "If it makes you feel better," she said while she chopped, sliced, and diced. "I'm hopefully moving soon."

He smiled.

"What?"

"You look excited whenever you talk about your new place. It's cute."

"I'm not cute. Take it back."

"Can't. Cuz you *are* cute."

"No. Cute's for . . ." She searched her brain. "Puppies and kittens."

"And sexy women who don't even realize they're sexy."

Shaking her head—and ignoring a serious tummy flutter—she plated three breakfast tacos and handed them over.

Kel looked down at the plate in surprise. "What's this?"

"Maybe I'm trying to be nice to you too."

His dark eyes warmed. "I didn't ask."

"I know. But I also know you love my food." Which she took great pride in. She was also a sucker for anyone who appreciated her, so she gestured to the stool in the corner. "Sit. If I know Caleb, it'll be the only time you sit all day."

He did and immediately dug in, letting out a rough, heartfelt groan, the sound of pleasure pulling at spots inside her she'd forgotten about. She wondered if he made that same sound when he was in bed with a woman.

Not that she was ever going to find out.

Unless . . . *that* was what he chose as his spoils from last night's bet. Because it would be rude to back out on a bet, right? Rolling her eyes at herself, she turned back to her prep work.

"Tell me about the condo."

"You've been to the building. You *work* in that building," she said. "You probably know more than I do."

"I like the light in your eyes when you talk about it."

More tummy squishing. "It's a great location. It's got a great view. And the kitchen . . ." She couldn't hold back a grin. "Once I get in there and start cooking, you'll have to come over—" She broke off as she realized he'd be gone.

His smile faded. "I would've liked to see you in it."

Their gazes met and held. She shrugged off the unmistakable sense of longing and kept working.

When he finished eating, he cleaned up after himself and then removed the knife from her hand before pulling her into him. Then he kissed her. It was a pretty great kiss, and when their tongues touched, she moaned.

Pulling back, eyes on fire, he took a deep breath, like it'd been hard to stop kissing her. "If you have any problems," he said. "Any at all, I want you to call me and let me help you take care of it."

"Always the cop."

He smiled against her mouth, taking her bottom lip between his teeth and giving it a naughty little tug that caused a secondary reaction deep inside. "Not always."

She had to bite back another moan. "Okay," she managed breathlessly. "So when you're not a cop or cowboy, you're . . . what? A Boy Scout?"

Cupping the back of her head, he held her still and kissed her again, taking his sweet-ass time as he took her completely apart, and she had her answer.

He was no Boy Scout.

"Thanks for breakfast," he said, and stuffed some cash into her tip jar before leaving.

When he was gone, she let out a long shaky breath and turned to eye the money. He'd left her twice as much as what she would've charged for the food he'd eaten.

Kel worked through lunch. There was a lot to do to get Caleb's security systems in place and up and running, and eight days of the two weeks he had here were already gone.

Caleb had given him an office to use when he wasn't onsite at any of the ten different projects he had going in the city. Kel was there now, neck deep in architecture and engineering plans, when a shadow fell across his desk.

Lifting his head, he found his sister.

Remy was bundled up and wearing one of those baby sling thingies, with Harper strapped onto the front of her, facing out. When she caught sight of Kel, she smiled a big gummy smile that allowed a long line of drool to escape as she began to bounce in excitement.

Heart. Melted.

"Hey, cutie," he said, rising to his feet as she squirmed and wriggled. Coming around his desk, he bent to press a kiss to the top of her head.

"And what about me?" Remy asked, taking a seat with a sigh of relief.

He pressed a kiss to the top of her head as well, making her laugh.

"What are you doing here?" he asked, leaning back against his desk. She, Ethan, and Harper had come over to Caleb and Sadie's every night he'd been there—except for last night when he hadn't been home—so they'd had lots of time together. "Everything okay?"

She stroked a hand over Harper's soft peach fuzz

and smiled. "Everything's great for me. I'm here about you."

"Why?"

She sighed. "There's no easy way to say this, so I'm just going to say it. I know about Mom."

Kel took a beat. "What?"

"I know that you ran into her at the diner where she's working these days. She took the night shift there because it pays extra and they're trying to save up to move a little closer to their only grand-daughter."

He blew out a breath. "I didn't know that."

"Of course you didn't. Because you didn't want to know. You know, she thinks you blame her for every-thing that's ever gone wrong in our family."

"What? Why would she even know to think that?"

"Because I was there when I told her."

Kel scrubbed a hand over his face and then slid his hands into his pockets. It was that, or kill his sister.

"Look," Remy said. "Mom wasn't perfect."

Kel rolled his eyes. He'd heard this speech before.

"But," his sister went on. "She's the only mom we've got. And she's trying hard. She's been trying hard for a decade now."

"You always did want to see the best in people."

"And why wouldn't I? It's not like I want to be old and grumpy like you."

"Ha ha," he said.

She flashed him a grin and unwound Harper from the sling before handing her up to Kel. "She thinks you hate her. Mom. Not Harper. Harper thinks everyone loves her."

He took the baby. "You need to stop meddling."

At his tone, Harper made a sound of distress, so he shifted her against him and stroked her back.

Harper immediately stopped fussing and gave out a little mew of happiness that did something funny to his heart. Then she yawned wide and set her head on his shoulder in a move so sweet that his chest actually went tight. Hugging her close, he kissed her head again. "Her scent. It's . . ."

"Crackalicious, I know. I think they come that way on purpose so we'll forget the hell they put us through and keep procreating."

Harper nestled her face into the crook of his neck.

He could honestly say he'd never given thought to settling down and having a family of his own. It just wasn't something he saw in his future.

But truthfully, he hadn't given a lot of thought to his future at all and what it might hold.

And yet standing there cradling his soft, sweet, warm niece, something inside him actually ached. "Does it always feel like this?"

Remy laughed. She laughed so hard she snorted, which started her laughing again, until she had tears running down her cheeks. Finally, she sniffed, swiped her face, and got herself together. "I'm tempted to say yes and then ask you to babysit, but I have this thing against lying my ass off to family." She shook her head. "She's just been fed and changed. This is the happiest she gets. Ever. The rest of the time, she's either pooping, throwing up, or screaming her fury to the world."

Kel looked down at the little angel in his arms. She yawned again, relaxing every bone in her body for a single beat before letting out an impressive fart.

Right into his hand.

With a blissful sigh, she then snuggled in again while—holy shit—his eyes literally watered and he gasped for fresh air. "How could something so small and dainty smell so bad?"

Remy grinned and snapped a pic of him with her phone and looked at it. "Aw. Hold on . . ." She thumbed on her phone for a second. "Okay, I just posted it on Instagram and tagged you, so brace yourself." She showed him the pic with the caption: *One of These Two Adorable Beings Just Farted . . .*

"Wow, seriously?"

"Hey, I'm still your baby sister."

She was the only person who could make him roll his eyes so hard they nearly came out of his head. And she was now yawning too, and he took a longer look at her. She seemed beat. "Listen, that loveseat's actually pretty comfortable. Why don't you lie down and close your eyes for a few minutes? I've got this."

Remy gave him a small smile. "You always say that. You've been saying it since the day Dad died. And you meant it. You always had my back, no matter what."

"Because we're family."

"No, it's because you care," she said. "You love me." Her eyes filled and he sighed, making her give a watery laugh. "Sorry. It's the baby hormones. They make me weepy." She met his gaze, her own still soggy but determined, and he braced himself.

Ah hell. "You didn't come here to have me hold Harper for you," he said.

"No."

He braced himself. "Just get it over with, Remy, say whatever you came here to say."

"I know about Mom."

"Yes, we just had that conversation. I ran into her." He shrugged. "Big deal."

She shook her head. "I mean I know about the thing she did."

"No, you don't."

"I do."

Kel looked into her eyes and saw sorrow and regret, but he still didn't believe she knew the real truth, that their mom had been cheating on their dad. No. There was no way she knew, because if she did, she wouldn't have such a close relationship with either their mom or her husband—the guy she'd cheated on their dad with. "Remy—"

"She told me years ago."

"Told you what exactly?" he asked carefully.

"About her and Henry."

Kel could only shake his head. "Why would she tell you?"

"I was turning twenty-one and I wanted a family birthday party. I *always* wanted a family birthday party, but it was so hard to get you and her in the same place at the same time. I knew I was missing a big piece of our puzzle. She'd always told me that I was too young to understand, but that year I refused to hear it. I told her I was a grown-up, legal, and I wanted the damn truth, even if you didn't. So she told me."

Kel stared at her. She was quiet, calm, and clearly worried about him, which was crazy. No one needed to worry about him, ever. But she was also accepting. "You're okay with it," he breathed in shock.

"Let's just say I made peace with it," she said softly. "And the reason I was able to do so was because I listened to her story, really listened, and got both sides—"

"You don't have dad's side. He's not here to tell it."

Remy shook her head. "You're the one who doesn't

have both sides, Kel. You acted as judge and jury, and you know what? I get it. We were kids and she left us. But she apologized to us. Or to me anyway. You weren't interested in talking to her about it. But it was a long time ago and I think it's time for you to make peace with it as well."

"I don't need you to tell me how to feel about this."

"Are you sure? Because you're acting like you're still ten."

"Look," Kel said, unusually frazzled. "I'll be gone soon enough, can't we try to just enjoy the rest of my visit while I'm here?"

"Oh my God. Seriously, if I hear one more time that you have to get back to Idaho . . ." She shook her head. "Just tell me this. What's holding you there other than sheer stubbornness? I mean grandma's been gone forever, and now grandpa's gone too. And you've got the ranch being managed by a solid team. Are you really not going to come and live near your family just because you're still pissed at Mom?"

He recognized a trap when he saw one, so he kept his mouth zipped.

"Caleb told me you're seeing someone, a friend of his. Does she know how screwed up you are about relationships?"

"I'm not screwed up about relationships."

"No?" she asked. "When was the last time you had one that worked?"

"My job," he said. "It's—"

"It's not the job, Kel, it's you."

The words were a not-so-surprising echo of what Janie had told him. But they didn't—couldn't—understand. They didn't know what his mom's early lies had done to him, how it'd been only further compounded by what had happened on the job he'd put ahead of his personal life for so long . . . "You don't understand," he said tightly.

"Oh, I think I understand plenty. You're nursing a grudge that's two decades old. And I get it, you were burned young, and that sucks. You can't trust your heart, and that also sucks. But have you ever tried looking for a better outcome?"

He opened his mouth to argue, but Remy shook her head. "Never mind, I'm wasting my breath," she said, standing up. "My own fault. I thought you'd grown up."

He was still standing there, pissed off and a whole bunch of other things as well when Remy gently took Harper from him.

"Maybe you should rethink being here at all," she said quietly, resetting the baby against her. "If it's so hard for you." And then, with a kiss to his jaw that belied the harshness of her words, she left him alone with his own thoughts, none of which were good.

It would certainly be easier for him to just go and forget how his mom had looked when she'd laid eyes on him. Forget the way Harper had felt in his arms. Forget how it was to have Caleb close again. Forget the emotions that had broken free when he'd had his mouth on Ivy's . . .

All of it, he could walk away from all of it, and maybe he should.

Chapter 16

Bust it out with every ounce you have left

Normally, Ivy left the truck in Jenny's capable hands by five in the afternoon, which still made it a twelve hour day for her, but tonight Jenny had a coffee date, so Ivy was up.

"You sure it's okay if I leave early?" Jenny asked for the tenth time.

"Go. Have fun. Take mace and a whistle, and make sure you text me when you get there and leave."

"Yes, Mom," Jenny said with a smart salute. "You do realize this is the only way to meet guys now, right? And that at some point even you, the hundred-year-old soul, is going to have to set up an online profile somewhere to get laid."

"Eh?" Ivy asked, cupping a hand around her ear, pretending to be ancient. "But I don't even know how to use The Facebook."

Jenny snorted. "See, you are old. No one our age uses Facebook anymore, except to check in with their grandmas. And even if you don't want a guy in your life right now, how about sex? And two of my best friends met their significant others on Tinder."

"Not happening," Ivy said.

"Then how will you meet anyone?"

Ivy thought of Kel, and how he'd literally just walked into her life. "If it's meant to be, it'll happen."

"That's oddly sage and Zen of you," Jenny said. "But you're never sage and Zen."

"Do you want to leave, or stay here and argue with me?"

"Bye," Jenny said and vanished.

It was seven p.m. before Ivy finished cleaning and closing up shop. She backed out of the food truck, concentrating on making sure the new lock was engaged. Then she looked around to make sure no one was watching and did her little deal with a small piece of tape, squatting low to get it down where no one would notice it.

Okay, so yeah, she was far more unnerved than she'd let on about the two break-ins. She'd have to be stupid not to be. Pushing to her feet, she turned to leave, and caught a shadowy outline of a man way too close. With a gasp, she jumped back a step, and nearly out of her own skin to boot. "Dammit," she said, hand to her chest. "You need a bell."

Kel stood there in a jacket against the night's chill,

a hoodie beneath it with the hood up, hands shoved into his jeans pockets. "And you need to be more aware of your surroundings."

That was just true enough to have her grimacing. She'd been too lost in thought. She'd clearly gotten too complacent, gone soft here in San Francisco, losing some of her edge, her survival instincts. That had to stop.

"I think we can do better than that for you," he said of the tape.

"It's effective enough." Turning away, she started walking down the sidewalk.

"Let me drive you home," he said, keeping her pace.

"I like to walk."

"You like to be stubborn."

"I like to be independent," she corrected, and pulled up her own hood, wishing she'd remembered gloves.

A bolt of lightning lit up the sky, the accompanying clap of thunder making her jerk as the first drop of rain hit her on the nose. And then another, and with a sigh she turned and found herself toe-to-toe with the current bane of her existence. "Okay, fine. I'll take the ride. Thank you," she added begrudgingly.

He flashed a smile. "It's because you're cold, right?"

"No." Cold, she could handle. But her hair was about to get frizzy, and that she couldn't handle.

"You hungry?" he asked in the truck a few minutes later.

"No. You?"

He glanced over at her, eyes dark. It wasn't hard to read his mind. Yes, he was hungry, just not for food.

And just like that, she was suddenly hungry too.

When he found a parking spot near her building, he turned off the engine.

She looked at him, not able to see much since now the only lighting came from the street traffic and surrounding buildings. But his outline was familiar and somehow . . . *comforting*, as was the feel of his gaze on her face.

For most of her life, she'd not given much thought to comfort, either needing or giving it. It'd been about survival, and comfort was a luxury.

But for over a year now, it hadn't been about just surviving. It was about learning to . . . well, *not* be like a feral cat. Learning how to be more open and make friends and . . . yes, dammit, find comfort in the life she was building for herself.

But taking in the man sitting next to her, the strength and warmth of him, she realized she most definitely wanted more than comfort tonight. "You're not sleeping outside again," she murmured.

His voice came back to her in the embodied dark, low, and a little gravely. "Are you inviting me in?"

"Well you did win the bet."

"This isn't going to be about the bet, Ivy."

"Yes, it is."

Not answering, he got out of the vehicle with her. As they walked toward her building, he was the one to call out a greeting to Jasmine and Martina, both sitting beneath two side-by-side umbrellas.

He'd remembered them, and as people, not as homeless nobodies.

And utterly without warning, she softened for him. She'd thought she wanted his body tonight, but suddenly she knew it was far more.

At her door, he crouched low and eyed her "alarm system." The piece of tape was in place. Still, he rose to his feet, held out his hand for her keys and then proceeded to clear the place.

When he was seemingly satisfied, he stood in the center of her postage stamp–sized apartment in that leather jacket, buttery soft faded jeans, and boots, hair damp from the rain, drops all over him. He liked to call her "Trouble," but the truth was, it was *him*. Every inch of him was going to be trouble, and she was looking forward to it.

He was watching her watch him, leaving her to it, calm. Patient.

Eyes hot.

"So," she said, mentally cracking her knuckles, trying to figure out how to get him closer and his mouth on hers. "Want to watch a movie?"

"Are you asking if I want to Netflix and chill?" He sounded amused, though that heated gaze of his was dark and serious. Very serious.

"Um . . . yes?"

He gave a slow shake of his head and came toward her, backing her up to the wall. Setting his hands on the wall on either side of her face, he leaned in and gave her what she'd wanted—one hell of a kiss. It started soft, questing, but when her arms wound around his neck and she kissed him back, he deepened the kiss. She heard herself moan as she fisted her hands in his hair. It wasn't enough, so she regrouped and slipped her hands beneath his shirt instead, touching his abs, feeling the hard muscles ripple in reaction. His skin was warm, the scent of him delicious, and . . . dangerous to her heart and soul. She simply couldn't be this close to him without losing her tenuous grip on her need and hunger.

He lifted his head and searched her gaze before his mouth curved very slightly and he backed up a step. "When you're sure," he said quietly, running his fingers along her jaw. "You'll say when." He dropped his hand from her. "'Night, Ivy."

She stared at his very fine backside as it headed toward the door, her heart still pounding, lips tingling from his kiss. She pulled out her phone, hit his number to call him, and watched as he got halfway out the door before his cell rang.

Pausing, he pulled it from his pocket and eyed the screen and then answered it as he turned back to face her, his lips curved as he found her on her phone as well.

"When," she said softly but firmly into her phone. She smiled. "And Merry Christmas."

Eyes on hers, Kel moved in close. "Are you my present?"

When she nodded, he took the phone from her ear and tossed it aside. Still holding her gaze, he tossed his phone as well, which ended up next to hers. Then he pulled her into him. "Can I unwrap you now?"

In answer, she shrugged out of her wet sweater and let it hit the wood floor with a thunk. She toed off her shoes and then waited expectantly.

As she knew he would, he got the message. With another small curve of those lips she wanted back on hers, he bent and untied his work boots and then kicked them off. His leather jacket went next and then his sweatshirt.

Then they stood there staring at each other. She didn't know about him, but her heart was racing, threatening to burst right out of her chest. She'd not lived like a monk, but she hadn't been with anyone in a while. She hoped it was like getting back on a bike, because she was pretty sure Kel was about to give her the ride of her life and she intended to measure up. With a deep breath, she pulled off her tank and unbuttoned and unzipped her jeans.

"Wait," he said, a soft but gruff tone as he moved closer. He unbuttoned his shirt and shrugged out of it. His T-shirt went next, all discarded in a heap on the floor with everything else.

She raked her eyes over his bare chest and then let her hands travel up to his sides, her fingers gently brushing his right side and the still healing bruises running down the length of him from shoulder to thigh. "The mechanical bull?" she asked in horror.

"No. Didn't get out of the way of a desperate-to-escape bad guy fast enough."

"My God," she breathed, horrified. "What did he hit you with, a baseball bat?"

"She. And it was a car."

She let out a breath and let her fingertips rest on a small, but thankfully much older scar on his right shoulder.

"Bullet," he said.

With a grim frown, she traveled down to another scar on his left flank, also old. She touched it and he shuddered a little.

"Knife."

She met his gaze. "I thought you were a small-town sheriff."

"I am."

"I figured that meant chasing bears out of Dumpsters and driving drunks home," she said.

He smiled. "There's plenty of that too." Bending his head, he brushed his mouth along her jaw to her ear, which he nipped lightly, drawing a sigh of sheer desire from her.

"There's a lot more to your job than I imagined," she said, ashamed to realize she'd not given it a lot of thought before. He'd chosen a career that meant walking into danger, where most people ran away from it. That took a certain type of man. A brave one, certainly. One who cared for others enough to risk life and limb.

While she was thinking this, he was busy sliding his big hands from her waist to push her jeans down past her hips. "You're just about the best present I've had in . . ." He shook his head. "A long time. I'm going to unwrap the rest of you now, Ivy." He lowered his head, his lips brushing her ear. "Slowly . . ."

She shivered. "I don't do slowly."

"I've noticed." When he had her jeans to her thighs, he cocked his head to take in the sight of her standing there in a black lace bralette and a matching black lace thong and let out a rough groan.

She put her hands over his to shove her jeans the rest of the way off, but he merely twisted his wrists and took her hands in his, bringing them up to his mouth to brush a kiss over her knuckles. Then he picked her up and set her ass onto the coffee table. Dropping to his knees before her, he slowly pulled her jeans the rest of the way off before tossing them aside.

When his hands settled on her thighs and gently urged them open, creating a space for him, she readily complied with a happy noise, because now, *finally*, they were going to get to the good stuff.

"Yes," he murmured on a rough laugh against her throat, making her realize she'd spoken out loud. "The good stuff is coming. And so will you."

She shivered in anticipation, making him groan. Belly-to-belly now, chest-to-chest, the inside of her thighs cradling his hips, he slid his hands up her arms, her throat, and into her hair.

And then he finally kissed her again.

The whole time moving so slowly she was at once quivering with anticipation and sheer frustration.

"Patience," he whispered against her mouth. Still amused, damn him.

Okay, yes, so she'd not been standing in line the day patience had been handed out, but seriously. How long could he drag this on for?

A long time, as it turned out. First, he kissed her until she was panting and writhing against him and rocking up into his hands every time they swept over her. And they did this with slow, purposeful intent, his thumbs stroking over the dainty little lace bra that wasn't doing much to keep her breasts contained, until she honestly couldn't remember why she'd held him off. Hell, she couldn't remember her own name.

Somehow she'd managed to get his jeans unbuttoned and filled her hands with what she desperately wanted inside her, and by his reaction, he felt the same.

He had a strap of her bralette down one shoulder, a mouth on her breast, his tongue and teeth teasing her nipple, whipping her into a whole new kind of desperate frenzy, when she couldn't take anymore. Tearing her mouth free, she fisted her hands in his hair and lifted his head.

His eyes were two hot molten pools of dark chocolate.

"What's the male version of a cock tease?" she demanded. "A vagina tease? Stop being a vagina tease!"

"What seems to be the exact problem?" he asked, his voice sex-on-a-stick.

Was he kidding? "We're still wearing too many damn clothes and you're not inside me!"

His hands slid to her ass, and thanks to the thong, she felt his warm, work roughened fingers squeeze bare cheeks as he rose, her clinging to him. She'd never been so grateful for such tightly enclosed living arrangements in her life because he had only to turn to climb onto her bed. Her back hit the mattress and when she felt him laughing, she looked up at him standing at the foot of the bed.

"You have so many pillows, I'm not sure I'm going to fit on there with you," he said.

Oh yes, he would, and to prove it, she began pushing pillows off the bed to the floor in earnest, in a hurry to get him where she wanted him most. This made him only laugh harder, which he was going to pay for. When she kicked the last pillow off, she got up on her knees and slid her hands south, wrapping her fingers around him and stroking.

He stopped laughing, nudged her flat to her back, and set a knee on the bed. With a smug smile, she bent her leg and put a foot to his chest. "Still overdressed, cowboy."

Taking the hint, he backed off the bed and stripped out of the rest of his clothes. When he was magnificently naked—and she did mean magnificently, the guy was a work of art—he once again put a knee on the bed. "Now who's overdressed?"

She began to tug her bralette off with haste. But here was the thing with bralettes . . . they didn't have any hooks. It was an over the head deal, which was fine if you were alone getting dressed in the morning. No one had to witness the stupid, awkward maneuvers one had to go through to get the thing in place.

Getting it off was just as ridiculous, but she did her best to mimic the easy, graceful way he'd stripped. Only she failed, because she got herself good and stuck halfway, with the bralette across her face, arms up. "Dammit. Don't look yet." She struggled harder for a beat and then froze when she felt his hands on her thighs, sliding northbound.

Okay, this was still going to work. He was going to help her.

But his hands stopped low on her hips, his thumbs hooking in the lace waistband of her thong.

"A little help?" she asked, somehow just by his touch utterly frozen in place with her hands above her head.

"Shh." He began to slowly—of course—so slowly she wanted to scream, drag her panties down at the very same time that his mouth captured a bared nipple. This had her struggling anew. She felt him smile against her, but that didn't stop her from *finally* freeing herself of the bra with a huff.

Still on a mission, Kel shifted a little lower, kissing and teasing his way down her body, making himself at home between her thighs, which he held open with those broad shoulders. But his mouth wasn't where she desperately needed it. Nope, he'd stalled at her hip, which he nipped with his teeth before soothing the spot with his tongue.

"Kel."

Again she felt him smile against her as he moved south, to the top of her thigh. And then her inner thigh. And then . . . finally, *and then*. He found the spot, the very best spot without any instructions, guidelines, or a treasure map. Her body tightened and her toes curled. A little unnerved by her shocking, over-the-top reaction to him, she froze for a beat.

Turning his head, he gently kissed her inner thigh. "Still with me?"

She bit her lip, glad he couldn't see her face from this position. "I think that you know that I'm very much with you," she managed as lightly as she could.

"You still want this?"

"Again, I think that's obvious."

Lifting his head, he met her gaze. She did her best to hold it. "I want to hear you say it, Ivy."

She drew a deep breath and gave him the utter truth. "I want you," she whispered. "*In* me."

"This first," he said huskily, stroking his fingers over her wet, quivering flesh. "I want you to be with me all the way."

"Where else would I be?" she asked, both his words and actions having her stomach doing that butterflies-on-crack routine again.

He flashed her a sexy smile and . . . went back to what he'd been doing. Which was that thing that had her breathing like she was trying to outrun a speeding train. It was good, so good she heard herself panting his name like a chant, a plea . . . And when their gazes met across her writhing torso, that was all it took for her to come.

When she could breathe again, she stared up at the ceiling and had to laugh, finding it exceptionally funny that this had been the best sex she'd ever had and he hadn't even gotten inside her yet.

Kel crawled up her body and licked the hollow of her neck where her pulse was still racing before coming into her field of vision, his eyes dark with heat and male satisfaction.

"Show off," she whispered.

"I've had over a whole week to fantasize about doing that to you," he said. "I suppose that freaks you out."

"No." She ran her hands down his body to wrap around what she was starting to think might be her favorite body part. "It makes me even more impatient."

At her touch, his head fell back. When she stroked, he groaned and kissed her hungrily before reaching to the floor for his pants, coming up with a condom. Watching him roll it on was a sexual act all in itself, so much so that she sat up and had to add her hands to the cause. He was just so beautiful. The cut of his body, the way he moved, the low timbre of his voice, how he looked at her, the feel of his hands as they caressed her into quite the state . . .

When he sank inside her, deep, her soft moan mingled in the air with his rough, heartfelt groan, and she thought it was maybe the best moment they'd ever shared.

He stuck to long, slow strokes at first, his body hard against hers, his mouth at her throat, then her ear, telling her how good she felt, the things he still wanted to do to her, the explicit words revving her up all over again.

As she lost herself in his arms, she felt it overtake him too. His eyes closed and he made a rough sound of pleasure that turned her on almost as much as the physical act itself. She knew the exact second he let go and surrendered, and she held on for all she was worth, stroking her hands over him, touching everything she could possibly reach.

After, he rolled to his side, bringing her with him to cuddle her close as he caught his breath. And that's when she knew she'd been wrong before, because this, *this* in-between moment was her favorite moment they'd shared.

Ivy had no idea how much later she came awake. It was still dark, but Kel was on his side facing her, head propped up on a hand, watching her sleep.

"Was I snoring?" she asked.

"Yes." He smiled when she gave him a shove, and not budging, he pulled her into his big warm body. He had her tucked beneath him, working his way down her body with his diabolically clever mouth when he suddenly froze and then quickly untangled himself from her.

"What is it?" she murmured, already missing his heat.

He put a finger to her lips.

Blinking to try to see him in the dark, it was her turn to freeze when she heard it.

The sound of someone rattling the knob of her front door.

Her heart knocked hard against her ribcage as old instincts kicked in. Rolling off the bed, she came up on the other side, her faithful baseball bat in hand, the one thing Brandon had ever given her, which she kept under her bed. "I've got this," she said. And in that moment, she meant it. She was ticked, completely pissed off about being messed with, and entirely over it.

Kel held up his hand and gave her an accompanying hard look, both of which very seriously and intensely said *stay*. His gun glinted in his hand as he turned to the door.

Right. He was good at this. This is what he did for a living. But she was pretty sure he didn't usually do it buck ass naked.

Chapter 17

Let's do double time

Kel got to the door just as it slowly began to open. Grabbing the intruder, he yanked him inside and shoved him up against the wall. The guy was of average height and build, but with a better than average ability to fight.

Good thing Kel was trained and also pissed off, because both worked in his favor. He held the asshole still and realized he could feel Ivy breathing down his neck. "Seriously? I told you to stay put."

"This is *my* apartment," she said. "No one tells me what to do."

Ignoring her, Kel held the guy face flat to the wall. "You picked the wrong place tonight."

"I'm not here to pick the place. I'm looking for Ivy," the guy managed to say.

Kel felt Ivy's surprise. "Why?" he demanded.

"Hey, man, let go."

Instead, Kel pushed him even closer to the wall. *"Why."*

Ivy flipped on a lamp and went hands on hips. She'd put on a shirt.

His.

Kel was pretty sure that was all she was wearing, which was still a whole hell of a lot more than he was. "Brandon," she said tightly. "The idiot's name is Brandon."

"Your brother?" he asked in stunned disbelief.

"The one and only." She didn't look happy at the reunion.

Which made two of them, because just as with Ivy's tales of this guy, something wasn't ringing true here. He turned Brandon from the wall. The guy had the same fiery red hair as Ivy, spiky on his head, as well as a scruffy beard, but it was his eyes that held Kel's attention. One was the same startling blue as Ivy's, the other green. He glanced at Ivy. "I thought he was in New York."

She nodded. "Me too."

"Hey, here's an idea," Brandon said, words muffled since his face was planted into the wall. "Maybe you could put on pants."

Kel let go of him and strode past Ivy to the bed, where he retrieved his jeans from the floor and pulled them on. When he'd buttoned them up, he realized brother and sister were standing there, just staring at each other. Not exactly the loving greeting of siblings who hadn't seen one other in a long time. Granted, *his* sister had smacked him upside the back of his head when she'd first seen him, but he'd deserved it.

Made him wonder exactly what Brandon had done to deserve that worried, wary expression on Ivy's face. "Two a.m. is an odd time for a visit," he said.

Brandon lifted a shoulder and went with an affable smile. One, by the way, that matched Ivy's.

Which she wasn't flashing now.

"Wanted to see my sister," Brandon said. "It's been a while."

Ivy was hands on hips. "What happened to New York?" she asked.

"Actually, it was Mexico . . ."

"You in trouble again?" Ivy asked.

"Who, me?" he asked and grinned.

Kel would bet all the clothes he wasn't wearing that Brandon had been in Mexico either finding trouble or running from it. "So if I was to look you up right now, there wouldn't be any outstanding warrants?"

Brandon laughed, but kept looking at Ivy. "Had no idea your tastes run to cops now. Kind of ironic, don't you think?"

Ivy cut her eyes to Kel for a telling beat, but hell

if he knew what it meant before Brandon continued. "We need to talk, sis. Alone."

"Hell no," Kel said.

"Kel," Ivy said softly.

He shook his head at her. "He was breaking in here, you realize that, right? And you've already had two other break-ins. What odds do you want to lay down that we just caught our guy?"

Brandon's easygoing vibe was still in play when he met and held Ivy's gaze. "Look, I just need to borrow your car. Like old times."

"The last time you borrowed my car you totaled it."

Brandon had the good grace to wince. "Yeah, that was my bad. But that was years ago. I've matured."

She snorted, and again Brandon smiled, in on the joke. "Okay, so that's unlikely to happen," he admitted.

Ivy shook her head. "It doesn't matter anyway because I don't have a car."

Brandon nodded and then sent her a long look, and at whatever had been silently communicated, Ivy turned to Kel.

"No," he said. No way was he leaving her alone with this guy.

"Listen . . ." She pulled him aside, and stepping very close, peered up into his face. "I want to hear what he has to say."

"Go ahead."

She gave him a pat on his chest, like she was soothing him. "He's my brother, Kel. He's not going to hurt me. He might be an idiot—"

The "idiot" in question snorted. He'd moved farther into the apartment, pacing around.

Ivy glared at him. "An idiot *and* a break-in artist," she added. "But he's not violent. It's okay, Kel. You can go."

"I'm not leaving you alone with him."

"Yes, you are." She went up on tiptoe and kissed him softly. Sweetly. "I'll be fine." She squeezed his hand. "Really."

Brandon came back toward them and made a point of looking at his wrist like he was eyeballing the time.

Ignoring this, Kel kept his eyes on Ivy. "You'll call me if you need me."

"Of course."

He shook his head. Then he strode toward Brandon and yanked her brother's backpack off his shoulder.

"Hey," Brandon said.

Kel opened the flap on the backpack and pulled out Ivy's laptop.

Ivy glared at Brandon.

"Oops." He shrugged and gave a rueful grin. "Sorry. Old habits."

Kel shook his head, scooped up the rest of his and Ivy's discarded clothes and tugged her with him to her bathroom. "Don't move," he warned Brandon. "And if you touch anything else, I'll remove your sticky fingers for you."

Brandon lifted his hands in the universal "I surrender" position.

Kel shut the bathroom door and waited until Ivy looked up at him. "So," he said conversationally, pulling on his socks. "He seems nice."

Ivy closed her eyes. "I'm sorry."

"Don't be. Not your fault. But you could've told me the truth about him."

She looked away.

He pinched the bridge of his nose and reminded himself that she'd clearly lived in a world where believing in people had gotten her nothing, and worse, possibly hurt. "How about your friends?" he asked. "You don't trust them with yourself either?"

This got him a response. Her eyes flashed with emotion. He just wasn't sure which one.

"You don't understand," she finally said.

"Then help me understand."

She went stubbornly mute, grabbed her clothes from his hands, and turned her back to him.

When the front door shut behind Kel five minutes later, Ivy dropped her forehead to the wood and took a second to get her bearings.

Easier said than done.

Her bathroom had enough standing room for one person, so it'd been cramped quarters as she and Kel had dressed in silence in there. A silence complicated by bare skin brushing bare skin, emotions still high from what they'd shared in her bed, and the adrenaline rush of her brother's untimely arrival.

Brandon.

Of course he'd shown up when he had. Because he'd made it his lifelong mission to make her life as difficult as possible.

Kel had instantly recognized she'd been telling tall tales about her brother. He'd been kind enough—or pissed off enough—not to press the issue right then. But he'd swing back to it later, she was quite certain.

Or maybe not. Maybe he'd decide to wash his hands of the crazy chick. She certainly wouldn't blame him.

Having no choice but to regroup and face one problem at a time, she drew a deep breath and turned to her brother.

"Sleeping with a cop? You've stepped up in the world."

"Why are you here?"

He cocked his head. "It was interesting to see the way you look at him though, when you don't think he's noticing. He makes you happy. Not a look I've seen on you much."

"He and I barely know each other," she said. "And you didn't answer my question."

"Happy's good, Ivy," Brandon said quietly, voice genuine. "It's not easy to find, not for people like us."

"It's not like that," she said.

"Hey, whatever you say."

She was not in the mood for this. Only a little bit ago, she'd been in Kel's arms with him deep inside her, reminding her what passion and hunger and desire felt like.

This, with Brandon, was a cold bucket of water, bringing back memories and feelings she thought she'd long ago put behind her. "It was you who stole from my truck and broke in here the other night, wasn't it?"

"Of course not."

She stared him down, doing her best to ignore certain facts. Like one, dammit, damn *him*, he was looking at her like she was somebody worth caring about, like he'd actually truly missed her. And then there was the undeniable fact that no matter what she wanted to tell herself, she'd grown up with him, been in the trenches with him. She knew him better than anyone, and knew that she'd been the only person ever able to ground him. To hold him accountable. To encourage him to stay on the right path.

Which he clearly hadn't. He had a hollow look to him, and a haunted one as well. He was too thin, like he hadn't been eating enough for weeks, maybe months, and he had what appeared to be a healing black eye and was favoring his right arm.

"How did you get hurt?" she asked.

"Fell down a set of stairs," he said on a shrug.

Her stomach tightened at the age-old anxiety over worrying about him and the trouble that followed him around like a bad cold. She moved to the front door and opened it, gesturing with a jerk of her chin that he should go.

He dropped his head and stared at his shoes for a long beat. When he lifted his head again, he shook his head. "Fine. I didn't fall down the stairs."

All this did was cement the anxiety in her gut. "This is why I dread your visits. I'm sorry you've found yourself some new trouble, but you've got to go."

"Ivy—"

"Why did you leave my fridge in the truck open? I had to throw away all the food."

His eyes revealed a quick flash of regret. "I'm sorry," he said very quietly. "I was starving and in a hurry. I was being followed."

"Followed by who? And *why are you even here?*"

He locked her front door. Then slid the security chain in place. "It's a long story."

"So start talking," she said, watching as he then moved to her windows and lowered the shades. "You're scaring me."

"You have no reason to be scared, you've got a big ape outside, ready to beat the shit out of anyone who hurts you." He turned to face her. "I need two things."

"No."

"A place to stay tonight," he said as if she hadn't spoken. "And . . ." He winced. "Okay, keep an open mind here, alright? I need to borrow some money."

"No *and* no," she said. "Besides, look around. I don't have any money."

He gave her a long look. "Since when do we lie to each other?"

Her eyes narrowed. "You've been snooping."

"Enough to know you have a deep savings account."

"That's the down payment on a condo I'm buying."

"A condo. Sounds a little fancy for us Snows."

That it was actually true made her defensive. "I want a home to call my own. I've always wanted that."

"I know." His voice had softened. "You always have more hope and faith than I did."

"Not hope and faith. It's called effing hard work, Brandon. If you used your powers for good instead of for fun, you could have whatever you wanted."

"So this condo. Tell me about it."

"It's a secure building, so I can stop being paranoid," she said. "The kitchen's . . . glorious. And there're great amenities, a gym, business center, pool . . ."

He smiled. "Sounds like it suits you."

"It does."

"I'm going to hope you've got room in your heart for both your fancy, new condo *and* for your brother."

She sighed.

"Can I stay?"

"You do remember last time, right? Two years ago when I was living in LA? You showed up and needed a place to stay. The next morning you were gone. And so was the money in my wallet and the cash I had in my hiding spot."

"Ivy, under the mattress isn't a hiding spot for cash. It's where you're supposed to keep the sex toys."

She pointed to the door. "Get out."

"Please, Ivy. It's an emergency."

She stared at him, trying to get a read on all he wasn't saying. But other than looking pretty serious at the moment—extremely unlike him—he wasn't revealing much. "What will happen if I kick you out right now?" she asked.

"Besides your boyfriend giving me the third degree when I hit the street? You don't want to know."

Dammit. She shook her head. "*One* night, that's it, no money. And I want Aunt Cathy's necklace back."

"You won't regret it," he said with clear relief. "What was for dinner?"

"I'm going to shower but there's food in the fridge."

Thirty minutes later she came out of the steamed up bathroom and stopped in surprise. Her brother was vacuuming. And by the looks of things, he'd also tidied up, including cleaning the kitchen. "Why are you here?"

He flashed her a sweet smile. "Made you some hot chocolate."

"Did you steal anything?" she asked him suspiciously.

"Not yet," he said with a look of innocence that she knew could fool the pope.

Great. So he'd been looking for something else of hers to sell for cash. Moving to a window, she pulled the shades aside and looked down to the street. Kel's truck was still at the curb. He'd meant it. It wasn't often that someone told her something and followed through or kept their word, so it was still a novelty.

Was he sleeping?

If not for their untimely interruption, they might've slept the entire night together, wrapped up tight and warm in each other. She'd never wanted such a thing before, but the idea of it with Kel sent shocking waves of yearning through her.

"So," Brandon said. "Where do you keep the booze?"

Chapter 18

If you want to see results,
you've got to stay with me

Two hours later Kel was still in his truck in front of Ivy's place. He was head back, baseball cap low over his eyes to cut the glare from the streetlamp on the other side of the street, but he wasn't sleeping. He was reflecting. On being back here in a city he'd left at age twelve after losing . . . well, everything, on whether or not he missed Idaho, on the fact that he and Ivy had pretty much decimated each other in her bed in the very best of ways and he still wanted more.

The way she'd felt wrapped around him, his name on those soft lips, along with everything else she'd done with that sweet, sexy mouth—

The passenger door opened.

"I could've been a murderer, you know," Ivy said and hopped into the passenger seat. "You can't just sit in an unlocked vehicle in this neighborhood, cowboy. It's dangerous."

He slid her a look, amused that she seemed to think he was naive. "I heard you coming."

"Why are you still here?"

"You know why."

"I agreed to call if I needed you."

"You don't do need," he said.

She lifted a shoulder in agreement to that fact. Then sighed and assumed his position, relaxing against the seat, tilting her head back. "You don't have to do this."

He hadn't moved a muscle, and he didn't now either, going still as stone. Did she mean be with her, or watching her back? "Define 'this,'" he said.

"Guard me. I've been watching my own back for a long time now. I'm good at it."

He looked over at her, but her eyes were still closed. "I've got no doubt of that," he said. And that was true. She was clearly capable, smart, wily . . . It was all sexy as hell. "Sometimes in life you meet someone," he said. "And suddenly you don't have to be alone all the time. You can share the burden. Relax your guard."

"For the few remaining days you've got here in town, you mean?"

This caused an odd stab of pain in his chest. "Sometimes you only get a beat in time. Sometimes you get a lot longer. But what you don't do is let it pass you by. Not when it's this good, Ivy."

She didn't respond to that. Her body appeared relaxed, but he knew better. He was starting to know her now and this was her false calm, the one that was only skin deep, the one she showed the world, while on the inside, she was scrambling.

He turned in his seat, lifting his hand to the back of her head, letting his fingers slip beneath her hair to knead at the tight muscles of her neck. "Do you want to tell me what's really going on with your brother?"

"That depends," she said.

"On what?"

"On if I'm talking to the man I just had sex with, or the cop." With that, she opened her eyes and turned her head to meet his gaze. "Because if I'm talking to the guy who just rocked my world . . ."

He let out a long shaky breath, filing that incredibly welcome compliment away for later. He had a decision to make, and in that moment, looking into her wary, guarded eyes, he knew there wasn't a choice. "Yes," he said. "You're talking to the guy who just rocked your world. Just as you rocked his."

She bit her lower lip, which didn't hide her small, quick smile. "Then I'd tell him that my brother makes bad decisions, but he promised one night and he'd be gone."

"Okay. And what would you tell the cop?"

She held his gaze. "That I haven't seen my brother in months."

So she was willing to lie for the guy. Not an easy pill for him to swallow. He'd spent some of his time sitting out here looking up her brother. Brandon was a convicted felon in three states. A lot worse than she'd made him out to be. "What do you have against cops?"

"A lot."

"On duty or off, I'm the same guy, Ivy."

"Then you're one of the rare ones," she said softly, and sighed heavily. "Listen, about Brandon. I . . . need to explain him."

"Not to me, you don't. You don't owe me anything." He wrapped a strand of her silky hair around a finger. "I know exactly how family works. You're not responsible for his actions, Ivy. Nor for the consequences of those actions."

She stared at him for a long beat, then let out a breath, along with an acknowledging nod. "I appreciate that. I'm not exactly used to caring what anyone else thinks. But I seem to care what you think," she admitted, not sounding too pleased about it. "My brother is the way he is because of how we grew up. No father figure, and a mom who slept the days away and was never home at night. There wasn't anyone to notice if we had meals or clothes to wear, or if we went to school. Brandon learned early on how to pickpocket, and it was thanks to that thieving that we weren't always hungry and didn't have to go to school barefoot."

Kel drew a deep breath, hating the picture she'd painted. "No one should grow up like that. But look at yourself, Ivy. You grew up in that same hell and you're not out there still thieving for a living. Don't make excuses for him."

"I'm not making excuses. I'm telling you why he does stupid shit. I was just smart and liked school. I loved reading and loved the library, and both kept me out of trouble. He didn't have that. He cut classes and hung out with bad kids, but honestly, when you move from school to school to school like we did, it's only the bad kids who want to befriend you anyway. It's not all his fault."

Kel reached for her hand, entangling their fingers and tugging lightly until she looked at him. "People make choices. You made good choices. He didn't."

"It's not that simple. And he's family."

She was defending Brandon because he was family, even though the guy had hurt her. In comparison, when his mom had hurt him all those years ago, he'd not only held on to the grudge, he'd nursed it, let it eat him alive, and used it as an excuse to not have a relationship with his family.

Ivy was watching him in the ambient lighting of the truck. "We all have our family ghosts," she said quietly. "Your mom's husband, is he a good guy?"

"Henry seems okay," he said, though in truth he didn't know much about him.

"But she's happy?"

He didn't know that either, and he didn't feel good about that.

"It seems like she is," Ivy said gently.

Kel closed his eyes. "You know who I'd rather talk about?"

"My stupid brother?"

"No. You." He opened his eyes. "Something's bothering me. You've got friends who care about you. Caleb, Sadie, and the others. Why make up stories about Brandon?"

She tossed up her hands. "I've always lied about Brandon. Call it . . . I don't know, wishful thinking."

"But why lie? Why just not talk about him at all?"

She looked away, out the passenger side window into the dark, wet night. "Did you know that until I landed here in Cow Hollow last year, I didn't really do the whole friendship thing?"

She looked like she felt alone, very alone, and his chest ached for her. "That's changed."

She shook her head. "I can't tell them now. It's too late."

He cupped her face. "They'd understand."

"I'm going to ask you for one thing, Kel," she said in soft steel. "That you don't tell them."

He'd have said that he'd never hold a lie for anyone, not ever again. He'd have sworn it. And yet here he was, looking into her big blue eyes filled with a vulnerability he knew she hated, and he nodded. "But no more lies, Ivy. Not between us. Promise me."

Staring at him, she hesitated and then slowly nodded.

He let out a breath and kissed her. She kissed him back, but when it got heated, she pulled free. "Go home," she whispered. "It's late and you have work tomorrow. It'll be okay. I've got this. Like I said, he's an idiot, but he's my idiot."

Feeling reluctant to do that, he hesitated. But she had that look on her face, the one that was in the dictionary under stubborn. "You've got to promise you'll call me if things go sideways," he said. "Or if things even *look* like they're going sideways. Or even the slightest chance of things going side—"

"I hear you."

"Is that a promise too? If you need me, you'll call?"

"Yes," she said. "But they won't. He's leaving in the morning. Nothing's going sideways."

"Okay." He still didn't let go of her. Couldn't. "You busy tomorrow night?"

She let out a small smile. "We already had a date, cowboy."

"I want another."

She cocked her head and studied him, and he did his best to look like the only thing she needed in her life. He must have succeeded because she smiled. "Is this because you're trying to avoid going to your sister's surprise baby shower?"

"No, that's the *next* night. Which reminds me, how do you feel about three dates in a row?"

She snorted. "You sure you want company to the shower? Filled with family? I mean, that makes me a witness."

He laughed. "There'll be no bloodshed." Probably. "And yeah, I want your company."

"Because you want to use me to deflect the attention off you," she said.

No, because he actually wanted to spend time with her, but that was more info than she needed right now. "Is that a problem?"

"Not even a little," she said, and he resisted pulling her onto his lap and showing her some gratitude of the naked variety, but only because they were in public.

Taking in his expression, she laughed softly. "You can thank me after."

Sounded promising.

Ivy woke up the next morning and looked over at the loveseat where Brandon had slept.

It was empty.

It took two seconds to look around. Brandon's backpack was gone. The mugs they'd had hot chocolate in late last night after she'd come back upstairs from talking to Kel were no longer in the sink, but washed and put away.

Brandon had cleaned up.

And then bounced.

He'd promised he'd stay only one night and he'd kept that promise. And at the thought, she felt both relieved and inexplicably sad.

Chapter 19

Just one more. Okay, two more. Three.

Ivy dragged herself to kickboxing class, where, not surprisingly, she got her ass handed to her by Tina.

"Your head's not in the game," Tina yelled.

True story.

Class had started with a warm-up and would end with a cooldown, but in between were several rounds of high intensity intervals. That's where they were at the moment, with Haley on one side and Sadie on the other, the three of them seriously lagging.

"Ladies," Tina called out. "When the going gets tough, ask yourself—what would Tina do? And then get your damn head in the game."

Haley, who'd had a few more dates with Dee and was looking happier than any of them had ever seen her, whimpered. "This is what I get for being a sex fiend. I'm too tired to get my head in the game."

Sadie bent over at her knees to suck in air. "I'm . . . going to have to tell Caleb . . . that we can't do it on the nights . . . I've got kickboxing class the next morning."

"Ladies!" Tina called out. "If you can't do it all night long and then handle this class the next morning, then I'm doing something wrong. Let's start over, from the top. One-two punch, jab, cross, and front kick. And . . . repeat!"

They all groaned and got to work.

Life at the taco truck that day was insanely busy, but thanks to Jenny's help, everything ran smoothly. The rain held off until Ivy had just started to walk home. In two blocks, she was soaking wet and frozen solid thanks to once again forgetting her umbrella.

Halfway home, Kel called.

"Hey, Trouble. How was your day?"

She found herself smiling for absolutely no reason. "Long."

"Yeah? You got enough left in you for dinner?"

She paused. Not because she didn't want to see him. She wanted that quite shockingly badly. "I'm wet, which means I'll have to change. And once I take off my bra, I won't want to go anywhere."

His voice lowered to a sexy timbre. "Even better."

She laughed. "Okay, so you're definitely a guy."

"Thought I proved that last night."

"Did you?" she asked innocently. "That was hours and hours ago and I'm not sure I can remember."

He paused. "You're flirting with me."

"Am I?"

"New plan," he said.

"What's that?"

"Leave your panties off too."

Suddenly she wasn't cold anymore. In fact, she was downright toasty hot as she disconnected and stared at her phone, pulse racing.

A flash of lightning had her quickly entering her building, and as she began to climb the three flights of stairs, she fantasized about all the things they might do to each other . . .

In the hallway in front of her door she stopped, and dripping a puddle around her feet, she took the extra beat to study her lock. Yes, she was flustered as hell, and also quite turned on. But she wasn't stupid.

The tape was not in place. Instead, it hung off the jamb about an inch from the floor. But for the life of her, she couldn't remember if she'd taken the time to set it before she'd left that morning.

Which meant she had no idea if someone—*Brandon*—had helped himself inside. Holding her breath, she unlocked the door and nudged it open with her foot, carefully peering in just as thunder boomed dramatically. But storms had never scared her.

People scared her.

One of the good things about living in two hundred and fifty square feet was that she could see her entire place in a single sweeping glance.

It was empty.

Still, she stayed on guard as she stepped inside and shut and locked the door behind her. Everything seemed exactly as she'd left it and she let out a long breath.

For the first time in his entire life, Brandon had really done what he'd promised and left. She tossed her purse to the couch and began to strip on her way to the bathroom and the hot shower she'd been dreaming about all day long. She was soaked to the bone and her clothes were stuck to her wet body. As she pulled them off, they hit the floor with a thunk.

She was at the bathroom door when her phone rang. It was Kel. "I miss you," he said in greeting.

She felt a ridiculously goofy smile curve her mouth. "Prove it."

"I'm outside your door with dinner."

She grabbed a small throw from the back of the couch. Wrapping herself up, she opened the door a crack, letting just part of her face show. "What's for dinner?"

His gaze slid southbound from her face. "You."

Liking that answer a lot more than she should, she stepped back enough to let him in, watching him shut and lock the door behind him. "Is your brother still here?" he asked.

"Nope, and if past habits are anything to go by, I won't see him again for a few years."

Nodding, he turned and took in the sight of her from head to toe.

"I'm still wet," she said softly.

His eyes darkened. "Are you?"

She shivered, and not from cold this time. Outside, the rain pummeled the roof and slashed at the windows. Inside, she was nearly overheating.

"Come here, Ivy," he murmured, setting the bag in his hand down and reaching for her. "I'm . . . starving."

Laughing, she held him off with a hand to the chest, which had her throw slipping a little bit, giving a quick free peep show that had him stepping into her and wrapping her up in his arms.

"And what if *I'm* . . . starving?" she asked.

Lightly tugging her wet hair so that she tipped up her face, he kissed her. A soft hello at first, which quickly turned into something else entirely. "Tell me now if you meant for food," he said huskily.

"I didn't mean for food," she said and tugged him to the couch.

He sank into the cushions, pulling her to stand between his spread thighs. And then, holding her gaze in his, he unwrapped her from the throw like he was unwrapping a most precious gift.

When the throw hit the floor, he let out a low groan at the sight of her. "You take my breath," he murmured in that voice that removed the knees from her legs. Cupping her bare ass in his hands, he urged her a little closer, taking his hot, wet, talented mouth on a tour. When he added his wickedly clever and diabolical fingers, she gasped and spread her legs to give him better access, which he took in such an erotic, sensual measure that she gasped again. "My legs . . . I can't stand."

His mouth busy at her breast, he tugged her so that she fell into him, arranging her so that she was straddling him, the inside of her thighs hugged up to the outside of his. And when he spread his wide, hers went with them.

"Please," she whispered, rocking into him, not even sure what she was asking. "Oh, please . . ."

Luckily he seemed to be able to read her mind because he pulled a condom from his pocket and handed it to her while he unbuttoned and unzipped and freed his essentials.

And goodness, his essentials.

She knew he liked slow and thorough to the point of torture, but she needed him now, so she rolled on the condom, rose up on her knees, and sank down over him.

His hands went to her hips, his fingers digging as his head went back, his eyes closing as he swore roughly beneath his breath. She knew *exactly* what he was feeling, because she was feeling it too, and it was so delicious, so . . . perfect, she needed more. So she began to move, wrenching some more low, reverent swearing from deep in his throat.

"You feel so good, Ivy. Too good. You've got to slow down or it'll be over before—"

She didn't slow down. She couldn't help it. There was something unbelievably erotic about being completely nude while he was still fully dressed. Still, she shoved up his shirt, because . . . well, *abs*. Watching them crunch and quiver every time she rose and fell on him was like a drug.

His hands gripping her hips, he slowed her rhythm, drawing out their pleasure in the way only he could, since he was the only one of them with any patience at all. When his head went back his eyes closed again, making a low sound of pleasure deep in his chest. She could ride this man forever, she thought. His hands were everywhere, stroking over her body, rubbing her lazily until she came with a shudder. After, he drew her down until she was low enough to kiss him, and tangling his hands in her hair, he sucked on her tongue as she moved.

"You're so beautiful," he whispered against her mouth. "I could stare at you forever."

Shockingly moved by his words, her hips stuttered to a halt, ripping a groan from him.

"Don't stop, God don't stop," he said roughly, his eyes glowing fiercely as his hands found her hips again, thrusting up to meet her. He felt so good, and his face when he came . . . well, she lost it again at the intensity.

Watching him recover was almost as good as the sex. When his breath returned to normal and his eyes cleared, he pressed one of her hands to his still thundering heart as he'd done once before. "If I tell you something," he murmured, "are you going to freak out?"

Her stomach tightened with nerves. "Of course not." Totally. She was totally going to freak out.

"I like you." He watched her face carefully, so she had to work at keeping it even. "A lot, Ivy."

The words both thrilled and terrified, and she bit her lower lip.

"What?" he asked.

"There's a big difference between liking the idea of someone and actually liking who they are," she whispered.

"I like both. Come here, Trouble, and let me give you my oral argument."

With a snort, she tugged her hand free.

Kel laughed and tucked her close before rolling her beneath him. And then he slid down her body and proceeded to give her the best oral argument she'd ever had.

It was another hour before Kel got around to cooking. *Cooking.* As in honest to God standing in her kitchen like he owned it, cooking her steak and baked potatoes.

"Wow," she murmured, once again wearing nothing but his shirt. She loved that he wore button-downs. She loved pulling up the collar and pressing her nose to the material so she could inhale his lingering scent.

She'd clearly lost her mind.

Kel, in nothing but low slung jeans, squatted down, balancing on the balls of his bare feet to check the potatoes he had in the oven. "You keep saying wow. It's good for a man's ego." Rising, he turned to the toaster because he was making cheesy bread too. His index finger repeatedly pushed down the level of the toaster.

Brushing his hand aside, she slammed the lever down, forcing it to stay in place. "It's temperamental."

"Like its owner."

She sent him a long watch-it-buddy look over her shoulder and he smiled like the big bad wolf, making good spots quiver. "And for clarification, I was saying wow because the steaks smell amazing and I'm ravenous," she said, hopping up onto the old Formica to sit cross-legged.

His dark eyes met hers. His hair was a mess thanks

to her fingers, and he seemed to have bite marks on his neck and shoulder. *Oops.* "Okay," she admitted. "It's not the steak. It's you."

He rose and expertly flipped the steaks. "Yeah?"

"To be honest, no one's ever cooked for me before."

He stopped and looked at her in surprise. "Never?"

She gave a slow shake of her head.

He set down the tongs and came to her, pulling her legs from beneath her so that they hung off the edge of the counter. Putting his hands on her thighs, he pressed them open, making a home for himself in between.

Then he kissed her. Long and deep and so sensually that she tried to get into his jeans again, but with a low husky laugh, he caught her hands.

"Didn't think a man as sexy as you would need such a long recovery time," she teased.

"Believe me, I'm recovered. But I'm going to feed you first."

She rocked into the proof that he'd indeed recovered. Fully. "I know something I could nibble on," she murmured huskily, but her stomach chose that moment to ruin the moment by rumbling, loudly.

Kel grinned. "Steak first." He gave her a hard, promising kiss and then he turned his back on her to return to the food. Which was when she saw the nail indentions on his back.

She sucked in a breath. "I hurt you. I'm sorry."

He pulled the steaks and plated them, adding the potatoes. "You didn't hurt me."

"But—"

He met her gaze. "I've been numb for a very long time, Ivy. I'm not numb tonight. Actually, I haven't been numb since the morning I met you, when you gave me that sweet sass at your taco truck, not to mention the best tacos of my entire life. I knew going in you had claws, but that's okay. I don't mind rough, and I don't mind pain if it means I'm feeling again."

Her mouth opened and then closed.

He gave her a half smile. "Did I just render you speechless?"

"I . . ." She shook her head, unbearably touched at his admission. "Yes, but don't worry, it won't last long." She shook her head again to clear it. "I've also never had a guy be so open and honest before."

He set the two plates on her tiny table and came for her, scooping her up and plopping her into one of the chairs. "Nothing personal, Ivy, but the men in your life have all been assholes."

She choked out a laugh. "Yeah. Maybe. Mostly."

He'd already poured wine. Handing her one of the glasses, he gently touched his to hers.

She held her breath, afraid he was going to say something too deep, too meaningful, and she felt panic seize her by the throat.

"To more stormy nights," he murmured, gaze on hers.

She let out her breath and felt warmth glide through her. Warmth that he'd given her and other emotions beat back the panic. Affection. Desire . . .

"To more stormy nights," she agreed.

Chapter 20

*When the going gets tough,
what would Tina do?*

The next day Kel was doing a walk-through of the new condo building. Caleb was with him and they were checking the plans to the actual build. Or at least that's what Kel was doing.

Caleb was fishing. "So. You and Ivy . . . ?"

Kel ignored this. They were on the fifth floor and Kel was taking notes on his iPad.

His silence apparently amused Caleb. "You're just not going to answer?"

"I wasn't aware that you'd asked a question." He stopped to do a radio check with his security team. Arlo was on the ground floor, Stretch in the basement.

Kel put away his radio while Caleb did a very impressive eye roll, which Kel had no doubt his cousin had learned from being raised by a mom and three sisters he lovingly referred to as The Coven.

"Your avoidance tendencies are top-of-the-line," Caleb said. "You and Ivy?"

Honestly? Kel wasn't sure what was going on, except that whatever it was, it was good. Very good.

"Okay, let me reword," Caleb said. "What do you *want* to be going on with Ivy?"

When Kel shook his head because he honestly didn't know how to answer, his cousin met his gaze. "Look, I know you've been burned, but it only takes one good one. You know that, right?"

"Ivy's got enough going on in her life, I don't intend to complicate it, or risk hurting her. Plus, I'm temporary, so . . ."

Caleb "coughed" and said "bullshit" at the same time. "You want to know what I think?"

"No."

"I think that *you* think you're a risk in the love game."

"I *am* a risk."

Caleb shook his head. "Just because you've had a few bad experiences doesn't make you a risk. And trust me, women are tougher than us. They can handle our shit. And if you don't think so, think about this—they take showers with the water temperature set to the exploding sun, by choice. She can handle

your shit, man. Unless you're not interested anymore."

Kel knew two things with certainty. One, he was
shockingly interested. And two, from the moment
he woke up until the moment he went to sleep, he
thought of her. And yeah, okay, much of that was
actually daydreaming about how it'd felt to be buried
deep inside her, her warm body wrapped around his,
panting his name like maybe no one had ever made
her feel as good as he had.

But the majority of it involved *more* than just
their physical attraction. Ivy had presented as a
closed book, a tough front against the world. But
from the night he'd found her after the truck break-
in, after those long dark hours they'd spent in the
close quarters of her working space cleaning up the
mess and talking, things had changed.

He'd seen a side of her, a vulnerable side that he
was getting loud and clear that she hadn't allowed
anyone else to see. It worried him, how she was surrounded by a close-knit group of wonderful people,
and yet she still held herself apart. And she did it in
such a way that none of them had seemed to even
realize it.

What would happen when he left? Would she go
back to being an island? Hell, who was he kidding,
she was *still* an island. Although . . . she'd trusted
him to help her. She'd trusted him in bed . . . and in
her shower. And on her counter . . .

But the way she tended to almost accidentally reveal some of her hard-knock past . . . it never failed to grab him by the heart and soul. The fact that she'd never had any sort of authority figure in her life, and that her brother seemed to screw with her life at every turn, and yet she'd still turned out as amazing as she had was nothing short of a miracle and a true testament to her strength and tenacity.

Growing up, he'd had his dad early on, as well as his grandpa, and he and Caleb had always been a team. He'd had people who had his back, who'd help him bury the bodies if he needed. Anything.

But Ivy had never had that.

He and Caleb were on the top floor now and Kel stepped forward. "That," he said, pointing to a closed door before thumbing through his iPad. "That's not on the plans. Why is it here?"

Caleb was on his phone scrolling through the stock market, probably making more money today alone than Kel would see all year. *"Caleb."*

"Oh, sorry, I didn't realize we were supposed to answer questions to each other, since you're avoiding mine."

"We're *working*," Kel said. "The talk should be about work. The door. What's up with that unmarked, undocumented door?"

Caleb sighed like he was greatly put out. "I added a roof access during the build. At the moment, I'm the only one with access. It requires a code to get through."

"I see the code pad," Kel said. "But you still haven't answered my question."

Caleb lifted a shoulder. "You know Spence."

Spence Baldwin was Caleb's occasional business partner and a good friend.

"He owns the Pacific Pier Building," Caleb said. "And one of his favorite things about it is the roof access. Only a select few have access to it, it's like a secret haven."

Kel took in Caleb's expression. "So . . . because Spence has a secret roof rendezvous spot, you need one too?"

"Of course."

Of course. Kel had to laugh. Caleb had grown up poor as dirt. But he now had more money than . . . well, possibly God, and though it hadn't changed who he was at the core, neither had he lost his competitive spirit. "If you truly want this space to remain private, we'll need to create individual codes for the people you allow access to. I'll need a list."

Caleb nodded. "Okay. And while we're up here discussing security . . ." He met Kel's eyes. "What's happening with your job?"

"Nothing, as I'm not there."

Caleb rolled his eyes. "When you get back."

Kel shrugged. "Same old, I expect."

"What if you didn't go back?"

"Why wouldn't I?"

Caleb shrugged. "Because you have a brand-new baby niece that might want to know her uncle. Because your sister misses you. Because my sisters miss you."

"And . . . ?" Kel asked.

"And hell. I miss you too, okay? Come on, man. Your grandparents are gone. You're living on the ranch, and I know you love it and probably miss it, but I also know that Donovan's shown you ranches for sale in Sonoma, an easy drive from here. Yeah, you've got the job in Idaho, but what else? There's nothing tying you there anymore. Stay here. Archer would hire you in a hot second for Hunt Investigations. Hell, the SFPD is hiring. And I don't even have to say I'd hire you yesterday."

"I don't need you to make up a job for me."

"Call my head of HR right now," Caleb said. "He'll tell you we've been looking for someone with your skills for months."

"Caleb—"

"Just think about it, okay? I've gotta go. See you tonight at the surprise baby shower, right?"

"Right," Kel said, but Caleb was already in the elevator, the doors closing, leaving so that Kel couldn't give him an impulsive, off-the-cuff answer, which would've been no.

Right?

Right.

But he could admit a part of him wasn't thinking no at all. He did love Idaho. He loved the wide open spaces. The peace of the ranch. The way at night you could see the entire universe in the sky, or so it seemed. The quiet . . .

But it didn't have Ivy.

He was still thinking of all this hours later after he'd left work, showered, dressed, and driven to Ivy's. He parked on the street where buildings butted up against the neighboring buildings without any space between. Where there was no peace and quiet, ever. And though dark had fallen, due to the vast city lights, he could barely make out a few faint stars.

Is that what he wanted?

His phone chirped with a text. Donovan, sending him more links to ranches in his area up for sale. One of them had a shot of the place at night.

There were stars, lots of them.

Tucking his phone away, he headed down the sidewalk, pausing in front of Jasmine and Martina. "How are you two doing tonight?"

They both look startled that he'd stopped to chat. "We're not doing anything wrong," Jasmine said defensively.

"I know." He held out a brown sack with the extra subs he'd bought at lunch and saved for them. "Are you hungry?"

The bag was snatched out of his hand so fast he nearly lost a few fingers.

"It's a turkey, bacon, and cheese club," Martina told Jasmine reverently after she'd pulled out the sub and examined it. "Nice."

"I like salami," Jasmine said.

Kel felt his mouth curve. "I'll remember that next time." He started up the path to Ivy's building.

"I told Ivy all men suck," Jasmine said, and Kel stopped and looked back.

Martina was bobbing her head in agreement.

Since they were both eyeing him, clearly waiting on a response, Kel nodded. "I agree. All men suck."

"She doesn't have men over," Jasmine said. "Ever. Near as we can tell, she doesn't let many in. But she let you in."

"Took some work," he admitted.

"See that you don't suck," she said.

And then they vanished into the shadows.

Kel turned to the building just as Ivy came out of it. She was wearing a soft-looking sweater that hugged her body to midthigh, jeans, and boots, and looked like the best thing he'd seen since he'd left her that morning, limp and boneless, sprawled facedown across her bed.

As if she knew where his thoughts had gone, she gave him a small just-for-him smile and met him on the path.

"I was coming up to get you," he said.

"No need."

He pulled her in to him and kissed her. "Is that because you didn't trust yourself with me near your bed?"

"Or my countertop. Or my shower. Or *anywhere*," she admitted freely and made him laugh.

But as they headed over to Remy and Ethan's apartment building, most of his amusement faded, leaving him with a sudden and raw case of nerves and anxiety.

"What's wrong?" Ivy asked.

"Nothing."

"You're nervous," she guessed.

"I said nothing. And I'm not nervous." But he was wondering why he'd ever agreed to this. The evening was going to be a nightmare, and Ivy would have a front row seat.

She turned to her passenger window. "Now who's the liar?"

He glanced over at her. She was still looking out the window, her posture stiff, radiating tension, and that was on him. Blowing out a breath, he reached across the console for her hand and gave it a gentle squeeze. "I should've warned you. When I'm walking into a situation I know isn't going to be pleasant, I get . . ."

"Quiet and broody?" she asked the window.

"I was going to say I turn into a dick, but that works too."

She snorted. Still didn't look at him, but she squeezed his hand back. "Well then, I guess I could also share that when *I'm* forced into doing something I don't want to do, I usually bail." Finally, she turned her head and met his gaze. "Which I believe makes you the better person. Because you might be feeling . . . dick-ish, but at least you're going. To be there for your sister, for your family."

"Actually, I'm going because Caleb threatened to hunt me down if I don't."

She laughed. "You're not afraid of Caleb."

Lucky enough to find a parking spot in front of Remy's building, Kel turned off the engine and turned to her. "How do you know?"

"Because I've seen you. You're like brothers. He loves and adores you. And I see why he wanted you here." She paused. "I looked you up. You've got an impressive record on the job."

This had him giving her a second glance. "Do I?"

"You know you do."

"I work in a small ranching town in Idaho, Ivy. I scare bears out of neighborhood parks. I help rescue runaway horses. I roust drunks off the sidewalks on cold winter nights so they don't freeze to the benches they're sleeping on and die."

"You helped a woman give birth a few months

back in a fast-food parking lot. At gunpoint. The place was being held up."

He gave her a look.

She shrugged. "Blame Caleb. He told Sadie and she told me while we were kicking each other's ass this morning at the gym. Most people are terrified of bears, drunks, and birthing babies, you know."

"I had very little to do with the actual birthing part."

"True," she said quietly. "But I have a feeling you'd face anything head-on and get through it. And look what happened to you not that long ago." She set a gentle hand on his side. "You could have died."

"But I didn't."

"But you could have. My point is that you're fearless."

He ran a finger along her temple, tucking a strand of hair behind her ear just for the excuse of touching her. "I'm afraid of plenty, believe me."

"Name one thing."

Walking away and losing you . . . "My sister's reaction to tonight, for starters. She hates surprises."

She held his gaze for a beat and there was a flicker of disappointment in her eyes before she smiled. "But the good news is that tonight wasn't your idea." She turned to get out and he caught her, pulling her back around to face him.

"What?" she whispered, then gasped as he pulled her over the console and kissed her.

She froze for a single beat before melting into him, sliding her fingers into his hair while letting out that soft sexy little sound she made when he kissed her deep, like she couldn't get enough of him.

"What was that for?" she asked breathlessly when he pulled free.

For letting me in . . . "For coming with me tonight. But brace yourself. It's going to be a bumpy ride."

Ivy wasn't about to admit she was also nervous as hell. This was Kel's family, which made it personal, which in turn made it intimate. She didn't do intimate. "It'll be fun," she said out loud for Kel's sake.

His smile was a little grim. "Yeah. And maybe hell will freeze over."

She looked at him and knew she'd been right to encourage him to come here. "I know this is hard on you. But things change. People change. And think of it this way. Your mom actually wants you in her life. Think about how you might feel if she didn't."

His gaze softened and he brought their joined hands up to his mouth. "Your mom doesn't know what she's missing."

Her heart skipped a beat. "This isn't about me."

"I'm okay," he said. "And though I appreciate what you're doing, you don't have to try and comfort me here. I'm a big boy."

"As I well know," she said and absorbed his

small laugh. "But also . . . I'm not all that good at comforting."

"Actually . . ." He sank his fingers into her hair and held her gaze. "You're much better at it than you think."

Her heart skipped another beat. At this point, she was going to get arrhythmia from her feelings for him. "Come on," she said, tugging him up the walk. "And hey, look at it this way, it can't possibly be as bad as you're imagining. Plus, don't look now but we've been spotted." She nodded her chin to the picture window of the small, pretty, and decorated for the holidays Victorian, where his mom stood looking out, smiling at them. When Kel tensed, Ivy tightened her grip on his hand. "Too late to run now. And smile. You look like you're headed to the guillotine."

He spared her a quick look and found her smiling. "You're enjoying this, aren't you?"

"Oh yeah."

They were quickly ushered into the house by Remy's husband, Ethan, who looked like a nervous wreck. "Tell me the truth," he said. "Am I crazy for allowing this? She's going to be surprised, and she hates surprises. And I hate our couch. I really don't want to be sleeping on our couch for the next ten years, which is how long she can hold a grudge."

Kel clapped him on the shoulder. "Look at it this way. It's too late to run now."

Ivy slid him a laughing gaze, and when he flashed her a grin, she felt her heart catch. Damn. He was potent.

"Great," Ethan muttered, making Kel laugh.

He had such a great laugh, one that somehow never failed to soften her from the inside out. As did watching his easy relationship with Ethan. She might not have had close relationships with any blood family to count on, but she could appreciate one when she saw it.

Ethan drew a deep breath. "Okay, so here's where we're at. We've got ten minutes before we all hide in the dark living room and give my wife the shock of her life."

Kel nodded and turned to tug Ivy into the kitchen to get a drink. They nearly ran right into his mom.

She clasped her hands tight and smiled bright. Too bright. She was clearly every bit as nervous as Kel. "Son," she said quietly. "I'm so happy you came."

Kel had gone still, showing no reaction at all. Unless you knew him. If you knew him, there was the slight tightness to his mouth and the purposefully blank eyes.

Ivy "accidentally" stepped on his foot.

He sucked in a breath, "Me too."

Ivy removed her heel from the top of his toes and smiled at him.

His mom's husband, Henry, came up beside her, sliding an arm around her, extending his other hand to Kel.

There was a terribly awkward beat of silence as they shook hands.

"Good to see you," Henry said. He looked down into his wife's beaming face and smiled. "Very good."

Kel's mom was barely holding it together, fighting tears of happiness, and Ivy ached for her. For Kel. For all of them.

Then Ethan was coming through, hushing everyone, turning off the lights. And a few minutes later, Remy walked in and they all yelled surprise.

Remy gasped and . . . burst into tears. "It's the baby hormones!" she wailed, hugging everyone. She cried all over Kel, who seemed to handle it like he'd done the exact same thing a million times before, just holding her tight and whispering something in her ear that made her sniffle and nod and hug him even tighter.

When Remy had gotten herself together, she turned to Ivy and squeezed her in a tight hug as well. "Thanks for bringing him," she said.

"Hey," Kel said. "Maybe I came of my own accord."

Remy laughed. "Okay, sure. But now that you've spent a few weeks back here in your old stomping ground, can we all hope that you're falling for this city again? Yeah? Maybe?"

"I don't know." Kel glanced over at Ivy and at the look in his eyes, she stopped breathing. "But I can tell you this. There's a lot of things about this place I *am* falling for."

Chapter 21

This is what you came for

A few hours later, Ivy was outside, sitting on the low brick wall bordering Remy and Ethan's small backyard. She was sky gazing when she felt Kel come up behind her. Nudging her hair out of his way, he pressed his mouth to the side of her throat.

Her eyes drifted shut, and she might have moaned.

He nibbled his way up to her ear, which he nipped, and her knees actually wobbled. Turning, she cupped his beautiful face in her hands and whispered, "If you want the same thing I do, then we're in the wrong place."

With a knowing smile, he shifted to sit next to her, his muscular thigh warm against hers.

Smiling, she voiced the question that had been bouncing around inside her head through a very rowdy dinner. "Are you seriously considering staying here in San Francisco?"

"Depends."

She turned to him. There wasn't much light, just a string of white lights crisscrossed from the four corners of the yard, but she could see his face and the way he was looking at her, like he was happy to see her, to be with her, and it made her breath catch. "Depends on what?"

"On a lot of things."

"Name one," she said.

He met her gaze. "You."

She stopped breathing, but did her best to play that off because just the thought that she meant enough to influence his decision scared the crap out of her. "Seems like a lot of power to give one person."

"Let me help inform your response," he said. "At the moment, your opinion matters more than anyone else's."

"But that can't be true. There's Caleb, who's like your brother. And—"

"I know what Caleb wants from me. What I don't know is what you want."

"But it's *your* life, Kel."

"Yeah," he said. "And I realize it's way early to say this, but I want you in it."

"Why?" she whispered, not sure if she was ready to hear his answer.

"Because you're important to me."

She'd never had anyone tell her such a thing before. And she must've looked as discombobulated as she felt because he smiled. "I told you I have feelings for you," he said, "but I didn't tell you why. You're the most unique woman I've ever known."

At that, she had to let out a little laugh. "I'm not sure unique's a compliment—"

"To me, it's the highest compliment," he said. "It means you're different, and I like different. You're also tough, sharp as hell, and a *huge* smartass."

She slid him a look that made him grin. "You're funny too," he said. "And also kind. And sweet."

"Okay, now you're just trying to piss me off."

He laughed and then his smile faded. "And resilient," he said quietly. "You're amazing, Ivy."

In spite of herself, she was unbearably moved by his words. And unnerved. "You've known me for all of . . ." She counted in her head. "Not even two weeks." And yep, she sounded a little panicked so she drew in a deep breath. "It's taken me longer to decide to trust a new pair of running shoes."

"It's okay," he said. "I get it. For you, it's all about trust, which takes time. There's plenty of that. I'm not going to rush you. I'm just asking if you're interested in me staying."

There were a lot of things happening on her inside. Pulse going a little too fast and too hard. Air backed up in her lungs. And then there was her heart, which was squeezed in both hope and fear.

Kel ran a hand up and down her back, waiting until she remembered that she knew how to breathe. "Too hard of a question?" he asked gently.

She closed her eyes. "No." She knew that when he left for Idaho it would hurt. But beyond that? She gave it a thought and knew the truth, even if she couldn't say it. "I wouldn't mind seeing where this might go," she admitted quietly.

He took her hand in his. "I like the sound of that," he murmured.

What she liked was the way he was looking at her, and his confidence in what they might have. Unable to stop herself, she reached out to touch him, running a hand up his chest, around the back of his neck to sink into his hair. "If I kiss you, is anyone going to be watching us out the window?"

"With my family? You never know." Standing, he pulled her up as well, turning them to the only tree in the corner of the yard. He tugged on something and a rope ladder fell down.

He gestured that she should start climbing and she blinked.

"It's a tree house," he said. "It was here when Remy and Ethan moved in. Remy won't go up there because she's afraid of heights. Are you afraid of heights?"

"No, just intimacy, relationships, and true love."

His teeth flashed white in the dark and he gave her a nudge.

So she started climbing. The tree house was one small room with a cut-out window street-side. There was one of those huge beanbag chairs that took up almost all the space, and a shelf on which sat a six pack of beer.

"It's Ethan's man cave," Kel said. He plopped into the beanbag chair, snagged her hand, and tugged her into his lap.

"How often does he come out here?"

"With a new baby? I'm guessing not much." He turned her to face him and his lips met hers in a kiss that went straight to DEFCON 5. The heat started in her core and spread outward and before she knew it, he had his hands under her clothes and she was practically purring. She could feel him hard and ready beneath her and shifted her legs to accommodate him, and was rewarded by a low masculine groan of pleasure that had her trying to get his jeans opened.

"Here?" he asked huskily, adding his hands to the cause.

"Here." She wrapped her fingers around him and started to rise up on her knees, but he stopped her.

"No condom," he whispered, voice strained.

They stared at each other.

Then she smiled into his eyes. "I think we can work around that." She began to slide down on his body but he caught her, pulling her up for a kiss that left her panting. Then he rolled in the beanbag, and it was a testament to his core strength and those delicious abs of his that he managed to tuck her beneath him so that she was on the bottom, him between her legs. He kissed her softly. "Ladies first," he whispered and shifted lower, adjusting her clothing as he went, freeing a nipple for his hot mouth, then a hipbone, which he nipped, making her jump and then moan when he soothed the ache with his tongue.

Then he was southbound, his hands moving her turned-to-jelly legs the way he wanted them. And the way he wanted them was draped over his forearms, his hands on her ass. This left her extremely exposed, but she wanted his mouth on her so badly, there was no room for modesty.

He took the longest moment in history to look his fill. "Gorgeous," he whispered.

She squirmed. "Kel—"

He used his teeth to pull the scrap of lace between her legs aside and then he put that amazing mouth on her.

They were outside, within shouting distance of his family. It was cold, and she was pretty sure her exposed nipple was going to fall off, but she didn't care because his mouth. God, his mouth. She tried to hold her breath, not trusting herself to be quiet, but then he added his fingers and she was flying.

When she came back to herself, she sucked in a breath. "Oh God," she whispered in horror. "Was I too loud? I'm so sorry—"

"You were perfect," he said.

With desire still pooled low in her stomach, she wanted, needed, to have her wild, wicked way with him. Pulling free, she shoved him to his back and climbed on top of him. Pressing her lips to the hollow at the base of his throat, she began to kiss her way down. Dropping to her knees, she licked her lips and leaned forward and—

"Kel?" a voice called up from the ground below.

Remy.

Ivy startled and fell over.

Kel picked her back up and then knocked his head back against the wall several times. "No worries on not having birth control," he muttered.

"My party has a happy ending!" Remy called up. "Ethan just pulled out a huge chocolate cake! It says Merry Christmas on it, but hey, that's what happens when you have a baby shower on Christmas Eve eve, right?"

Ivy's eyes met his and she put a hand over her mouth to stifle a laugh because she was pretty sure she was thinking the same thing as he—that while *she'd* gotten her happy ending, he'd been shafted.

Because of cake. "Coming," he called, and Ivy snorted as she fought to right her clothing.

"Well that was *almost* true," she whispered. "You were *almost* coming."

Much later, Ivy and Kel were leaving the party when Remy caught up with them. "Hey," she said to her brother. "Can I have a sec?" Remy glanced at Ivy. "Do you mind? I'll be quick."

"No problem," Ivy said and moved down the front steps to give them privacy.

But it turned out Kel's family wasn't a quiet bunch.

Remy took Kel's hands in hers—Ivy suspected so he wouldn't walk away—and looked right into his eyes. "You didn't say goodbye to Mom."

"Sure I did."

"You didn't."

"I waved," Kel said.

"Lame," Remy said. "And also pretty rude."

He shifted on his feet. "Remy—"

"I've seen you looking at all the family pics, Kel. And I know you realize you're not in most of them."

"Any," he said. "I'm not in *any.*"

"And who's doing is that?" Remy asked, then pulled him in for a hug before he could answer. "Just think about it, okay? Promise me, Kel."

Ivy wasn't trying to eavesdrop, but she couldn't

help it. The way his sister loved him and had his back . . . it grabbed her by the heart and squeezed.

Ethan appeared behind Remy with Harper asleep on his shoulder, drooling down his back. He and Kel hugged goodbye, and not one of those silly male half-handshake, shoulder bump things, but a real hug without a care in the world as to what that might say about their masculinity.

As far as Ivy was concerned, it was the cutest, warmest, sexiest thing she'd ever seen. But then Kel lifted little Harper and kissed her on the tip of her tiny nose before burying his face in her neck and breathing in her sweet baby scent.

Ivy's ovaries actually sobbed a little.

But it was more than that. He had something here, something she'd never had, something she'd only recognized because of movies and TV. And it didn't make her feel envious so much as . . . warm and fuzzy. And something else too. Seeing him allow his emotions to show, seeing him easily give love and affection to those he cared about . . .

Yeah. He'd never been as sexy to her as he was right that moment.

Remy hugged him goodbye and then came down the steps to do the same to Ivy. "Take good care of him," his sister whispered. "He doesn't know it, but he could use someone to watch *his* back for once."

Ivy pulled back and met her gaze.

"He's always been the one of us to hold it together," Remy explained. "For the whole family. When my dad died, who held it together? Kel. When my mom had her breakdown and stayed away for a bunch of years, he held it together, and me. He's always held me together. And my grandparents too. He helped me get into college, helped Grandpa keep his ranch, helped my grandma through her grief. Because that's who he is, our protector. The keeper of our hearts. But he's never allowed anyone to do the same for him."

"Remy—" This from Kel in a low, exasperated tone. He said a firmer goodbye and walked Ivy to his truck, a hand at the small of her back.

She loved the touch. Needed more. Far more. Watching him love his family tonight had turned her into one big bundle of need.

"You okay?" he asked, opening the passenger door for her.

"Yes. Why?"

"Because you just moaned. When I touched you."

She glanced up at him and bit her lower lip.

He met her gaze and stilled, his eyes heating as they held hers. "Let's go," he finally said, a husky quality to his voice now. "There's something I want to show you."

"I really hope that's a double entendre," she said as she slid into the truck.

He laughed and . . . didn't drive her home. Instead, he took her over the bridge and north.

"Where we headed, cowboy?" she asked, watching the city vanish in her side mirror.

"Sonoma."

She turned from taking in the dark rolling hills to stare at him in surprise. "Wine country?"

"Also horse country."

She blinked and he flashed her a smile in the dark, intimate interior of the truck. "Are you looking for another cowboy bar?" she asked. "I'm not sure I'm up for bull riding tonight." Because it wasn't a bull she wanted to ride . . .

"My buddy Donovan owns a ranch up here. He's been wanting to expand, but doesn't have the capital. A ranch right next to his just went on the market."

"But you just said he doesn't have the capital."

"He doesn't." He slid her a quick look. "He's looking for a business partner."

She blinked again. "You want a horse ranch."

"I have a horse ranch."

There was a warmth in her chest now. She wasn't quite sure, but she thought maybe it was hope. "So . . ."

"What I don't have is a horse ranch near San Francisco. What I do have is my own capital from years of being badgered by Caleb to invest wisely."

She sucked in some air. "And you like San Francisco."

"A whole lot," he said. "But more than the city, I like who's in it."

"Your family."

"Yes." Eyes on the road, he reached out and took her hand. "And . . ."

"Cowboy bars."

"Ivy."

She let the warmth spread. "Me," she breathed.

"Yes."

Forty-five minutes from the city, they were leaning against the front of his truck. The headlights were still on, revealing what looked like endless land. The stars above had never seemed so bright. "It's beautiful," she said quietly in the night air. "You'd live out here?"

"No," he said, surprising her. "At least not full-time."

She turned and looked at him. Cupping her face, he smiled. "I find I'm feeling the city again. It's exciting there, and I want to work with Caleb." He ran the pad of his thumb over her lower lip. "But I like this for an investment. Donovan would run the day-to-day. I'd oversee and manage."

"You like to manage a lot of things," she said. "Your sister said you're naturally bossy."

He smiled. "What about you, do you think I'm bossy?"

"You can be." She smiled back. "In bed. Which, just FYI, is the only place I like you a little bossy."

Pulling her into him, he kissed her for a good long time. When he lifted his head, she was shocked to find they were still out in the middle of nowhere. "Home," she said. "Bed."

"I'm not the only bossy one." He nipped at her lower lip. "And FYI . . . I like you bossy wherever you want."

The tension in the air on the drive home was palpable, and all erotic heat. She didn't speak, and neither did Kel, he just drove with a quiet intensity that had her all revved up. She watched his hand on the wheel, the sinewy muscles of his forearms whenever he moved, and utterly unable to contain it, a small sound of longing escaped her.

Kel glanced over at her and then took a second, longer look. "What are you thinking about?" he asked, voice low. Sexy.

"The ways I intend to pay you back for the tree house."

His eyes darkened and heated, and he picked up the speed a bit, swearing roughly beneath his breath when she put a hand on his hard thigh. After that, there was touching, lots of touching, and by the time Kel found a spot near her building, Ivy was near combustion.

After pulling the keys, Kel put a hand on her arm, warm and steady. "Wait for me."

Everything about him was warm and steady, and

she'd never considered those traits a turn-on before, but in Kel they were incredibly arousing. She watched him round the front of the truck as he came to her side to let her out, nerves on fire for him. When he opened her door, she slid down, making sure to rub up against him, enjoying the response she got.

They practically ran up the three flights of stairs. She was winded, but not from running. They stumbled inside together, wrapped up in each other, mouths already fused. Kel kicked the door shut, hit the lock, and then pressed her back against the wood.

Which was as far as they got before they jumped each other.

When Ivy could breathe again, she lifted her head. She was flat on her back on the floor, naked. Kel was in the same state next to her, except he had one sock still on, which made her laugh.

At the sound, he turned his hand toward her. His gaze softened as he smiled, completely comfortable in his own skin. "You'd laugh at a naked man?"

"When all he's wearing is one sock."

"That's because you tore my clothes off in your desperation to get to my good parts, and you forgot to take it off."

"I was not desperate," she corrected. "I'm never desperate."

"Baby, you were *desperately* desperate."

"Oh please," she said, even while doing a little quiver at the endearment and also while knowing that okay, yeah, she'd been *desperately* desperate.

"You begged."

"I absolutely did not beg," she said.

He just smiled at her, and she remembered panting his name with a whole bunch of "oh pleases" and "don't stops" . . . Fine. So she'd begged. "Don't get used to it."

He wrapped his fingers around her wrist and tugged. Tucking her into his side, he looked into her face, his own unusually revealing.

It's not that he was as guarded as she, but he wasn't exactly an open book either. Life and the job he'd chosen had given him a dark side, an edge, and knowledge that people were not innately good. He'd put walls up. Understandably, she thought.

But those walls were down now, and knowing it was for her felt like both a gift and a curse. Because surely he'd expect the same from her, complete openness, and though she wanted this with him, she wasn't sure she even knew *how* to be open and vulnerable with someone. At just the thought, she went a little cold, and shivered.

With a low murmur of regret, he pulled her closer, sharing his body heat, his expression lazy and satisfied, like a big wild cat.

"My bed is so close," she managed to say, pointing to it, still unable to get up.

"And yet so far . . ."

She laughed, and he smiled as he managed to stagger to his feet. "So that's funny too?" he asked.

"What, that you're so old you can't get me to my bed?"

"You're just baiting me in the hopes that I'll carry you," he said.

"Is it working?"

"Yes, but you're going to pay for calling me old." Scooping her up and flinging her over his shoulder, he carried her fireman style to the bed.

Where he then proved just how not old he was.

Several times, just to make sure it stuck.

Kel came awake at the soft vibration of his phone from an incoming call. Never good at one in the morning. Reaching past a sleeping Ivy, he grabbed his cell from her nightstand.

It was Caleb. "What's wrong?" Kel asked.

"Someone broke into the condo building and got into a fight with Arlo, who was just taken to the hospital by ambulance. I'm heading there now, but the site's unsecured—"

"On it," Kel said, already on the move, off the bed, snatching his clothes from the floor where he'd dropped them and pulling them back on. "Arlo?"

"Took a hit to the back of the head. Looked bad. I don't know anything more yet."

"And the asshole who got the jump on him?"

"Gone, but there's blood here that isn't Arlo's. He told the medic he got a shot off, so hopefully the guy's injured bad enough to end up in a hospital too so we can get him."

"Keep me posted," Kel said and disconnected, shoving his feet into his shoes.

Ivy sat up. "What's wrong?"

"There's a problem on the job."

"Problem?"

"Someone broke into the new building," he said, shoving his things into various pockets.

"Oh no," she breathed. "Damages?"

"Arlo was hurt, he's on his way to the hospital now."

"Oh my God."

She looked so horrified he came back to bed, and with a hand on either side of her face, leaned in and kissed her quickly.

Ivy fisted her hands in his shirt to hold him still for another second. "Come back after," she whispered against his mouth. "When you can."

Their gazes met, and in hers, he saw a deep concern and worry. He stroked the pad of his thumb over her lower lip, kissed it again and then did what he didn't want to do, what he was starting to realize he would never want to do—leave her.

Chapter 22

Let's do this

Ivy turned over in her bed for the hundredth time since Kel had left at one a.m. It was now three a.m. and he still hadn't returned, though she'd gotten a text with an update on Arlo's condition. Stable. She drew relief from that, which backed up in her throat at the sound of someone at her door.

Not Kel. He wouldn't be making that odd scraping noise. He'd have let her know right away it was him, knowledge that had her heart in her throat.

Rising from the bed, she grabbed her handy, dandy baseball bat and reminded herself that she was a badass tough chick who could handle herself.

That's when the knock came, just a single, almost soft, knock. Swallowing hard, she moved to the door and took a look through the peephole.

Nothing.

When the knock came again, she nearly jumped out of her skin.

"Ivy, it's me. Open up."

"Brandon?" she gasped. What the hell . . . She yanked open the door and there he was, sitting on the floor.

Bleeding.

"Oh my God," she said and dropped to her knees.

"Merry Christmas a few days early."

"What the hell happened?" she demanded.

"It's just a scratch," he said, sounding far away. "Help me inside and shut and lock the door."

At the real fear in his voice, which she'd never heard, not once in her life, not even the time he'd accidentally set their trailer on fire and they'd nearly burned along with it, she got behind him, hooked her hands in his armpits, and dragged him over the threshold.

Then, because she hadn't been born yesterday, she left him to go shut and lock the door. Turning back to Brandon, she found he'd scooted his way farther into the room, and still on the floor, had his head tilted back on the couch cushions, eyes closed.

Crouching over him, worried about all the blood and where it was coming from, she started patting him down, arms, chest—

"It's my thigh," he murmured in a faraway voice. "Bullet went all the way through. At least I'm pretty sure."

Pushing back to her feet, she rushed to her bathroom to scrub her hands and grab her first aid kit from beneath the sink, along with a spare towel. With shaking hands, she then ran to her freezer and grabbed the vodka before moving back to Brandon.

"Okay, start talking," she said, dropping to her knees. It took a pair of scissors to cut off his pants leg to the point where she could see what she was doing.

"Just like old times," he murmured, head still back, eyes still closed. "How many times have you patched me up?"

"Too many to count," she said tightly, taking in the fact that yes, the bullet had indeed gone straight through. Using the towel, she applied direct pressure to stop the bleeding.

Brandon sucked a breath in through his teeth and moaned.

"You're so stupid."

He was grating his teeth and trying to hold still, but failing. "I know."

"And dumb," she added.

"I know that too."

She held firm, watching his face as she did, wondering what the hell he'd done, knowing he wouldn't say. After a few minutes, she cautiously peeked beneath the towel.

She'd slowed the blood flow down. "A Band-Aid's not going to do it this time, Bran. You need an ER."

"No."

She lifted her head and he dropped his, meeting her gaze. "You can't take me to the hospital."

"Why not?"

"Because I fucked up." He paused, and closed his eyes again. "Fucked up bad."

"What did you do?"

He didn't answer.

She opened the vodka and poured it over his wound.

"Jesus," he gasped. "Jesus H. Christ . . ."

"Breathe. And start talking."

"I need to vanish."

"So you've said. And yet here you are."

"This isn't funny."

"No shit," she said.

"I mean I *really* need to get out of here."

"Well I'm all for that," she said, gesturing for him to get up and go.

He looked at her. "I need twenty grand to do it."

Her mouth fell open. "Are you kidding me?"

"No," he said seriously, more seriously than she'd ever seen him. "And we both know you have it."

She just stared at him. "What the hell happened tonight?"

"It wasn't my fault."

"It's *always* your fault," she said. "Tell me."

He shook his head. "I needed money to pay off . . .

some people. When I couldn't get it together, I tried to . . . acquire some stuff to sell. But I ran into trouble during the . . . acquisition. Now I don't have the . . . stuff, I don't have the money to pay the people I need to pay, and plus, the trouble that I ran into is likely to cause *more* trouble. So if I want to keep my kneecaps—and I do, I really, really do—I need to vanish for a while." He paused. "A long while. And I need money to do that."

"The twenty K."

"Yes," he said.

She gaped at him. But not for long because there was a knock at her door. She rushed to it, thinking it was Kel, he'd finally come back.

But it wasn't Kel.

It was two very large guys who looked like they ate a lot of burgers and steroids, and little else. One had a whole bunch of hair. Everywhere. The other was bald as a cue ball.

"Can I help you?" she managed to ask, keeping the door cracked so only a sliver of her showed as she slowly reached, trying to grasp the baseball bat she still had leaning against the wall from Brandon's first visit.

"We're looking for Brandon Snow," Unibrow said.

"Who?" Dammit, she needed a longer arm, she couldn't quite . . . reach . . . the bat.

"We know he's your brother," Thug Two said.

She kept an even expression on her face, stretching out her fingers. "I haven't seen him."

"Really," Unibrow said, heavy on the doubt. "Because he says you're going to give him the money he owes us."

"Well that's funny," she said, feeling anything but amused as her fingers finally laid purchase on the bat, which she gripped like a lifeline. "Because I don't have any money."

"That's too bad," Thug Two said. "Because if you don't, we'll have to take it out of his flesh. You sure he isn't inside?"

"*Quite* sure—"

Before she could finish the sentence, Unibrow gave the door a hard shove. It bounced off Ivy's face, and while her vision faded for a second, it was enough time for Unibrow to hold the door open and get a look inside.

Ivy turned to look as well, her face throbbing, but still prepared to use the baseball bat she was holding behind her back. For once she was gratified that her apartment was small enough to take in with one glance. Her couch was empty. The blanket was even gone. The bathroom door was open, and also empty. No one in the kitchen either. "See," she said, trying not to sound shocked to the core.

Where the hell was Brandon?

That's when she saw it. One of her two windows

was open, the lace curtain blowing in the night breeze. Jesus. If Brandon had crawled out the window, he was on an eight-inch ledge four stories off the ground. With a bullet wound.

"He's not here," she said faintly, brandishing the baseball bat in front of her like she was warming up for the big leagues. "Now get out."

Thug One stepped back just out of reach of the bat, but didn't look particularly scared. "He's got twenty-four hours to pay up." He pointed at her. "Or we'll be back for you."

Ivy stood there at the door, watching to make sure they left. When they'd vanished down the stairs, she shut and locked her door and ran to the window just as Brandon fell back inside.

"Shit," he gasped, hands clutched to his chest. "While you were having a casual—and *very* long— conversation with those assholes, my life was flashing before my eyes."

"Well excuse the hell out of me," she snapped. "I was very busy lying my ass off! I thought you'd left me alone with them."

A genuine look of regret crossed his face. "I get I'm a huge fuckup, but I wouldn't have ever left you alone with them to fend for yourself," he said quietly.

"Who are they?"

"You don't want to know."

"You're right, I don't," she snapped. "But seeing

as they're going to come back for me if you don't pay up, I figure I *should* know."

Guilt and more regret were in his eyes as he met hers. "I've made a few mistakes."

"You think?"

"I'm sorry, Ivy."

She blew out a breath. "Okay, let's see if I've got this right. You either gambled poorly, *or . . .* you won and blew your earnings, and now the people you owe money to are making you do their dirty work since you can't pay them. You brilliantly figured stealing something to cover your losses would work, but you failed. You nearly got caught, got shot for your efforts, and now you're not just on the run from the guys you owe money to, but probably from the cops as well. How am I doing?"

"Pretty good," he said weakly.

"Oh my God, Brandon."

"Please, Ivy. You can help me out of this."

Kel had told her that people make choices. That she'd made good choices and her brother hadn't. She'd never thought of things that way before, but he was right. She'd chosen to put down roots. She had a nice group of great friends, her own business, and she was buying her first home. She also had Kel—one of her very best choices to date.

Brandon hadn't chosen any of those things. Or her. And in fact, he'd chosen her now only because he needed something. "The way I see it," she said quietly. "You have two choices. One, you can stay here with me and face what you've done, meaning confess and face the consequences for whatever went down tonight, including jail time, if that's the sentence. I'll be at your side, rooting for you. It'll be a fresh start, a clean start with a new slate, just like I've made for myself here."

"You aren't naive enough to think it's that easy."

"Oh, it won't be easy," she assured him. "But I want a long future. And it'd be nice to have you in it under those circumstances."

"I'm not sure us Snows have any sort of future," he said quietly.

"You're wrong, Brandon. You can have a future. All you've got to do is live on the straight and narrow for the first time in your life."

"Or?" he asked tightly. "Door number two?"

"You can walk out right now and run, but if that's your choice, you can't ever come back." Her throat went tight. "Not ever, Brandon."

He stared at her. "That's harsh."

"Is it? I've got something here, something good. And instead of being my brother, all you do is threaten it. If you run from this, we're done."

He took a long swig of the vodka and set it down. Again his head went back against the sofa. "Okay," he said.

"Okay what?"

"Okay, I'll stay, if you want. Which is far more than I deserve and we both know it."

"You'll turn yourself in?" she asked doubtfully. "You'll deal with whatever happens next?"

"With you by my side," he murmured. "You forgot that part." He opened his eyes and looked at her.

She nodded and he gave her a very weak smile. "You're a good sister," he said quietly.

She let out a slow breath and felt herself relax for the first time since he'd shown up on her doorstep. For once, he was going to do the right thing, and the relief left her exhausted. Or maybe that was just the events of the evening. "And I want Aunt Cathy's necklace back."

He grimaced.

"Tell me you didn't sell it."

Now he closed his eyes, as if looking at her disappointment and hurt was too painful for him. "I'm sorry."

Grounding her back teeth into powder, she got him onto her couch and beneath a blanket, where he promptly passed out cold. It was nearly dawn now. Not wanting the bloody towels to stain, she ran them downstairs to the basement where they had a communal washer and dryer. She needed to go to work soon, she thought, shoving the towels into the washing machine and adding soap.

And something else she had to do? Talk to Kel.

She'd promised after Brandon had shown up the first time that she'd contact him if she heard from her brother again. She reached for her phone in her back pocket before realizing she'd left it upstairs in her apartment.

Damn.

She climbed the stairs and entered her apartment, immediately knowing something was off.

Her couch was empty.

Brandon was gone.

"Shit!" She ran through the place, which didn't take but a second, trying to figure out if anything was missing. Her laptop was right there on the table.

In fact, just then it lit up with a notification that her PayPal transfer had gone through.

Except she hadn't made a PayPal transfer.

Whirling around, she looked for her phone. She couldn't find it, and she froze in place. Where had she left it? When had she had it last?

She couldn't remember. Hell, she could barely function. Brandon had used her laptop to transfer himself *her* twenty thousand dollars.

She sank to a chair on wobbly knees and didn't know who she was more furious with—her brother, or herself.

Both, she decided, and on her laptop went straight to PayPal to put in an immediate dispute to the transaction. Then she called her bank and did the same. After, numb, she looked at the time. Six a.m. She ran downstairs and went searching for Martina and Jasmine. She found them sipping coffees and discussing homeless etiquette.

"I mean, this here alleyway between the buildings is ours," Jasmine was saying. "Until we say otherwise. So no, she can't stay here."

"She's your sister and it's the day before Christmas Eve," Martina said.

"Fine, whatever. But I still get the good stoop."

"Do either of you have a phone?" Ivy asked.

"Girl, what do you take us for?"

"Right," Ivy said on a wince. They were homeless, they didn't have money for phones. "Sorry."

"Of course we have phones. We're civilized." Jasmine gave her a long look. "You got man trouble?"

"Men *are* trouble," she said.

"Amen to that."

Ivy looked down at Jasmine's phone and realized she had a problem. While Kel was in her cell as a contact—which she'd changed to *Bad Decision*—she didn't actually have his number memorized.

Nor Caleb's.

Nor anyone's.

"Are you okay?" Martina asked.

No. Not even close. "Yes. Everything's fine."

"You don't sound okay."

"I'm tougher than I look."

"You are," Martina said easily. "But just remember even the tough need someone at their back. And you've got that anytime you need us."

She nodded and swallowed the ball of emotion in her throat. "Thank you." She handed back the phone. "I've got to go." She needed to get to the job she'd created for herself, the one she now needed more than ever. Upstairs, she opened her laptop. She didn't have it set up for messages, so instead of texting, she had to e-mail.

She didn't know Kel's e-mail addy.

But she knew Caleb's. So she sent him a quick e-mail that she'd lost her phone, and if he could let Kel know, that would be great, thanks.

Thirty minutes later, she was at the truck and in the middle of prepping when a noise at the back door had her turning in hope, a smile already curving her lips. Kel, she thought. Caleb must have gotten his e-mail and let Kel know her phone was missing, and he'd come to make sure all was okay.

But it wasn't Kel.

It was Unibrow and Thug Two. With one hand, she automatically reached for the phone in her back pocket, the one she no longer had.

Dammit.

Luckily she happened to have a massive chopping knife in her other hand and she waved it in front of her in what she sincerely hoped made her look as fierce as the mother of all dragons.

None of them said a word. But Thug Two pointed to his eyes and then to Ivy.

They were watching her.

Great. Just great. She went to point to her eyes to signal she'd be watching them right back, and nearly took out her own eyes with the knife.

She'd been in the same city for a whole year and apparently in that time, she'd lost all her hard-earned survival instincts. By the time she managed to put a menacing, try-me expression on her face, she was alone.

But what if they'd come when she hadn't been alone. What if she'd had customers, or if she'd been with her friends? What might've happened?

Her hands were still shaking, and now so was the rest of her as she turned the OPEN sign to CLOSED. She needed to call Kel, but she also needed to solve her problems and fast, before anyone, including herself, got hurt.

Chapter 23

Leave it all here

Kel spent the long hours of the night dealing with the local authorities for Caleb, and going over the site. Whoever had broken in wasn't a novice. He'd managed to avoid surveillance cameras, or destroy them by spray painting the lenses, all while revealing only a dark hoodie, no facial features.

No visual or evidence of an accomplice.

It turned out that the hit Arlo had taken to the back of his head had been because he'd been shoved and had fallen, hitting the concrete floor. It wouldn't have been so bad except that he'd been the one in a million who developed an unexpected brain swell, requiring surgery.

When Kel was finally allowed in to talk to him in the predawn early morning, he took a seat next to the bed.

"Merry Fucking Christmas Eve," Arlo said.

Kel had to smile. "How you feeling?"

"Better than I look."

"Good. You went over and above the call of duty on this one."

"I tagged the fucker," Arlo said. "Tell me you caught him." He looked at Kel's face and swore. "Follow the blood trail. He was bleeding like a mother fu—" He broke off when his nurse poked her head in.

"Everything okay in here?" she asked.

Arlo gave her a sweet wink. "Yes, ma'am."

"You're supposed to be resting."

"Resting is my favorite activity."

The nurse rolled her eyes and left.

"Can you describe him?" Kel asked.

"Late twenties to early thirties," Arlo said. "Red hair that needs a cut, scruffy wannabe hipster beard. His left arm was tatted up."

Kel had started to write down the description, but at this he stilled and lifted his head. "Did you see his eyes?"

"Yeah. One blue, one green. Weird as hell. He'd covered the ground floor security cameras with spray paint and was on the second floor. He'd broken into the business office and gym. He had a stack of laptops and tablets. Somehow he knew that was the only floor that had anything of value in it yet."

The business center had just been stocked with

computers, the gym with state-of-the-art equipment. One week from now at least ten of the units would've had people and valuables in them, as this coming weekend the place was opening to the first round of owners.

How had Brandon known to hit the condo building? That answer was easy. Obviously Ivy, who'd gotten the intel from none other than Kel's own mouth.

The question was . . . why had she told Brandon, and had she known what her brother was going to do? Was she in on it? And how had Kel not seen that coming?

In his professional world, his life had depended on him remaining calm and steady in any situation. After years on the job, where cool thinking was a requirement, it had become habit, which he'd transferred to his personal life as well.

But he didn't feel calm now. He felt everything but calm. In fact, he felt sick. He had no idea if Ivy had known what Brandon was going to do, but it was his job to find out. And while he expected to screw up in relationships, he wouldn't fail on the job, not ever again.

But just the thought of Ivy gave him a chest pang. Hours ago, he'd left her warm and soft and sated in her bed, thinking she was a balm on his past and the key to both his present and future.

Now he didn't know what to think. Brandon had

broken into the property and he'd hurt Arlo in the process, giving Kel bad flashbacks to what had happened in Idaho. He pulled out his phone and texted Ivy: Have you seen or heard from your brother? And then went back to giving his attention to Arlo while he waited on her response.

"I caught him at the second floor entryway," Arlo said. "I pulled my gun and told him to put his hands up and hit his knees. He did, so I moved close to secure him, but before I could, he whirled on me and he had a bat. Came out of nowhere."

"Was there any exchange of words first?"

Arlo looked a little sheepish. "I might have said something, yeah."

"Like?"

"Like . . . " He grimaced. "Go ahead, punk, make my day."

Kel shook his head. "Watching too many movies."

"Yeah." Arlo's smile faded. "I also said I was going to make sure he rotted in jail because I was tired of punkasses like him thinking all they had to do was take what they wanted instead of earn it."

"Arlo—"

"I know. I goaded him and he reacted faster than me." Arlo shook his head. "Turns out, *I'm* the punkass."

Kel's phone buzzed with an incoming text from Ivy. Nothing.

Kel texted: Let me know if that changes. And then he shoved the phone away. "This wasn't your fault," he told Arlo, rising to his feet. "Rest up, okay? That's your only job right now."

Arlo let him get to the door. "Caleb had me trained at Hunt Investigations before you arrived. Then you came and trained all of us as well. And in the heat of the moment, I disregarded all training. I failed, Kel. And I'm sorry."

Kel made sure to make eye contact. "Not your fault," he repeated. Because it was very likely his, for once again believing his heart when he knew better. He left the hospital and ignoring notifications of missed calls and texts, he drove straight to The Taco Truck because this couldn't wait.

The truck wasn't open.

Heart pumping, blood pressure up at stroke level, he went to Ivy's place.

The ladies gave him a long cool look and didn't return his greeting. Not a good sign, he thought, heading up the walk. He jogged the stairs, motivated by adrenaline and worry and temper—never a good combo for him. By the time he got to her floor, he was telling himself that Ivy was an innocent pawn because she'd never be involved in anything like this, no matter that Brandon was family.

Ivy opened the door to his knock, her face revealing nothing. "I need to talk to you."

"Are you okay?" he asked.

She paused as if surprised he'd ask her that question. Which was a shocking commentary on her low expectations of the people in her life, and he had to take a deep breath and force himself from pushing his way inside and snatching her up against him and holding on tight.

Ivy stood in her doorway, not knowing exactly what to say to Kel. Was she fine? No. Was she going to be fine? The jury was still out. But she couldn't say either of those things, so she nodded. "Yes, I'm . . . fine." Ish. "Is Arlo?"

"He will be." Kel's eyes tracked to behind her, where on her small coffee table sat her first aid kit, the contents scattered, along with the wrappings of gauze in a pile off to the side.

She knew very well it wasn't hard to add two plus two to get four and she braced herself when he finally met her gaze again.

"Brandon was here," he said tightly.

"Yes. That's what I needed to talk to you about."

"Did you know he broke into the condo building and attacked Arlo?" Kel asked.

She gasped, feeling like she'd just been hit by a train, which for the record would have hurt less. "No!"

He let out a slow exhale, like he was trying to be very careful what he said. "Are you sure, Ivy? Because the bat seems like a family signature. Are you sure you didn't know what he was going to do?"

She stared at him in utter shock. "Are you kidding me? Of course I didn't know!" She shook her head, stunned but also angry. And not a little hurt to boot. Never a good combination for her. "How could you ask me such a thing?"

"Because you're siblings." Again he looked past her to the first aid kit. "And because he was most definitely here."

She felt sick. "Are you going to come in?"

"Are you going to implicate yourself in a felony?"

She closed her eyes for a beat, and he swore beneath his breath before nudging her aside so he could come in.

Turning from him, she locked the door and slid the chain into place.

"Isn't that a little like locking the barn door after the horse has escaped?" he asked.

She turned to face him. Not all that long ago, he'd been buried deep inside her, making her feel things she'd never felt before. Ever.

Now he stood a mere foot from her and yet he might as well have been on the moon for the space and distance between them. "There are things you don't know," she said.

"Then you should have told me."

"I tried. But my phone's . . . missing. When I realized it, I went downstairs to use Martina's phone, but I couldn't remember your number. Or Caleb's."

"Okay." He crossed his arms and studied her, impenetrable. "What exactly were you trying to tell me?"

"That Brandon came back," she said. "After you got called away. He'd been shot. He told me that he needed money to pay some people off, but he didn't have it. So he'd done something stupid."

"Like break into a building for all the new, expensive equipment to fence," Kel said. "When he pushed Arlo, Arlo fell and hit his head, requiring surgery for a brain swell."

She looked away. "I didn't know. I didn't know he was going to do any of that."

"But the only way he knew about that building and what was in it was if you'd told him."

"The first time he showed up, that night you were here, after when we were talking, I told him about my condo and the great building it was in. He joked about me stepping up in the world." She met his gaze. "I had no idea he'd use that info the way he did."

"He needs to turn himself in, Ivy."

She had to laugh. "And you think I can get him to do that?"

"You two are a whole lot closer than I thought," he said. "So yeah, I do think you can get him to do that."

She shook her head. "He's . . . he's paranoid about prison."

"He nearly killed a man while looking for a quick buck. He's going to have to get over his paranoia and face the consequences."

"I know," she said, more quietly now, hugging herself because he was keeping his distance on purpose, which possibly made her heart hurt more than it already did, and it hurt pretty damn bad. "Near as I can tell," she said, "he either made some bad bets, or he conned someone he shouldn't have out of a lot of money. He's desperate to pay them off, nearly as desperate as the guys he owes are to get their money back."

His eyes sharpened. "What do you mean?"

"They came here looking for him and then showed up again at my truck."

There was a muscle jumping in his jaw now. "And?" he asked tightly.

"They didn't do anything," she said. "But they made it clear he needs to pay up or they'll get it another way."

"And I assume they think that other way is through you."

She looked away. Yeah, that was what they assumed alright, and she was so on edge it was like her childhood all over again.

"Ivy, this is bad."

"And you think I don't know that?"

"How could you let him back in?"

"Well, one, I didn't know what he'd done. And two, he's my brother, Kel."

"You housed a criminal."

She tossed up her hands. "I didn't know!"

"It doesn't matter. You hid him. And when I texted asking if you'd seen him, you replied that you hadn't."

She blinked. "Wait. What?"

He shook his head and turned to the door, but she grabbed his arm and pulled him around. Okay, so he allowed her to do it, and she took the smallest bit of comfort in that.

Or she would have, if she wasn't vibrating with fury and a pierced heart, both nearly bringing her to her knees. "I didn't send you a text," she said.

He pulled out his phone and showed her a short conversation between him and . . . her phone.

"What?" he asked when her mouth tightened.

"Brandon has my phone," she said. "I think he took it when I went down to the basement. He must have texted you back pretending to be me in order to throw you off the trail."

"That's pretty ugly."

She nodded. She knew.

He blew out a breath. "I'm fighting a bad case of déjà vu here," he said.

Lifting her head, she stared at him as the hits kept on coming. "You don't believe me," she breathed.

"I believe in facts, Ivy. Cold, hard facts. And at the moment, they're stacked the wrong way."

She couldn't help it, she gaped at him. "Against me, you mean."

He just looked into her eyes, his own not giving anything away.

"Wow," she said, reading him loud and clear, words or not. Heartsick, shaking with it, she turned to the door and opened it. "You need to go now."

Chapter 24

If you want it bad enough, make it happen

Of course he didn't leave, Ivy thought. Nope, he just stayed right where he was, looking like everything she'd ever wanted and had never gotten.

He wasn't giving much away but it wasn't a big leap to assume he blamed her for what Brandon had done, and she got it. She blamed herself too. But he needed to go, now, before she lost it. "Please leave."

Kel shut the door, but he didn't leave. His expression was formidable. Remote.

The cop was in residence.

If someone had asked her yesterday if she could be surprised by anything life had to offer, she'd have said no way. She'd been through too much. Seen too much.

But Kel thinking she might be involved in Brandon's

scheme surprised her. And hurt. It left her feeling extremely raw and vulnerable, two emotions she'd hoped she'd left behind a long time ago. She'd built walls, protective walls, so she couldn't ever feel vulnerable again.

But Kel had gotten through.

How ironic then that it hadn't been her to screw it all up.

But Brandon. Not that this was a huge surprise. He'd probably never meant it when he agreed to turn himself in. He'd just needed her to be stupid enough to believe it. Once again, he'd blown up her life, and the worst part was, she'd let him. She'd literally handed him everything he'd needed in order to do it.

She might as well have hurt Arlo herself. So as much as she wanted to demand that Kel get the hell out so she could nurse her emotional wounds in private, she couldn't until she gave Kel everything she knew so that he could make this right.

Heartsick, she met Kel's distant gaze. "What do you need from me?"

"Tell me again exactly what happened when he showed up here," he said.

"He was bleeding. Said he'd been shot." She swallowed hard, fighting tears. "I tried to get him to go to an ER, but he refused. So I got my first aid kit and did what I could. I told him he had two choices. He could stay and turn himself in, and I'd be there for him, or he could leave and never come back."

Kel didn't seem at all moved by any of this. In fact, it was like he was a robot. Zero reaction. "And he said?"

"He said he'd stay," she whispered. "I ran down to the basement to throw the bloody towels in the washer. While I was down there, I reached to pull my phone from my pocket to text you that Brandon was here and he'd been shot. But it wasn't there. I didn't realize until I got back upstairs that he'd taken it."

He held her gaze for a long beat, but said nothing.

She drew a deep breath and finished. "When I got back, he was gone. And that's when I knew he'd probably never really considered staying and turning himself in. I think he took my phone with him, which didn't make sense until I got a PayPal notice on my laptop that my transfer had gone through."

"What transfer?"

She looked away, she had to. She hated the way he was looking at her almost more than she hated having to admit this part. "He transferred a large chunk of money from my account to his. He had to have used my phone to do it. And then he probably received your text and responded as me to keep you off his tail."

He stared at her. "He took money from you."

She nodded.

"How much?"

She closed her eyes.

"Ivy."

"Twenty thousand," she said quietly. "It was what I'd been saving for my down payment on the condo."

He let out a long breath and waited until she looked at him to speak. "Did you call the authorities? Anyone?"

"I contacted PayPal to start a dispute on the transfer," she said. "I was able to do that from my laptop."

"Okay, but what about Brandon. Did you call the police when he showed up with a bullet hole?"

She held his gaze with difficulty. "No."

"You do get that's why he wouldn't go to the ER, right? They'd have to report it."

"You have to know that if I'd been aware that Brandon had hurt someone, I'd have been the first person to turn him in," she said shakily.

She could see the doubt in his eyes, and her heartsick turned to anger. "I did promise I wouldn't lie to you."

"Doesn't mean you meant it."

Like a dagger to the heart that she had never meant to give him access to. "If you're done with the interrogation, I'd really like you to leave now."

He closed his eyes for a beat. "Ivy," he said low and pained. Like *she'd* hurt *him*.

"I don't understand what you want from me," she whispered, hugging herself.

"Honesty."

"I've given you that, even when it hurt and was humiliating," she said. "But it's not enough, is it." She grabbed her bag and keys. "I'm tired of feeling like I'm not enough. For once, I want the person in my life to be what I need them to be."

"And what did you need me to be?"

"It no longer matters."

"It does," he said, sounding very serious.

The words escaped her mouth before she could filter them. "I want someone to have my back without question."

"I think I've done that."

"Really?" she asked. "Because you think I withheld information from you, on purpose. You accused me of hiding my brother, of lying to you via text." She held up a hand when he would have spoken. "I know. I get it. I can see how it looked to you, but you have the facts now. At least all the facts that I have. And yeah, I made a mistake, a big one. But that mistake wasn't lying. It was believing in Brandon when I knew better. And I did know better."

Kel blew out a breath. "He's your brother and you wanted to believe in him."

"It was stupid," she said. "And I won't do it again." Once again. And with that, she walked out of her own place.

Completely wrecked.

It felt like she'd lived a year in just today alone, but

unbelievably it was only eight in the morning. And yet all she could think was . . . Kel hadn't believed in her, and in doing so, he'd played right into her worst fears. That once again she didn't have anyone at her back.

On the street, she ran to catch the bus to the Pacific Pier Building because she wasn't up for walking. She was pissed off and still shaky, and . . . so, so unhappy. But hell, she'd been unhappy before. She would live.

In the meantime, she needed to earn money, now more than ever, since she clearly wouldn't be getting her condo. Or anything anytime soon.

She felt the threat of tears and willed them away. God, she'd been so stupid. It was her fault a man was in the hospital, not to mention that she'd allowed her brother to draw her into this mess. The worst part was, she knew she'd ruined not only what she'd had with Kel, but also had most certainly destroyed any trust Caleb had had in her. And ditto for the friends when they found out. And they would find out, this building didn't hold its secrets. Hard to believe she'd found that refreshing.

She'd actually started to believe that this life could be hers. But the joke had been on her . . .

When she got off the bus, she walked through the courtyard of the building, heading directly for the coffee shop. No way could she possibly face customers without caffeine. Caffeine would bolster her up and allow her to get through the day without losing it completely.

Something she refused to do.

She strode up to the counter and gave Tina her order. "A tall, nonfat latte with caramel drizzle. And if you could make it more like a scoop than a drizzle, that'd be great."

Tina nodded. "You weren't at class."

"I know."

"Bad day already?" Tina asked.

"*Bad* doesn't begin to cut it."

"Give me a minute, darling."

And in the promised minute, Tina reappeared with a jasmine green tea and an organic banana oatmeal muffin. "Strong is what happens when you run out of weak."

"Um . . . what?"

"Trust me," Tina said. "Mama knows best. That tea's going to rejuvenate you instead of send you to an early grave, and you look like you're down a quart so the muffin's going to fill your tummy and give you energy and life." She paused. "Man problems?"

"Is there any other kind of problem?"

Tina smiled grimly. "Not that I've ever found."

Chapter 25

*Strong is what happens
when you run out of weak*

There'd been many times in Kel's life where he'd felt he'd been wronged. It was rare for him to feel like he was the one doing the wronging. He just didn't operate that way. He followed his own moral code and instincts, and they'd rarely steered him off base.

Work first. He'd promised himself this after the last fiasco, he would never again put anything ahead of work. Certainly not emotions.

So that's what he did. He turned himself into an unfeeling machine to handle the situation calmly and thoroughly. He gathered all the evidence and facts he had at his disposal, and now he was going through it all with Caleb.

While simultaneously ignoring a very unwelcome

feeling tightening his chest with each minute that ticked by.

Regret. So much fucking regret.

But there wasn't time for that right now. This was the job, this was *his* job, and that's just the way it had to be.

They were going over all the known intel at their disposal; the surveillance feeds, Arlo's recounting of what had happened, and also Ivy's.

When Caleb heard about the two assholes who'd gone to her apartment and then her work, he scrubbed a hand down his face. "We need to put a guy on her 24–7 until this thing is finished."

"Already done," Kel said. "She's now in your security rotation until one of us says otherwise."

"Does she know?"

"What do you think?" Kel asked.

"I think she'd have our balls in a sling if she thought we were spending money protecting her," Caleb said.

"Which is why she doesn't need to know. Also, we have manpower out looking for Brandon. He's going to give his sister back the money he stole from her if it's the last thing he ever does."

"Agreed." Caleb rose from his chair and moved to his floor to ceiling windows to stare out at the city.

The reflection of his grim expression moved Kel to stand as well. "I feel like I failed you on this one."

"You've never failed me," Caleb said.

"Arlo being in the hospital suggests otherwise."

Caleb turned to him. "Did you hit him?"

Kel shook his head. "You know what I mean."

"Yeah, I do. You feel the need to control every single situation so that it goes your way. But life's annoying like that, man. You *can't* control everything. Believe me, I've tried. Ask the women in my life, they'll tell you, especially Sadie." He shook his head. "Which means I had to let go of a lot of shit I didn't want to let go of."

"But Sadie never put your job in jeopardy," Kel pointed out. "None of them closed themselves off to you at every turn. You had it easy."

Caleb laughed. He laughed so hard he had to sit down. "Let me correct that notion right now. Sadie was more closed off than Fort Knox. It took patience, cunning, and every ounce of brainpower I had to make her fall in love with me, and in the end I nearly screwed it up by not trusting her." He gave Kel a direct look. "I'd say don't do that, but it seems like I'm too late."

"You want me to trust the woman who hid stuff from you too?"

"Self-protection is something I understand all too well, and so should you. And it's all a moot point anyway, because in spite of everything that happened between Sadie and me, I wanted her anyway. Every minute that she's in my life, she makes it better. Her smile, the way she looks at me, hell, the way she laughs at me. She . . ." He trailed off, searching for the words.

Kel groaned. "If you say she completes you—"

Caleb pointed at him. "That's the one."

Kel shook his head.

"Don't believe me?" Caleb asked, amusement fading. "Then think about what it will feel like when you go back to Idaho and leave what you have with Ivy in your dust."

Kel had thought about nothing but . . . and it still didn't change facts.

Caleb's brows went up. "Are you kidding me? You're going to go back?"

"I was *always* going to go back, Caleb. You know that."

Caleb shook his head, not accepting this. "You're looking at that ranch in Sonoma."

"As an investment."

"I call bullshit," Caleb said. "You're really going to walk away from the best thing to ever happen to you—and for what? A job that betrayed you?"

"It wasn't the job. It was the people."

"So stay and work for people who'd never put you second to a job."

"It's not that simple," Kel said.

"Yeah, it is, but you're too stubborn to see that." Caleb shook his head again. "So are you going to be a total dick and just ghost her, or are you going to try to work things out first so that you can at least try the long-distance thing?"

"It's not up to me."

"Really?" Caleb asked, heavy on the disbelief. "You think she should come to you? Because she's not humiliated enough that her brother screwed things up in a very large way, affecting you, me, and her entire life here, the life she's worked so hard to get for herself?"

It was Kel's turn to stare out the window now, blindly, into the city.

"You fell in love with her," Caleb said.

"You can't fall in love in two weeks."

"I fell in love with Sadie in one night."

Kel shook his head. "That was you."

"What, and you're immune?" Caleb studied his cousin. "No, that's not it," he said slowly, not sounding happy. "You think you don't deserve it."

"More like I don't want it."

"But you admit you fell in love."

Kel hadn't articulated it to himself quite that bluntly, but there was zero doubt that Ivy had gotten to him. She'd gotten inside his head, inside his heart, even down to the primal part of his soul. She'd bypassed all his defenses and brought something to life deep inside him that he'd kept hidden and protected. "It was a mistake," he said.

"What a load of horseshit."

"You're friends with her," Kel said quietly. "I understand that. I don't expect you to cut her out of your life. I'm asking you to understand what I have to do."

"No, don't give me that crap," Caleb said. "You're not owning up to a mistake, and you're not making a hard choice either. You're covering your ass and protecting your heart, the way you did with your mom, the way you had to do at work, and now with Ivy. But unlike you, I don't cut someone out of my life simply because they're the hard choice." He let out a mirthless laugh. "You're an idiot, Kel. You could have a life here, a really great one that includes family, a job, and the love of a good woman. Instead, you're . . . hell, I don't even know. You need to figure out why you think you don't deserve the good stuff." Caleb's phone buzzed. He eyed the screen and shook his head. "I've got to go. But I'm asking you, as someone who cares about you very much, to think about it, really think about what you're doing."

Kel did think about it. He thought about nothing else as he drove through the city. Did he really think he didn't deserve love?

Maybe. Maybe deep down, he blamed himself for what had happened between him and his mom. For what had happened on the job.

For what had happened between him and Ivy.

Being alone had become easier than facing his own mistakes and regrets. Something he figured Ivy knew a little about, seeing that she was alone too, also by choice. She had friends, but she let them in only so far. They cared about her, but he wasn't sure they understood her.

Kel understood her. An outsider always recognized another outsider.

Not that it had mattered. None of it was supposed to matter. But somehow, when he hadn't been paying attention, things had changed. And now he needed her on a level so deep and basic it was primal in a way that felt dangerous to his heart and soul.

And he was tired of fighting it.

He'd made mistakes. A lot of them. He knew the only way to make things right was to start at the beginning and fix what he could. Which was why, thirty minutes later, he ended up walking through a mobile home park with his GPS app. Dark had fallen, but it wasn't hard to find his way because most of the homes had been lit to within an inch of Christmas's life. The park was a decent one. There were tiny little yards, most of them well kept. Clearly there was a sense of pride of ownership here.

His mom and Henry lived at the end of the middle row in a double-wide. There was a small living

Christmas tree on the porch with a string of sparkly
lights twinkling. He'd just reached out to knock on
the door when Henry opened it.

"Hey," he said to Kel in genuine surprise. He
looked past Kel, obviously searching for someone,
probably whoever had dragged Kel out here against
his will.

"I came alone," Kel told him.

Henry looked even more surprised at this. "You
did?"

"Yeah. Do you mind if I come in?"

"Sure." Henry nodded, but didn't move out of the
doorway, blocking Kel's entrance. He paused a moment and then grimaced. "Listen, here's the thing.
Your mom . . . she's . . . well, to be honest, you make
her nervous, when all she wants to do is connect with
you. And when she's nervous, she feels she trips all
over herself with you."

"She has no reason to be nervous around me,"
Kel said.

Henry gave him a long look.

"Okay," Kel said, feeling like an asshole. He was
starting to get used to it. "I've been hard on her."

"I don't need an apology from you, nor do I deserve one," Henry said. "I just need to you to respect
my woman of twenty plus years and treat her with
basic kindness."

"That's enough, Henry," Kel's mom said, coming

to the door, gently nudging her husband aside with a small I've-got-this smile.

To Henry's credit, he stepped back, letting her take the lead.

"Would you like to come in?" she asked Kel.

Which is how he found himself in a small but warm and cozy kitchen accepting a mug of tea.

He hated tea.

"Go ahead," his mom said, finally sitting across the narrow table from him, still looking calm though her hands were clenched. "Say what you've come to say."

She was braced for him to continue to be an asshole, he realized, and he sighed, scrubbing a hand down his face. "I didn't come here to fight with you, Mom."

She blinked and straightened. "You didn't?"

"No." He sipped the tea and nearly scalded off his tongue.

"Here." She moved to the freezer and dropped two ice cubes into his mug.

She'd done the same thing for him when he'd been little and she'd made him hot cocoa after school. The flashback was so real it took him back to another time.

When they'd been family.

"I've not been . . . open to talking to you. I was wrong to not listen to what you've wanted to say to me."

She stared down at her own tea for a long moment.

When she lifted her gaze, her eyes were filled with regret and sadness. "I've been waiting for this for so long. I actually had lost hope of it happening."

He grimaced and started to say something, but she put her hand on his. "There's a few things I want you to know. Will you listen?"

He nodded.

"Your dad and I . . . we were best friends. From middle school. By the time you kids came along, we were more like siblings ourselves. We each knew it. But neither of us wanted to miss out on raising you and Remi. So we agreed to stay together until you two were raised and off to college. We both wanted that. We still liked each other, very much. In fact, we loved each other. We just weren't . . . in love."

Kel stared at her. "Are you saying you had an arrangement?"

"Yes." Dropping her gaze, she went back to watching her tea like it was the most fascinating thing. She wasn't comfortable talking about this.

"So there was never a secret to keep. Not that it's an excuse for what happened, for what you saw—"

"Mom." He winced, not wanting to think about his mom having an active sex life. "That's not what I—You sent us to Idaho." He shook his head, hating that he felt like a kid all over again. "And you never came for us. You didn't come back around until I was eighteen and no longer cared."

She met his gaze straight on. "First, I'm going to hope that's not true, that you still care, deep down inside. And second . . . I'm sorry. I've said it before and I'll keep saying it. I wish I hadn't stayed away so long, but I had to." She shook her head. "I wasn't okay, Kel. I had a breakdown. I was depressed and anxious and could barely care for myself, much less you and Remy. I know you don't remember your maternal grandma, but she suffered from depression and anxiety too, and it can be hereditary." Her eyes filled and she was clasping her hands tight. "It took me a shamefully long time to get it together—"

"Mom." Kel's gut clenched, even as his heart seemed to swell so that it was too tight to fit into his chest. He put his hand over his mom's and squeezed. "There's no shame in needing to take care of your mental health. I didn't know—"

"I know." She swiped at her tears. "For the longest time, I didn't want you to. By the time I was ready to face you kids again, you were grown up. You no longer needed me."

But Remy had. Plus, Remy had forgiven, readily. Easily. If anyone should be ashamed, it was him. He held his mom's hand. "I'm sorry. I'm so sorry. I should have listened sooner."

"You're here now," she whispered. "Now is all that matters. Family is all that matters."

Kel's gaze landed on the walls, upon which, just

like at Remy's place, picture after picture was hung. Pictures of Remy, Remy and Ethan, and of course Harper. His mom was in many of the pics, as was Henry. Through holidays. Birthdays. Family dinners. Outings . . .

And that's when it hit him just how right his mom was. Love was about showing up. Love was about being there for the people in your life during their darkest moments and doing your best to understand and support those people through whatever course their life took.

Without judgment.

He'd failed there, big time. He'd failed his mom and his family.

And he'd failed Ivy. He'd listened to her, but not taken the time to understand the choices she'd made.

"Are we going to be okay?" his mom asked in a soft whisper.

"Yes."

With a soft sob, she flew at him to hug him so tight he could scarcely breath. He started to attempt to extract himself, but he realized she was shaking and crying, and with a sigh, he wrapped his arms around her. "It's okay, Mom. Please, don't cry."

She sniffled and tried to control herself. "Will you stay for pancakes?"

"Will you stop crying?"

"I'll try."

"Then I'll stay."

She smiled through her tears and turned happily to the stove. Kel exhaled slowly, trying to find his bearings in a world gone upside down.

Henry was watching from the doorway and gave Kel a single nod of approval. And why that felt like so much more, he had no idea. But he stayed. And he ate his weight in pancakes.

Chapter 26

If you never change, you'll never change

There was always a lull at The Taco Truck between lunch and dinner, usually around two in the afternoon. Typically, Ivy used that time for a quick but thorough cleanup and restocking. She'd not expected a lot of customers today on Christmas Eve, but for whatever reason, business was heavy. She and Jenny were working like crazy when Jenny's phone rang. It was Caleb, and it was for Ivy.

She stepped out of the truck to talk to him. "How is he?"

"Devastated," Caleb said. "I'm not sure I've ever seen him like this."

Ivy paused. "Arlo's devastated?"

"No, Kel is." Now it was Caleb's turn to pause. "Sorry, I just assumed that's who you meant."

"I want to know how Arlo is," she said tightly. "Is he really going to be okay?"

"Yes," Caleb said gently. "He is."

She let out a long, shuddery breath. "You're sure?"

"I promise you. He's going to make a full recovery."

She nodded, then realized he couldn't see her, and sighed. "Caleb, I'm so sor—"

"Don't you dare apologize to me."

"But my brother—"

"Baby, this was not on you."

She closed her eyes. "I appreciate you saying that, but Brandon . . . he wouldn't have done this without me opening my big mouth."

"You're supposed to be able to open your big mouth around family," Caleb said and then paused. "I called because earlier today, thanks to an anonymous tip, the police apprehended two guys for B&E, felony theft, and some other stuff. They spilled their guts to reduce charges." He paused again. "They implicated Brandon," he said quietly. "And that, along with Arlo's statement, sealed it. There's a warrant out for Brandon's arrest."

"Okay," she said just as quietly. "Thanks for letting me know."

"The police are probably going to want to talk to you. Don't say anything unless your lawyer's with you."

"I don't have a lawyer."

"Yes, you do. He'll be in touch. And Ivy . . ." She heard the regret and sympathy in his voice. "If Brandon's caught, he's going to go away for a long time."

"I know," she said. "But he's not coming back. He knows he detonated everything here and he's not stupid. His healthy sense of self-preservation will keep him gone."

"I'm sorry," Caleb said quietly.

"If I can't say it, neither can you."

"Got it," Caleb said. "Now . . . about your condo."

"It's no longer mine."

"We'll work something out."

"No," she said and then softened her voice. "You have no idea how much it means to me that you'd do that, but it's not fair. I'm going to start over and get there. On my own."

"Ivy, I understand, believe me, but it means you'll miss out on getting into this building."

And here she'd thought she couldn't hurt more than she did. "I know."

"But—"

"It's okay, Caleb. I have to do it this way. For me."

He sighed. "I get it. I don't like it, but I get it."

She bit her lower lip. "So . . . Kel's devastated?"

"Yes. Did you think he wouldn't be?"

She wasn't sure what she thought. "He's not alone there."

"So give him a chance to fix it."

"He had it, but he didn't want it. He's not the right one for me if he doesn't want me as is, Caleb," she said softly.

"Ivy—"

"Gotta go," she said softly and disconnected. Wincing, she shoved the phone away and turned back to her truck, coming to an abrupt stop at the sight of the girls huddled around one of the picnic tables. Molly, Sadie, Tae, and Haley and Dee—who were sitting very close together.

No. She was not ready for this, so she sneaked into the truck. She adored them, even loved them, but she was pretty sure that by now they knew what had gone down. And she wasn't ready to come face-to-face with the consequences of her lies.

The phone buzzed an incoming text. It was a group text, with all the girls on it.

SADIE: Come back! We're waiting for you!

MOLLY: **I saved you a muffin. And none of that healthy shit either. I've got the double chocolate chip muffins.**

At that, Ivy stuck her head out of the truck. Everyone waved her over and with a sigh she went.

When Molly caught her eyeballing the table for

the muffins, she smiled. "Oh, I lied. Just wanted to make sure you were getting the texts."

"Wow. That was mean." But Ivy sat. "What's up?" she asked, as if she didn't know. First rule of the Screwup Club—play innocent.

"Tina told us she saw you at the coffee shop earlier and that you looked like shit," Sadie said. "She said that men are scum."

"They are," Ivy confirmed.

"Yes," Tae said. "And?"

"Hey, wait a minute," Molly said. "Not *all* men are scum. Lucas made me breakfast just this morning."

"Was that because you'd done him a favor first?" Tae asked.

Molly went a little red in the face. "Maybe. In the shower. But it took him longer to make me breakfast, so really, I'm the winner."

"Not if you have sore knees," Sadie said.

"If you fold up two washcloths and set them on the tile before you start the shower," Dee said, "problem solved."

Haley blushed tomato red.

Sadie took Ivy's hand, looking her in the eyes. "I want to tell you something, without you getting all fidgety and weird and trying to escape with some dumb excuse so you don't have to talk about your feelings."

"I don't do that," Ivy said.

Everyone snorted in unison and Ivy sighed. "Fine. I suck at feelings. Whatever."

"You don't suck at feelings," Sadie said. "If anything, it's the opposite. Did you know that ever since you started seeing Kel, you've been . . . happier?"

Everyone nodded.

"And more open," Sadie said. "You smile, and it goes all the way to your eyes."

Ivy started to immediately pull back, both her hand and in fact her entire body, but she froze.

She was fidgeting.

Dammit.

"You do that," Sadie went on. "Because, as I suspect, as *we* suspect . . ."

Again everyone nodded.

". . . That you're feeling things . . . things you're not used to feeling."

Ivy blew out a breath. "You're not wrong."

"We thought maybe you'd want to talk about it," Haley said gently.

"It's okay if you don't want to," Sadie said, just as gently. "But from experience as someone who denied all emotions for too long, I can tell you that facing them head on like a badass bitch is the only way to go. Otherwise, they chase you, follow you, haunt you, and believe me, those suckers can outpace you, I swear. You need to just get in front of them and turn and fight."

"I've been fighting all my life," Ivy said. "I'm tired of it. I wanted someone to fight for me. For once."

"Tell us what happened?" Sadie asked quietly.

"You mean you don't already know?"

They all looked at each other.

They knew.

But Sadie held Ivy's gaze and spoke for the group. "We want to hear it from our friend. We want to know what you want us to know so we can help. Or just stand at your back. Whatever it is you need."

So . . . she told them. For the first time in her life, she opened up, starting with her childhood and how she'd walked away from that as soon as she could. She told them about coming to San Francisco last year and first working for the guy who owned the taco truck, and then with Caleb's help, buying the truck. She told them about managing to scrimp and cut out all extras in her life in order to put away half of the down payment for her condo, and how Caleb had intended to match her half in exchange for her continuing to cater for him as needed.

They all nodded and made encouraging noises whenever she hesitated, wanting her to go on.

So she did. She went on to the hardest part. She told them about Brandon, about the lies she'd told them all over the past year. That she'd made up stories about Brandon being such good family because she hated the truth.

Sadie squeezed her hand. "Oh, honey, I wish you could've told us. I'm sorry you went through all this alone."

"I was ashamed," Ivy admitted, willing herself not to cry. "After hiding so much from you, I couldn't tell. Not even when Brandon showed back up and I knew I was in trouble. It's all on me. I let him back into my life, and he hurt a good man and ruined my relationship with . . . well, everyone." She lowered her gaze. "I appreciate you listening to me. Having you guys as friends this past year has meant so much to me. I was the new girl, and not a single one of you made me feel like I wasn't wanted, or left out." She stood up. "But now I really need to . . ." She made a vague wave toward her truck.

Sadie caught her hand. "You know we love you, right?"

Ivy had to swallow hard. "I lied to all of you. Friends don't lie."

"I lied to everyone when my girlfriend was cheating on me a while back," Haley said. "I told everyone I was fine. That was a huge, big fat lie."

Tae nodded. "We only found out she wasn't fine when we found her in the courtyard drunk, sobbing out her troubles to the firepit while wearing only one shoe."

"Hey," Haley said. "I didn't have any coins on me so I'd thrown my shoe into the fountain to make a wish. Plus, I *thought* I was talking to Old Man Eddie. But he'd fallen asleep on me."

Old Man Eddie might not live in the alley anymore, but he was still the keeper of the firepit. He had lots of sage advice—on the days he wasn't eating his homemade marijuana brownies.

"I've lied too," Sadie said. "By omission. Before I got together with Caleb, I was afraid to let people in. Thought they wouldn't like me. I pushed away anyone and everyone who tried to be my friend."

Haley nodded to Ivy. "Yep. She did that. Big-time."

"And I was the 'I'm okay' girl," Molly said. "Which was a huge lie. I just never wanted anyone's help because I didn't want to be vulnerable."

"I've lied too," Tae said and then paused. "I know I've been away for a while, and I came back without really telling anyone why. It's because I got a divorce. It was bad, and I'm broke. That's why I'm living with my brother at the marina. I tell people it's all good, but it's not. The relationship was toxic and dangerous to my mental well-being, and I'm still working on being okay."

Sadie slipped an arm around her. "All of us are working on being okay. You're not alone." She met Ivy's gaze. "And neither are you. None of us are. We have each other."

"I'm so grateful for that." Haley smiled a little sadly. She looked at Dee, who nodded at her. "I've never told any of you before, but my family doesn't approve of my so-called chosen lifestyle. So really, you're all my family. Knowing that we all love each other unconditionally has gotten me through a bunch of stuff."

Ivy felt her throat tighten. "I've not had much luck with unconditional love and happily-ever-after fairy-tale stuff. In fact, you might say I'm really bad at it."

"But life's *not* a fairy tale," Molly said.

"And if you lose your shoe at midnight, you're drunk," Haley added sagely.

They all laughed at that. "But the good thing about that," Sadie said, "is that true friends will get you home regardless. We're that kind of friends, Ivy. The ride or die kind."

"I'm not especially good at that either," Ivy managed. "You're all my first ride or dies."

"No sweat," Sadie said, and squeezed Ivy's hand. "Me too."

Ivy looked into her eyes. "Did Caleb tell you about last night? That Brandon broke into the new condo building with the intention of stealing computers and equipment to sell for cash?"

"He told me that it happened, and that one of the security guys was badly hurt, but he didn't tell me it was your brother. Is that what happened between you and Kel?"

"How do you know something happened between me and Kel?" Ivy asked.

"Because from the day he arrived, you've been smiling like none of us had ever seen," Sadie said. "The two of you seemed perfect together. But now you look like someone stole your best friend."

Ivy drew a deep breath. "Let's just say he didn't take any of what happened very well. I lied to him about Brandon. And once he showed up, I continued to lie. Kel didn't like Brandon from the start, but I kept telling him that he wasn't a bad guy. An idiot, yes, a bad guy, no. But then Brandon broke into that building and hurt an innocent man. And . . ." She drew a deep breath. "That's not all. He used my phone to make a PayPal transfer, stealing money from my savings account. Before I figured that out, he fled."

"Oh my God," Haley said. "But why would Kel get mad at you for that? None of that was your fault."

"I was the one who told Brandon about the condo building. I was excited about buying one and he seemed excited for me." Ivy shook her head. "Now I know he was just excited about figuring out a solution to his money problems."

"But you didn't know he'd do what he did. It wasn't your fault," Sadie said firmly. "It's all on your brother, honey. Not you."

"I appreciate you saying that, but I made mistakes. I didn't turn him in when I could have. And then there was the thing with my phone. Brandon had it when Kel texted me asking if I'd seen my brother. Brandon texted him back, pretending to be me, saying I hadn't. But I have no way to prove that."

"I know Kel," Sadie said. "He's a logical, rational guy. Whatever his gut reaction might have been, when he thinks about everything, he'll understand."

Ivy shook her head. "I think that maybe love isn't for me. It's just too . . . hard."

"None of us had an easy go of it with love," Sadie said. "Well, except maybe Molly."

Molly snorted. "You cannot be serious. I almost blew the best thing to ever happen to me by nearly getting Lucas killed, remember? Listen," she said to Ivy. "If you believe nothing else, then please believe this. The right guy will believe in you when it counts. I'm not saying Kel isn't the right guy, because I happen to think he is. I just also think he's running scared on this thing with you. But that's because of his own past, nothing to do with you."

Kel had definitely been burned before, in a big way. And Ivy had played right into his fears. She got that. They were both pretty screwed up. Didn't make it any easier to take. A few people were approaching the order window of the truck, so she got to her feet. "I've gotta go. The dinner crowd's starting to show."

"Don't forget tonight," Haley said.

"Forget what?"

"It's Christmas Eve," Molly said. "And there's a

group of us who always get together at the pub for Christmas Eve."

Ivy knew that the tight-knit group of friends who worked and lived in the building always celebrated this night together, it was tradition. The pub was closed to outsiders, and until now, that had been her. Just a year ago, she'd watched from the outside, wondering if she'd ever be a part of anything like this.

She realized she'd come a long way. "I signed up to serve food at the Mission Homeless Center for a few hours after work," she said, which she'd done for more than purely altruistic reasons. She hadn't wanted to be alone.

"No problem," Sadie said. "We'll come volunteer with you, then we'll all go to the pub."

"I don't know," Ivy said quietly.

"Oh, you've got to come," Haley said. "It's my turn to put up the star. I mean, I might have to fight Spence for it, he seems to think it's his turn, but he's wrong." She looked at her watch and stood. "Shoot. I've got to get going too."

Everyone else rose to go as well, and Ivy tried to just keep breathing. Her two least favorite emotions—heartbroken and loneliness—were already swamping her again. Her brother was gone, probably really headed to Mexico this time, and he wouldn't be coming back.

And Kel . . . well, that was over, and though she'd

known it would be, and had told herself she was prepared for it, she wasn't. But she managed a smile and
saw everyone off and then went back to work. She
told herself what was done was done, and in truth,
she wasn't sure she'd do anything different.

But when she and Jenny closed up a few hours
later, Ivy made a point to walk by the fountain in
the courtyard. She took a ridiculous beat to try and
figure out which quarter on the bottom of the copper bowl was hers, but of course she couldn't. So she
just glared at the whole fountain. "Do you feel good
about yourself?" she asked it. "Giving people false
hopes? Because I don't feel good about it. You suck."

"So you wished on the fountain."

At the craggily old voice next to her, Ivy craned
her neck and took in Old Man Eddie standing there
grinning.

At her dark look, he laughed and lifted his hands
in surrender. "Hey, just making conversation. But
just so you know, the fountain never fails."

"It failed," she said flatly. "It's just a stupid myth."

"What did you wish for?"

Feeling stupid, she hedged. "If I tell you, it can't
come true."

"Now *that's* a stupid myth," he said. "Tell me. Did
you wish for your one true love?"

"No." She blew out a breath. "I wished to believe
in true love."

He nodded sagely.

"What?"

"Well," he said slowly. "Don't kill the messenger, but . . ."

"But what?"

He smiled. "Seems like you believe in true love now, if you're pissed off at the thing for not dropping it in your lap."

She stared at him as the truth of his statement hit home. "Dammit."

He laughed and pulled a coin from his pocket and tossed it to her. "Maybe it's time for wish number two," he suggested, and walked away.

Ivy really wanted not to throw the coin in the water. But in spite of what had happened between her and Kel, she realized that suddenly, or maybe not suddenly at all, she really did believe in love. When exactly that had happened, she wasn't sure. So . . . with her heart tight and aching in her chest, she let go of the coin. "Thanks for helping me believe," she whispered. "No regrets."

At least not on that . . .

Chapter 27

We start together and end together

Thirty minutes later, Ivy stood behind a table slicing turkey and ladling gravy. She was at the Mission Homeless Center, wearing a red apron and matching hat, doing her best to look festive while on the inside she felt like the Grinch.

At the table to her right was Sadie, dishing out scoops of side dishes such as corn, stuffing, salad, and rolls. To her left was Tae, handing out dessert, which was cupcakes. In an identical assembly line just across from her, Molly and Haley were serving as well. There was a crowd of people making their way through the lines for a free Christmas Eve dinner and a few minutes inside, safe from the icy night.

There were other volunteers as well, everyone working in sync to keep things moving. There were a lot of people and Ivy was able to keep herself busy with orders. She didn't even look up until she heard the unbearably familiar voice.

"I'd like to make a special request."

Ivy jerked and spilled gravy down the front of her apron. It was Kel, of course. No one else could evoke so many feelings within her without even trying.

He was in a hoodie with a jacket over that, hood up against the chill. Dark sunglasses on his face. All she could see was his unsmiling mouth. Her mind stuttered, but the rest of her did not. Specifically, her mouth. "No special requests allowed."

"It's just that I lost something," he said quietly, removing his sunglasses and pushing off his hood. "Something, some*one*, who means a lot to me." He shook his head. "Actually, she means everything to me."

Her heart took a good hard leap against her ribcage. "What are you doing here?"

"Can we talk?"

Her chest felt tight. Way too tight. "It's hot in here," she whispered. "Is it hot in here?" she asked all the people standing *way* too close.

"Honey, that's called a hot flash," an elderly woman waiting in line said. "Are you going through the change?"

"Edna, she's like twelve," the woman next to the first one said. "She's not going through the change.

And how much longer before you refill the mashed potatoes? I can't stand on my feet too long, I get the veins."

Ivy was having a hard time processing and just stared at Kel.

"I was wrong," he said before she could speak. "About a lot of things, as it turns out. But mostly about how I reacted."

"The mashed potatoes?" the woman asked again, impatiently.

"Hush, Amelia," Edna said. "Can't you see she's in the middle of something? Hot Stuff here's trying to apologize. A man apologizing, can you imagine such a thing?"

Ivy's heart was in her throat. She was trying to remember if anyone had ever apologized to her before, especially a male, but nothing was coming to mind. And that alone was boggling.

Kel hated airing his feelings, she knew that. And yet here he stood, in front of a hundred homeless people and also her friends, who'd all stilled and were staring at them.

"Maybe we should talk about this later," she whispered, which didn't matter since she could now hear a pin drop in the unbelievably crowded hall that only moments before had been at deafening levels. "After I'm done working here."

"You'd deprive an old woman of this Hallmark

moment?" Edna asked in horror. "I haven't been wooed since 1965. Don't take this away from me, honey."

Kel drew a deep breath and took Ivy's hands. "Later won't work," he said. "I was wrong to let you think I blamed you, for any of what happened. And I should never have let you run off without saying that to you."

"What did you do?" Amelia asked. "Cheat on her?"

"No," Kel said, still holding Ivy's gaze in his own. "Worse. I let her think I didn't trust her."

"Well that was dumb," Edna said. "She's serving the homeless on Christmas Eve. She's trustable."

"She is." This from Sadie, who gave Kel a hard look. "And she deserves better."

Ivy shook her head. "Sadie—"

"No, it's true," Kel said. "I have this thing that I do. I don't let people in past my guard."

"That's a man thing," one of the ladies said. "They're chickenshits."

"That's true too," Kel said, still holding Ivy's gaze. "I was the biggest chickenshit of all."

"You've got to speak up," Amelia demanded. "I can't hear very well, and since I'm not getting my mashed potatoes anytime soon, the least you can do is talk loud enough for us all to hear."

Kel's lips twitched, but his eyes remained very serious as he spoke to Ivy. "In the past, a lack of communication and dishonesty has gotten in the way of my relationships. And I used that past to blow this—you and me—up."

Ivy bit her lower lip and grimaced. "Well, I did my fair share of meeting you halfway there," she admitted.

With a real smile this time, he stepped into her, apparently not caring that he was now hugging up to the gravy spill. "No, this is on me, Ivy. I was wrong, and I'm sorry."

"Wow," Edna said. "He also admits when he's wrong. That's a rare breed."

"That's true," Sadie said.

Ivy glanced over at her and Sadie lifted her shoulders, silently letting Ivy know she was at her back no matter what. The warm fuzzy that the gesture sent through her was new and very welcome. And maybe also made her far braver than she might have been if she'd still been alone. Braver, and more honest. "We've *both* been burned by our past, in a big way," she said to Kel. "Maybe too burned."

"No," he said. "I don't believe that." He slid a hand to her waist, the other skimming down her arm to gently and slowly remove the very sharp knife she still held. "Earlier you said you felt like I was looking for something, and you didn't know what it was."

She nodded.

"It's you," he said. "*You're* what I'm looking for. I

made mistakes, a lot of them. I should have believed in you, I should never have doubted your intentions. That was my . . ." He glanced at the ladies. "My chickenshit-ness doing the talking for me. It had nothing to do with you and everything to do with me and my own fears. You gave me your love and I burned that love to the ground. I'll never do that again." He bent a little at the knees so they were eye-to-eye. "Never," he said with a seriousness she'd not seen from him before. "And I should admit, I've probably got a lot more mistakes yet to make."

She found a smile. "Ditto."

He smiled too. "Maybe we could learn and grow together."

She stared into his eyes. "Maybe. And maybe we could also . . ."

"Anything," he said. "Name it."

"Start over?"

He stared at her and then smiled and held out a hand. "Hi. I'm Kel O'Donnell. I'm new to town, love spicy tacos, *and* the woman who makes them. Also . . ." He pulled an iPad from his inside jacket pocket and showed her a document. "I wanted to deliver this personally."

She stared down at what appeared to be a purchase agreement for her condo, the same exact deal as she'd had, only the down payment had been marked paid. "What's this?"

"Your deal went through today."

She stared up at him. "How? My deposit's gone."

"It's worked out," he said.

She eyed the paperwork again and realized he'd made the down payment for her. "Are you crazy, you can't buy a woman you're just sleeping with a condo."

"If it freaks you out, consider it a loan until PayPal reverses Brandon's transaction. Caleb's attorney said he could make it happen, things are just being held up because of the holiday. And," he said, softer now. "We're more than just sleeping together." His mouth curved in amusement at the collective gasp in the room, though his eyes remained serious and on hers. "Much more."

"But why," she said, still gaping. "Why would you do that?"

"Because I wanted to."

She shook her head. "It's not your fault that I lost the down payment, Kel. It was mine. I trusted when I shouldn't have."

"I know. And watching you start to trust me in spite of everything you've gone through and then losing that trust because I was an asshole, kills me."

"You can't buy it back."

"I know that too. I intend to earn it."

"That's going to be hard to do from Idaho."

He didn't say anything, so she looked at him and

found his expression softened. "At least you didn't say impossible," he said quietly. "And I know we could've made that work somehow. But I'm not going to be in Idaho. I'm not going back, at least not to stay. I want to be here, and I want to be with you."

"But your whole life is in Idaho."

"Actually, my whole life is right here."

She didn't move. And she'd forgotten how to breathe again.

"I thought I knew myself," he said. "I thought I knew what the rest of my life was going to look like. But things change, things get messed up, things blow up in your face, and sometimes it feels like there's no light at the end of the tunnel. But I was wrong about that too. Because as long as you've got someone to wade through the bad shit with, someone who loves you, nothing else matters."

"*Kel.*"

At the wealth of emotion in her voice that she couldn't have hidden to save her own life, he cupped her face, tilting it up to his. "You're that person for me, Ivy. I want to fall asleep to the rhythm of your breathing and wake up with you right there, getting mad at me for hogging the blanket, even though you're the blanket hog."

"Are you saying I snore?"

"Just lightly," he said, grinning while she glared at him. "I want to hear you laugh when I burn my tongue on your tacos because I can't wait for them to cool, I want to dance in a honky-tonk cowboy bar with you stepping on my toes—" He smiled when she snorted. "But most of all, I want to share my life with you. I promise to always have your back, and stand at your side, and I also promise to be worthy of your trust and heart. I love you, Ivy."

She heard a few soft "aw's" and Amelia's "honey, you'd better hold out for a big-ass diamond!" But she couldn't tear her gaze off Kel's. "That sounded an awful lot like wedding vows."

He shrugged. "White dress and a license or not, I meant every word."

Her mouth fell open. "Are you saying you'd marry me?"

"I'm saying I'm in for whatever you want."

She was stunned. "That's . . . a lot of power."

He smiled, and it was a beautiful smile that stole her heart. Nope, not true. He'd stolen her heart the very first moment she'd laid eyes on him.

Be smart.

Be brave.

Be vulnerable.

Her aunt's words bounced around in her head as they always did, but suddenly she got it, she knew what her aunt had meant. So she went up on her tiptoes, wrapped her arms around Kel's neck, and kissed him, hard.

Their audience erupted with hoots and hollers, and slowly she pulled back. "I love you too, Kel."

He let out a breath like he'd been holding it for too long. And then he kissed her again, softly this time, his arms tight around her and feeling like . . . home. "It's Christmas Eve, and I have big plans for you. So what do you say we get back to serving and finish up?"

"We? You're going to serve too?"

One of the women handed him a red apron, which he put on without hesitation. And then, while she was still gaping at him, he nudged her over and began serving mashed potatoes and gravy.

At the end of their shift two hours later, he was still going strong and making small talk with everyone who came through the line.

Ivy and her friends were still working too, the lot of them spattered with food.

Kel didn't have a speck on him.

They made their way back to the Pacific Pier Building and the pub for their annual Christmas party. The pub was all decked out for the holidays with twinkling lights strung across the brass lanterns hanging from the rafters. The vibe was antique charm and friendly warmth.

Everyone moved toward the bar but Kel took Ivy's hand and held her back. They stood next to a beautifully decorated tree, beneath a large beam from which hung mistletoe.

Ivy glanced up and smiled. The last time they'd stood beneath mistletoe she'd told him not to even think about kissing her. She sure wouldn't mind if he was thinking about it now.

He tilted his head up too, and as if he could hear her thoughts, his mouth quirked. He slid a hand to the nape of her neck, his thumb grazing soft, sensitive skin just beneath her ear. He kissed her, long and warm and intimate. When he pulled back, he gave her a smile that had her falling in love with him all over again. "I've got something for you," he said.

"Oh. Oh, but I don't have your present—"

"It's not from me," he said. He took her hand and turned it palm up to drop something in it.

She opened her fingers and gasped.

It was her aunt Cathy's necklace. She stared at it, throat tight as the implications hit her. "He said he didn't have it anymore."

"It wouldn't be the first time he's lied to you."

She pressed the necklace to her heart. "No."

"But I happen to know he went back to the pawn shop and bought it back." He lifted a shoulder. "He finally put you first."

Nodding, she smiled through a thick throat. "I'm worried about him. I know that's stupid."

"It's not." He looked at her for a long moment. "I was asked not to tell you this, but I'm not going to start our life together with a lie."

Time stopped as she stared at him. "What?"

"He turned himself in, Ivy. A few hours ago. He was the anonymous caller that allowed us to get the bigger fish, by the way. He's being charged and processed. He's pleading guilty and cooperating fully. He says he wants to do his time so he can have a fresh start with a clean slate."

"Oh my God," she whispered, stunned.

"That's how I got the necklace. He wanted you to have it. And this." He handed her a folded piece of paper that turned out to be a handwritten letter.

Dear Ivy,

I know I'm probably the last person you want to hear from right now, but I had to write this. Had to make sure you know that when I was bleeding in your living room and you were doing everything in your power to save my sorry ass, that it did something to me.

It made me realize that I wasn't hurting just me by my lifestyle, but you too. I dragged you into my mess and you could have been hurt. Thank God you weren't.

I'm sorry. I know those two words don't mean shit, but I intend to back them up with actions. I mean, obviously it's going to be a while before I can prove myself. But I won't forget you or what you've done for me.

You said if I left, I was no longer your

*family. And I deserve that. But I'm going to
hope like hell to make amends and change
that.*

*Forever your brother,
Brandon*

Ivy lifted her head. "I want to see him."

Kel shook his head. "You can't, at least not yet.
Soon as it's possible though."

Brandon had turned himself in, for her. Shock
and grief spilled into regrets. And relief. "He finally
chose me. I actually . . . have a brother."

Kel nodded and his gaze softened as he stroked
a strand of hair from her face. "That's not all you
have."

She marveled over that as Kel pulled her into him.
"I have you."

"You have me," he agreed huskily, pressing his
lips to her temple.

This was greeted by cheers and catcalls, reminding her they had an audience. An audience filled
with people who loved and cared about her, which
gave her such a feeling of joy, her eyes prickled with
happy tears.

He'd warmed her from the inside out. And she figured, hoped, that while nothing was a guarantee, it
was worth the risk. He was worth the risk.

He tilted her head up to look into her eyes and said,

"*You're* worth the risk," making her realize she'd spoken out loud. "I've never felt like this for someone, Ivy. Never."

Her breath caught at the way he looked at her, held her. "Me either. But we started so fast, what if we . . . burn out?"

"Not going to happen," he said fiercely. "We started strong, we stay strong." He pulled back just enough to shoot her a melt-her-heart smile. "I'm all yours, Ivy. For as long as you'll have me."

Which was going to be a good long time, she thought happily, and then she pulled him down for a kiss to seal the deal.

Epilogue

Five years later

Ivy stood against the farthest fencing of Kel's—their—Sonoma horse ranch, staring out in wonder and surprise as tiny little snowflakes drifted from the sky. It never snowed here, *or* in the city where she and Kel spent most of their time, and she couldn't stop smiling.

"Look, Kenzie," she whispered to the three-month-old in a baby carrier against her chest. "It's snowing for Christmas Eve."

Her baby girl wasn't at all moved by the snow, or her mama's excitement. Nothing disturbed Kenzie when she was napping. Ivy ran a finger over the baby's forehead and felt her entire being soften as it always did whenever she looked at her daughter.

The daughter who looked exactly like Kel, right down to the satisfied smile on her face as she snoozed.

She loved it here. Kel had taken her to Idaho, plenty

of times, and she loved it there too, but he'd taken the job with Caleb and sold the Sunshine property.

They were a California family now, splitting their time between the city and her still beloved Taco Truck—which had a legal permit now, thank you very much—and here.

And here . . . owned her heart.

She heard the crunching of footsteps coming her way, two sets. Knowing it was Kel and probably Donovan, she didn't take her eyes off the gently falling snow.

Two strong warm arms came around both her and the baby, and Kel kissed Ivy's jaw. "Cold?"

"Not at all. The horses okay?"

"Yes. One of your Christmas presents came early."

She looked down at Kenzie, now lovingly cradled in her daddy's hands. "I don't need any presents."

"We'll call it the present that you didn't think you need then," Kel said.

Curious now, she turned, and time stopped.

Brandon stood there, looking leaner and entirely uncertain of his welcome. "Hey," he said. "I see you kept your cop."

"I married him," she managed through a raw throat.

This had become their standard, teasing greeting over the past five years whenever she'd visited him in prison. But she hadn't been this year because of a difficult pregnancy.

"You're out early," she whispered.

"Good behavior." He lifted a shoulder. "I've been practicing."

Swallowing the lump in her throat, she nodded. "It's good to see you."

Some of the worry left his eyes and his shoulders dropped from where he'd held them practically up to his ears. "You don't have to say that."

"I mean it."

He held her gaze with his mismatched eyes. "Part of my early release was contingent on me having a place to stay and work. Kel got me a job working for him and Donovan. I'm going to live in the employee barracks on Donovan's property." He paused. "If that's all okay with you."

Ivy thought she was choked up before, but she could scarcely draw a breath, overwhelmed with love and affection for her amazing husband. She looked up at him and hoped she conveyed her love and affection and gratitude back, because she couldn't speak.

With a smile, Kel leaned in and gave her a quick, warm kiss.

"I love you," she managed to whisper.

"I know," he whispered back before lifting his head and looking at Brandon. "I think it's safe to say it's okay with her."

"Very okay," she said and reached for Brandon, pulling him in for a hug. When little Kenzie mewled her protest, Ivy pulled back with a laugh. "Meet your niece, Kenzie Snow O'Donnell. She's as impatient and feisty as her mom."

Brandon stared down at Kenzie in awe. "Wow." He seemed choked up. "She's . . . amazing."

Just as choked up, Ivy nodded. "Guess us Snows have a future after all."

Brandon let out his first smile. A small one, and it felt a little rusty, but totally genuine. "Didn't see that coming."

She looked up at Kel, knowing her heart was in her eyes. "I didn't either. But I met someone who made me see anything was possible."

Kel smiled down at her. "To our future," he said softly.

"To our future." And once again she kissed him to seal the deal.

Keep reading for a sneak peek at the next
women's fiction novel from Jill Shalvis

ALMOST JUST FRIENDS

Arriving January 2020
Pre-order now!

Chapter 1

"Chin up, Princess, or the crown slips."

Piper Manning closed her eyes and plugged her ears against the horror. She'd known this would happen even as she'd begged against it, but sometimes there was no stopping fate. *You've survived worse. Just push through it. Pretend you're on a warm beach, vacationing, and there's a hot surfer coming out of the water. Wait, scratch that. A hot Australian surfer coming out of the water, heading for you with a sexy smile—*

Someone tugged her fingers from her ears. Her best friend and EMT partner, Jenna. "It's over," she said. "You can look now."

Piper opened her eyes. No warm beach, no sexy surfer. She was still at the Whiskey River Bar and Grill, surrounded by her coworkers and so-called friends, and way too many birthday streamers and balloons, all mocking her because someone had thought it'd be funny to do it in all gloom-and-doom black.

"You do realize that turning thirty isn't exactly the end of the world?" Jenna said.

Maybe not, but there was a reason Piper hadn't wanted to celebrate. She'd just hit a milestone birthday without being at any sort of milestone, or anywhere even close to a milestone. Certainly nowhere near where she'd thought she'd be at thirty.

"Hey, let's sing it again now that she's listening," someone called out. Ryland, no doubt. The hotshot firefighter was always the group's instigator.

And so everyone began singing again, laughing when Piper grimaced and did her best not to crawl under the table. Truth was, she'd rather have a root canal without meds than be the center of attention, and these asshats knew it. "It's like you all want to die," she muttered. But someone put a drink in her hand, and since she was off duty now for two days, she took a long gulp.

"I was *very* clear," she said when the alcohol burn cleared her throat, eyeing the whole group, most of whom were also first responders and worked with her at the station or hospital in one form or another. "We weren't going to mention my birthday, much less sing about it."

Not a single one of them looked guilty. In fact, they ignored her. "To Piper," Ry said, and everyone raised a glass. "For gathering and keeping all us misfits together and sane."

"To Piper," everyone cheered and drank, and then thankfully, conversations started up all around her so that she was finally no longer the center of attention.

Her friends, God love them, were all used to her ways, which meant they got that while she was touched they'd all remembered her birthday, she didn't want any more attention. Easily accepting that, they were happy to enjoy the night and leave her alone.

"Did that hurt?" Jenna asked, amused.

"What?"

"Being loved?"

In tune to the sounds of the bar behind them—someone singing off-key to Sweet Home Alabama, rambunctious laughter from a nearby table, the slap of pool balls . . . Piper rolled her eyes.

"You know one day those eyeballs are going to fall right out of your head, right?"

Piper ignored this and went back to what she'd been doing before being so rudely interrupted by all the love. Making a list.

She was big on bullet journaling. She'd had to be. Making notes and lists had saved her life more than once. And yes, she knew she could do it on a notes app on her phone, but her brain hadn't been wired that way. Nope, she was annoyingly old school, so she had to write that shit down by hand to make it stick.

She had pages dedicated to:

Calendars
Grocery Lists
Future Baby Names (even though she didn't
    plan on having babies)
Passwords (okay, password, single, since
    she always used the same one—
    CookiesAreLife123!)

And then there were random entries, such as:

Life rules
—Stop eating entire bags of Cheese Poofs in
    one sitting.
—Don't cut your own bangs no matter how
    sad you are.
—Never ever EVER under any circumstances
    fall in love.

She had a bucket list of wishes. Oh, and a secret *secret* bucket list of wishes . . .

Yeah, she probably needed help. Or a little pill.

Jenna leaned over her shoulder and eyed the open page. "New journal?"

Her vices were simple. She didn't drink much, never smoked, but . . . she was an office supply 'ho. A never ending source of amusement to Jenna because Piper was also a bit of a hot mess when it came to organization and neatness. Her purse, her car, her office, and also her kitchen always looked like a disaster had just hit. "Maybe."

"How many journals have you started and either lost or misplaced since I've known you, a million?"

Piper didn't answer this on the grounds that it might incriminate her.

Jenna played with the pack of stickers that Piper had tucked haphazardly into the journal. "Cute. But I feel like stickers are cheating."

"Bite your tongue. Stickers are everything." So were pens. And cute paper clips. And stick-it notes . . .

"Stickers? Come on. There are far more important things than stickers."

"Like?" Piper asked.

"Like food."

"Okay, you've got me there."

"Or sex," Jenna said.

"Since it's been awhile, I'll have to take your word on that."

"Well, whose fault is that?" Jenna nudged her chin at the journal. "What's today's entry?"

"A list for figuring out what's next on fixing up the property." Which was the house and cottages on

Rainbow Lake that Piper and her siblings had inherited from their grandparents. "It still needs a lot of work. I'm in way over my head."

"I know." Jenna's smile faded. "I hate that you're going to sell and move away from Wildstone."

Wildstone, California, was Piper's hometown. Sort of. She'd moved here at age thirteen with her two younger siblings Gavin and Winnie, to be raised by their grandparents. But in the end, Piper had done all the raising. It'd taken forever, but now, finally, her brother and sister were off living their own lives.

And hers could finally start.

All she had to do was finish fixing up the property, then she'd sell and divide the money in thirds with her siblings. With her portion, she'd finally have the money and freedom to go to school and become a physician's assistant like she'd always wanted.

So close. She was so close that she could almost taste it. She squeezed Jenna's hand. "Don't worry. I'm coming back to Wildstone after school."

Where else would she go? Her only other home had been following her parents all over the world, providing healthcare wherever they'd been needed the most. But her mom and dad were gone now. Her family was Gavin and Winnie, and everyone in this room.

"But why the University of Colorado?" Jenna

asked. "Why go so far? You could go right here to Cal Poly."

Piper shook her head. Staying wasn't an option. She'd been stuck here for seventeen years. She needed to go away for a while and figure out her life, who she was if she wasn't raising her siblings. But that felt hard to explain, so she gave even her bff the excuse. "U of C is one of the really strong schools for my program. And I think I'll like Colorado."

Jenna looked unconvinced, but she was a good enough friend to let it go.

"Don't worry," Piper said. "I'll be back."

"You'd better." Jenna read the journal over Piper's shoulder. "You sure make a lot of very responsible lists. I can't even make a shopping list."

"That's because you don't go food shopping. You order in."

Jenna smiled. "Oh, right."

"Paint samples!" Piper remembered suddenly, and wrote that down. When you ran your world, everyone in that world tended to depend on you to do it right. That's how it'd always been for her. She'd been in charge whether she liked it or not.

"You know you're a control freak, right?"

Piper chewed on the end of her pen. "I'm forgetting something, I know it."

"Yeah," Jenna said. "To get a life."

"What do you think I'm doing here?"

Now it was Jenna's turn to roll her eyes. "Everyone else is talking about the hot new guy in town, and you're over here in the corner making a shopping list."

"Hot guys come and go."

Jenna laughed. "Yeah? How long has it been since you've had a hot guy in your life, or any guy at all?"

Piper looked across the bar to where Ry was currently chatting it up with not one, but *two*, women. Her ex was apparently making up for lost time.

"Well, whose fault is that?" Jenna asked, reading her mind. "You dumped him last year for no reason, remember?"

Actually, she'd had a really good reason, but it wasn't one she wanted to share, so she shrugged.

"You need a distraction. Of the sexy kind," Jenna said. "You carry that journal around like it's the love of your life."

"At the moment, it is."

"You could do a whole lot better." Swiveling in her barstool, Jenna eyed the crowd.

"Don't even think about it."

"About what?" Jenna asked innocently.

"Fixing me up."

"Would that be so bad?" Jenna asked, softer now, putting a hand on Piper's writing arm. "You're the one always fixing everyone's life, everyone but your own, of course. But even The Fixer needs help sometimes."

It was true that she'd gone a whole bunch of years now being the one to keep it all together. For everyone. Asking for help wasn't a part of her DNA. But Jenna did have a point. Today was her birthday, a milestone birthday at that, so she should do at least one frivolous thing, right? She turned the page of her journal and glanced at her secret bucket list.

—Take a cruise to Alaska.
—Get some "me" time every day.
—Learn to knit.
—Buy shoes that *aren't* nursing shoes.

"Okay, seriously, I'm worried," Jenna said. "You're sitting at your birthday party eyeing a list about buying nursing shoes?"

"About *not* buying nursing shoes," Piper corrected. "And this isn't my party."

"It's your party. And if you'd told Gavin and Winnie about it, they'd be here helping you celebrate too."

Just what she needed, to give her twenty-seven-going-on-seventeen-year-old brother and her not-quite-legal-to-drink sister a reason to party. "I told them not to come. Gavin's busy at his job in Phoenix, and Winnie's working hard on her grades at UCSB."

"They're lucky to have you, I hope they know that," Jenna said genuinely. "You work so hard,

Piper, keeping all of you going. But today, at the very least, you should have some fun."

"I hear you. But keep that . . ." She pointed to the sign hanging above the bar. ". . . In mind, yeah?"

The sign read:

WARNING:

ALCOHOL MAY MAKE THE PEOPLE IN THIS PLACE APPEAR BETTER LOOKING THAN THEY REALLY ARE.

Jenna laughed, but wasn't deterred from glancing over at the closest table to the bar, where three guys sat.

"Oh, no," Piper said. "Don't you dare."

But then she was grimacing because Jenna dared. "Who here is single?"

Two of the guys pointed to the third at their table.

"You?" Jenna asked him.

He took a beat to check Jenna out. Tonight her partner was channeling Beach Jenna with her wild blonde hair rioting around her pretty face, her athletic build emphasized by tightly fitted fancy yoga gear. "Yeah," he said with a smile. "I'm most definitely single."

"Good. Because my friend here . . ." Jenna turned to gesture at Piper, who'd been trying to sneak off, but froze in the act of getting off the barstool when they all looked at her.

"It's her birthday," Jenna said.

"She's hiding in the corner writing in a book," the guy said doubtfully.

"Yes, well, we can't all be perfect, right? Look, she's friendly . . ." Jenna grimaced and made a correction. *"Ish.* And she's got all of her shots and is potty-trained to boot. I mean, yeah, sometimes she hides out in bars writing in her journal. Or in her pantry closet inhaling an entire bag of Cheese Poofs while thumbing through Pinterest, but hey, who doesn't, am I right?"

Looking alarmed, the man turned back to his friends.

"Gee," Piper said dryly. "And you made me sound like such a catch too."

Jenna shrugged. "Maybe he's just not a Cheese Poofs fan."

"Yeah. That's definitely it."

"Don't you worry," Jenna said. "I'm not done."

"Please be done."

But Jenna was now eyeing the man who'd just taken a barstool a few seats down. *That's him*, she mouthed to Piper.

Who?

New Hot Guy!

Piper sneaked a peek. He was in military green cargos and a black Henley that hugged his long, leanly muscled body. He had dark hair, dark eyes, and dark scruff, all of which went with his quietly dark expression that said *Not Feeling Social*.

Jenna stood as if planning on another round of Let's Embarrass Piper, but Piper grabbed her. "*Don't you dare!*"

Jenna just smiled and looked at the man. "Hey."

He nodded at her.

"So . . . you're a guy."

"Last time I checked," he said dryly.

Jenna jerked a thumb to Piper. "It's my best friend's birthday."

Hot Guy's gaze locked on Piper.

"She's made herself a list," Jenna said.

Hot Guy eyed the still open journal as Jenna assisted by turning it his way for ease of reading.

Honest to God, Piper had no idea why she loved this woman.

Hot Guy read the list and then rubbed the sexy scruff on his jaw. "Is this for you or your grandma?"

Jenna snorted. "Hey, that's her nickname, actually. *Grandma*."

"Some wingman you are." Piper snatched up the journal and closed it.

"What does 'me' time entail?" Hot Guy asked.

"I'm pretty sure it involves batteries," Jenna answered helpfully.

"Okay," Piper said and pointed at Jenna. "You know what? You're cut off."

"Notice that she didn't answer the question," Jenna said to Hot Guy. "She's good at that."

"It doesn't involve batteries!" Piper snapped. No way was she going to admit she'd meant a nap.

Jenna took the journal back, flipped the page, and added something to Piper's supposedly *secret* list:

—Get laid.

Then she drew an arrow pointing at Hot Guy, who nodded in approval. "*Now* you've got a list."

"Keep dreaming, buddy," she said before turning back to Jenna. "And you. Are you kidding me? You wrote that in *ink*." Which meant it couldn't be erased. And Piper couldn't rip it out either. She couldn't just rip out a page from a bullet journal, it went against how she'd been coded. She supposed she should be grateful Jenna hadn't turned to the next page and revealed her secret *secret* bucket list.

"Don't let her bad attitude scare you," Jenna said to Hot Guy. "She's all bark and no bite."

"I like bite," Hot Guy said, and his and Piper's eyes locked again. His were an intense, assessing hazel, a swirling, mesmerizing mix of green, brown, and gold. He was good looking, but so were a lot of men. He was leanly muscled—also not all that uncommon. But he had a way about him that created an odd fluttering in her belly. It took her a long moment to recognize it for what it was—excitement. Which made no sense. None. Zero. Zip. She wasn't looking for anything, and he . . . well, he was obviously both sharp and witty, but his eyes seemed . . . hollow, and he hadn't cracked a smile.

She stared at him thinking maybe they were kindred perpetually-pissed-off-at-the-world spirits. One thing for sure, he didn't seem uncomfortable in the least as she studied him. In fact, he didn't seem the sort to be uncomfortable in any situation.

Around them, the bar was filled with music, talking, laughter . . . the sounds of people having a good time. Someone called out for Jenna to join a dart game. Jenna slid off her stool. "Okay, so, I'm going to abandon her now. Feel free to play the gallant gentleman swooping in to save the birthday girl. Night, Piper."

"That's Grandma to you," Piper called to her back, and when Jenna laughed and kept walking, Piper pulled out her phone and thumbed in a text.

Hot Guy seemed to be very slightly amused, though still no smile touched his lips. "Bet you just told your wingman that you're going to kill her."

Gallant Gentleman her ass. Dark and Dangerous, maybe. She shrugged. "I might've mentioned she shouldn't close her eyes when she goes to sleep tonight. But yours is better. Hold please." She typed a new text: *Don't forget, thanks to my dad, I know a ton of ways to kill someone with my pen.*

"Nice," he said, reading over her shoulder.

"You find violent tendencies nice?"

He shrugged. "Being able to defend yourself is smart."

She paused. "You know I was just kidding about the pen thing, right?"

He cocked his head and studied her. "Were you?"

She sat back, staring at him. She *had* been just kidding about the killing Jenna thing. But *not* about knowing how to do it with a pen. No one had ever, not once, called her out on that threat as being real.

"Your dad military?" he asked.

"Was," she said. "He's gone now."

He gave a single nod, like he got it at a core level. "I'm sorry."

She supposed it was his genuine and clearly understanding reaction that had her doing something she rarely did. She said more. Unprompted. "We lived overseas in some seriously sketchy places. He made sure I knew how to defend myself and my siblings."

He gave another nod, this one in approval, and it had her taking a second look at him, at the calm steady gaze that withheld any personal thoughts, at the way he sat at rest, but with a sense of tightly harnessed power. And then there was his build, which suggested he could handle whatever situation arose. "You too," she said quietly. "You were military too."

He studied her right back for a long beat, assessing. "Still am."

When he didn't say anything else, she arched a brow, waiting for more, but it didn't come. "Let me guess," she said. "It's a secret. If you told me, you'd have to kill me."

The very corners of his eyes crinkled. Yeah, she was most definitely amusing him. "I'm actually a DEA agent, but also Coast Guard."

"How do you do both?" she asked.

"I was active duty for twelve years. Been in the Reserve for two. My DEA job schedule allows for the times I'm in training or activated."

She thought her parents had lived dangerous lives. This guy had them beat. And considering what had happened to her mom and dad, she had less than zero interest in him, no matter how curious she was. Where was a hot easy-going surfer when you needed one? "How often do you train or get activated?"

"My unit trains three days a month. We get activated at will." He shrugged, like it was no big deal that he put his life on hold at what she assumed was short notice to go off to save the world.

"The DEA doesn't mind you leaving at the drop of a hat?"

"They knew that when they signed me on." He shrugged again. "I had the skill sets they needed."

"What skill sets are those?"

He gave her another of those looks, and she

smiled. "Right. *Now* we're at the 'you'd tell me, but then you'd have to kill me' part."

With a maybe amused, maybe bemused shake of his head, he lifted his drink in her direction. "Happy birthday."

She blew out a sigh. "Yeah. Thanks."

He gave a very small snort. "You're really not a fan of birthdays."

"No. Nor parties."

"I'm getting that." He was looking at her list and she put a hand on the page to prevent him from flipping to the next page, which was even *more* revealing. Still, she braced herself for an inevitable comment, probably about the getting laid thing.

But he surprised her. "It's way too cold in Alaska," he said. "If that were my list, I'd be aiming for a South Pacific island."

"Let me guess—preferably deserted?"

He met her gaze. "Maybe not *completely* deserted."

Her stomach did a weird flutter, and that scared her. She didn't want to feel stomach flutters, not for this guy. "If you're flirting with me," she said slowly, "you should know I'm not interested."

"Good thing then that I'm not flirting with you," he said, completely deadpan.

She didn't know how to respond to that. Reading social cues was not her strong suit. Feeling awkward, which was nothing new for her, she slid off her barstool and tucked her journal inside her jacket.

How was it that they were surrounded by people, her people, and music and talking and laughter and yet . . . for those past few moments it had felt like they were all alone?

"You out?" he asked.

"I think it's best if I call it a night."

He rubbed his jaw again, and the sound his stubble made did something to her insides that she refused to name. "I could at least buy you a drink for your birthday."

"Thanks," she said. "But there's a big storm blowing in. So I need keep my wits about me."

"Doesn't have to be alcohol." He glanced around them at the full, rowdy bar. "Are you a first responder like all your friends?"

"Yes. I'm an EMT."

"Well, I'm the new guy," he said. "Zero friends. You going to desert me like Jenna deserted you?"

She actually hesitated at that, until she caught that flash of humor in his eyes. "You're messing with me."

"I am."

She wasn't sure how to respond. It'd been a long time since she'd felt . . . well, anything. Just beyond him, she could see a group of her friends playing pool. CJ, a local cop, was winning. After Jenna, CJ was one of her favorite people. He glanced over at her, caught her eye, and gave her a chin nudge.

Guy speak for "Are you alright?"

She nodded and he went back to pool. Ry was still flirting with two women, and she had to wonder. What was the worst thing that could happen if she let her hair down and enjoyed herself for a few minutes? After all, it *was* her birthday. "Maybe just one drink," she said.

Hot Guy nodded to the bartender, who promptly ambled over. "A Shirley Temple for Grandma here on her birthday."

Piper laughed. She shocked herself with it, making her realize how long it'd been.

Hot Guy took in her smile, and *almost* gave her a small one of his own. "Or . . . whatever you want."

She bit her lip. What did she want? That was a very big question she'd tried very hard not to ask herself over the past decade plus, because what she wanted had never applied. In her life, there were *need-to-do's* and *have-to-do's* . . . and nowhere in there had there ever been time for *what-Piper-wanted*.

Which was probably why she made lists like it was her job.

The bartender's name was Boomer, and she'd known him for a long time. He was waiting with a smile for her to admit the truth—that she loved Shirley Temples. But she didn't admit any such thing. She just rolled her eyes—honestly, she was going to have to learn to stop doing that—and nodded.

Boomer slid a Shirley Temple in front of her. She

took a big sip and was unable to hold in her sigh of pleasure, making Hot Guy finally *really* smile.

And oh boy, it was a doozy.

Just a little harmless flirting, she told herself. There was no harm in allowing herself this one little thing.

Which was when the power flickered and . . . went out.

She wasn't surprised, but by the collective gasp around her, she could tell everyone else was. Boomer hopped up onto the top of the bar. "Storm decided to hit us early and she's gonna be a doozy! Calling it a night!" he yelled out to the crowd. "Everyone go home and stay safe!"

In the ensuing chaos, Hot Guy grabbed Piper's hand and tugged her along with him, not towards the front door with the mass exodus, but through the bar and out the back.

Where indeed, the storm was moving in with a vengeance, given that the wind slapped them back against the wall.

"Nice work getting us out so quickly," she said breathlessly. "How did you know about the back door if you're new here?"

"I always know the way out."

That she believed. She took in the night, which was the sort of pitch black that came from no power anywhere and a dark, turbulent sky whipped to a frenzy by high winds.

"The rain's gonna hit any second," he said, not sounding thrilled about that.

This tugged a breathless laugh from her. "Chin up, Princess, or the crown slips."

He turned and gave her a dry wtf look. She'd bet her last dollar he'd never once in his life been called a princess before. "Sorry," she said on a grin. "That was an automatic response. My dad used to say that to me whenever I complained about the rain. Do you know how often it rains in Odisha, India?"

"I'm betting less than Mobile, Alabama," he said, "where I spent six months with my unit training the Maritime Safety and Security Team, and we never once saw anything but pouring rain. Emphasis on pouring."

"Six months straight, huh?" she asked sympathetically. "Okay, you win."

His lips quirked. "Ready?"

"As I'll ever be."

And with that, he took her hand and was her anchor as they ran through the wind to her beat up old Jeep. She was actually grateful since the gusts nearly blew her away twice, saved only by his solid, easy footing. Actually, the man moved like he was at the top of the food chain; quiet, economical, stealth movements that if you knew what he did for a living made perfect sense.

She and Jenna waved to each other from across

the lot, and when Jenna gave her a thumbs-up, Piper shook her head.

"Thanks for the drink," she said, having to raise her voice to be heard over the wind.

"I'll follow you home to make sure you get there okay."

"Not necessary, I'm fine." Because no way was she falling for that line. There was flirting, and then there was being stupid. "And anyway, as a local, I should be checking on you to see if you get home okay."

He laughed. And as it turned out, he had a great one, though she had no idea if he was so amused because he was touched by her worry for him, or because it was ridiculous, since clearly he could handle himself.

"I'm good," he finally said. "Drive safe." And then he stepped back, vanishing into the darkness.

*G*ive in to your Impulses!

These unforgettable stories only take a second to buy and give you hours of reading pleasure!

Go to *www.AvonImpulse.com* and see what we have to offer.

Available wherever e-books are sold.

AVONIMPULSE

IMP 0811